D0198132

FEATHER

BOOK ONE

AbrA EbneR

Text Copyright © 2009 Abra Ebner

All rights reserved. Except under the U.S. Copyright act of 1976,
no part of this publication may be reproduced, disributed, or transmitted in any
form or by any means, or stored in a database or retrieval system, without the
prior written permission of the publisher.

Crimson Oak Publishing

Pullman, WA 99163
Visit our website at www.CrimsonOakPublishing.com

the characters, events, and locations portrayed in this book are fictitious. Any
similarity to real persons, living or dead, or real locations is coincidental and not
intended by the author.

Ebner, Abra, 1984 -
Feather : A novel / by Abra Ebner

Cover Design and Layout Done by the Author herself.

www.FeatherBookSeries.com

Summary: Love spans and eternity, at least for Edgar and Estella. As She fights
to figure out her past, she finds something much more. There is a whole world
of history about her and her complicated special life. Estella comes into her
own in her first great adventure, in the life she was born to live, and die for.

printed in U.S.A

2 3 4 5 6 7 8 9 10

For my friends -

Love hits us all, if not in this life,
then maybe the next.
Have hope.

CONTENTS

THE RAVEN
Edgar A. Poe, 1845

Once upon a midnight dreary, while I pondered weak and weary,
Over many a quaint and curious volume of forgotten lore,
While I nodded, nearly napping, suddenly there came a tapping,
As of some one gently rapping, rapping at my chamber door.
`'Tis some visitor,' I muttered, `tapping at my chamber door -
Only this, and nothing more.'

Ah, distinctly I remember it was in the bleak December,
And each separate dying ember wrought its ghost upon the floor.
Eagerly I wished the morrow; - vainly I had sought to borrow
From my books surcease of sorrow - sorrow for the lost Lenore -
For the rare and radiant maiden whom the angels named Lenore -
Nameless here for evermore.

And the silken sad uncertain rustling of each purple curtain
Thrilled me - filled me with fantastic terrors never felt before;
So that now, to still the beating of my heart, I stood repeating
`'Tis some visitor entreating entrance at my chamber door -
Some late visitor entreating entrance at my chamber door; -
This it is, and nothing more,'

Presently my soul grew stronger; hesitating then no longer,
`Sir,' said I, `or Madam, truly your forgiveness I implore;
But the fact is I was napping, and so gently you came rapping,
And so faintly you came tapping, tapping at my chamber door,
That I scarce was sure I heard you' - here I opened wide the door; -
Darkness there, and nothing more.

Deep into that darkness peering, long I stood there wondering,
fearing,

Doubting, dreaming dreams no mortal ever dared to dream before
But the silence was unbroken, and the darkness gave no token,
And the only word there spoken was the whispered word, `Lenore!'
This I whispered, and an echo murmured back the word, `Lenore!'
Merely this and nothing more.

Back into the chamber turning, all my soul within me burning,
Soon again I heard a tapping somewhat louder than before.
`Surely,' said I, `surely that is something at my window lattice;
Let me see then, what thereat is, and this mystery explore -
Let my heart be still a moment and this mystery explore; -
'Tis the wind and nothing more!'

Open here I flung the shutter, when, with many a flirt and flutter,
In there stepped a stately raven of the saintly days of yore.
Not the least obeisance made he; not a minute stopped or stayed he;
But, with mien of lord or lady, perched above my chamber door -
Perched upon a bust of Pallas just above my chamber door -
Perched, and sat, and nothing more.

Then this ebony bird beguiling my sad fancy into smiling,
By the grave and stern decorum of the countenance it wore,
`Though thy crest be shorn and shaven, thou,' I said, `art sure no craven.
Ghastly grim and ancient raven wandering from the nightly shore -
Tell me what thy lordly name is on the Night's Plutonian shore!'
Quoth the raven, `Nevermore.'

Much I marvelled this ungainly fowl to hear discourse so plainly,
Though its answer little meaning - little relevancy bore;
For we cannot help agreeing that no living human being
Ever yet was blessed with seeing bird above his chamber door -
Bird or beast above the sculptured bust above his chamber door,
With such name as `Nevermore.'

But the raven, sitting lonely on the placid bust, spoke only,
That one word, as if his soul in that one word he did outpour.
Nothing further then he uttered - not a feather then he fluttered -
Till I scarcely more than muttered `Other friends have flown before
-

On the morrow he will leave me, as my hopes have flown before.'
Then the bird said, `Nevermore.'

Startled at the stillness broken by reply so aptly spoken,
`Doubtless,' said I, `what it utters is its only stock and store,
Caught from some unhappy master whom unmerciful disaster
Followed fast and followed faster till his songs one burden bore -
Till the dirges of his hope that melancholy burden bore
Of "Never-nevermore."'

But the raven still beguiling all my sad soul into smiling,
Straight I wheeled a cushioned seat in front of bird and bust and
door;
Then, upon the velvet sinking, I betook myself to linking
Fancy unto fancy, thinking what this ominous bird of yore -
What this grim, ungainly, ghastly, gaunt, and ominous bird of yore
Meant in croaking `Nevermore.'

This I sat engaged in guessing, but no syllable expressing
To the fowl whose fiery eyes now burned into my bosom's core;
This and more I sat divining, with my head at ease reclining
On the cushion's velvet lining that the lamp-light gloated o'er,
But whose velvet violet lining with the lamp-light gloating o'er,
She shall press, ah, nevermore!

Then, methought, the air grew denser, perfumed from an unseen
censer
Swung by Seraphim whose foot-falls tinkled on the tufted floor.
`Wretch,' I cried, `thy God hath lent thee - by these angels he has
sent thee

Respite - respite and nepenthe from thy memories of Lenore!
Quaff, oh quaff this kind nepenthe, and forget this lost Lenore!'
Quoth the raven, `Nevermore.'

`Prophet!' said I, `thing of evil! - prophet still, if bird or devil! -
Whether tempter sent, or whether tempest tossed thee here ashore,
Desolate yet all undaunted, on this desert land enchanted -
On this home by horror haunted - tell me truly, I implore -
Is there - is there balm in Gilead? - tell me - tell me, I implore!'
Quoth the raven, `Nevermore.'

`Prophet!' said I, `thing of evil! - prophet still, if bird or devil!
By that Heaven that bends above us - by that God we both adore -
Tell this soul with sorrow laden if, within the distant Aidenn,
It shall clasp a sainted maiden whom the angels named Lenore -
Clasp a rare and radiant maiden, whom the angels named Lenore?'
Quoth the raven, `Nevermore.'

`Be that word our sign of parting, bird or fiend!' I shrieked upstarting
-
`Get thee back into the tempest and the Night's Plutonian shore!
Leave no black plume as a token of that lie thy soul hath spoken!
Leave my loneliness unbroken! - quit the bust above my door!
Take thy beak from out my heart, and take thy form from off my
door!'
Quoth the raven, `Nevermore.'

And the raven, never flitting, still is sitting, still is sitting
On the pallid bust of Pallas just above my chamber door;
And his eyes have all the seeming of a demon's that is dreaming,
And the lamp-light o'er him streaming throws his shadow on the
floor;
And my soul from out that shadow that lies floating on the floor
Shall be lifted - nevermore!

PREFACE

The Gods once created a being far greater than anything in existence. These beings, the highest form of human life, were closer to the Gods than even the Angels, and their beauty far more appealing than any earthly creation.

The Gods, upon seeing such a beautiful creation, grew jealous. The being needed no love, longed for no power, and hungered for no nourishment of either mind or soul. Their flawless creation was angelically perfect, and therefore appallingly wrong, for nothing could be more perfect than the Gods themselves.

As the being flourished, troubled by nothing, the Gods grew dark and vindictive. Fueled by their hatred, they plotted, and the plan they constructed was horrid, inhumane, and dark. They chose to split the perfect soul for eternity, fore the Gods thought themselves ultimately endangered by their creations' power and strength. In one swift movement, they ripped the being apart, creating two hearts; both sharing one soul.

One half was the creator, the life and energy of the Earth, and the mother of man. The other half was the power and protection, a warrior of worlds. In this, they created Male and Female.

As the Gods schemed in their eternal greed, they chose to make their creation a game, no more than mere pawns for their enjoyment. As punishment, they scattered the beings among the humans of Earth, both halves separated and eternally locked in hunger and longing for the love of their shared soul.

The female half was the holder of their life, the emotion and beauty of the soul. In her, she protected this delicate power, never abusing its energy, and forever giving to the Earth and nature. Despite her possessions, she was lonely and lost in love - weak, sad, and alone.

The male half, the powerful half, was left lifeless and drained of the energy only the soul could give him. In the male's life on Earth, he searched for his strength, the female, and the power he could ultimately gain from it. Their lethal lust for that soul was so great, that it drove them into madness, anger, and despair.

Upon meeting their soul mate, the male half was found hungry and vicious, murdering his other half in his greed, and ultimately leading to their demise. But despite their vicious love, many survived long enough to understand their power, and in finding each other, they unlocked the secret to their lives.

Together, the two halves created a whole, a life force greater and more powerful than anything on Earth. Though eternally tormented by jealously and hunger, they were better together than apart, the ultimate test of eternal love.

A NEW DAY

"Estella, take this."

Heidi thrust a thick envelope toward me as tears of sadness filled her eyes. Her hand was trembling and weak as it floated in the air between us.

I looked at the envelope with caution.

"Oh, no!" I shook my head, my face contorted into a sad frown. "Heidi, no, I couldn't." I squeezed my eyes shut, unable and unwilling to accept the gift.

"Please, Estella." She paused, her voice breaking. "I just want to see you happy. I am old and tired. My life is ending and yours is just beginning."

Heidi walked toward me with a determined look on her face. The envelope was still stubbornly held out in front of her. Her eyes pierced mine, and I could see she loved me like her own.

I grabbed the small, manila package between my trembling fingers, treating it with delicate care. The contents were beyond what I could ever deserve, but the needs reflected in Heidi's eyes ran deep, and I found myself unable to say no.

"Thank you." I looked at the ground as a familiar sadness pierced my heart.

Heidi leaned in and hugged me, her thin arms squeezing the breath from my lungs.

"I'm sorry I couldn't have been more of a mother to you," she whispered, her breath hot as it fell across my ear. She sounded responsible, as though the fact of my absent parents was her fault.

She was crying now, and I felt her tears seeping into the shoulder of my blouse.

"Heidi, you are the closest thing to a mother I've ever known. Don't think any less of yourself." I put my arm around her frail shoulders as she trembled against my chest, the guilt in me rising as I forced back my desire to stay, to save her from her lonely life.

She pulled away, a determined look now filling her tear-stained face. She was strong, I knew this, but she hated to say goodbye.

"You go, make me proud," she said bravely. "And find your happiness." Heidi patted both of my shoulders with surprising strength, her nails digging into my skin.

"I promise I will come back as soon as I can." I tried to smile as I bent to pick up my last bag, but try as I might, I couldn't summon the action.

15

Heidi followed me to the car in her housecoat and slippers as I threw the last bag in the back seat of the old, rusty, green Datsun. I was finally able to afford the car after my summer working at the Market downtown. I did everything I could to scrape enough money together, to make my escape from the city.

Heidi's eyes had dried and I looked at her with nostalgic love and admiration as I climbed into the car. The old vinyl seats yawned against my sweaty skin, and I winced at their searing heat. I squeaked the door shut, slamming it with as much force as I could muster before putting my hands on the plastic wood grain steering wheel. She waved to me with hopeless vigor as I coaxed the vehicle to life and forced it into reverse.

"I will visit soon!" I yelled out the window as I drove off. "The college is not too far."

Heidi took a small step forward as she waved goodbye one last time. I would miss my foster mother, but this was my time to make something of my sad life. The upbringing she had given me was more than I could have hoped for, but something inside me was driving me away, pushing me to another place.

As I drove down the crowded streets, the shadows cast by the towering buildings of downtown Seattle always left me somewhat disappointed. The tiny house where I had been placed when I was ten glared at me in my rearview mirror as it disappeared between the apartment complexes of the west side.

I took a deep breath, exhaling with a heavy heart. I had

decided the city was not for me. After years of adoption and rejection, I couldn't stand its cold cement and moist, dirty air any longer. Why the city had let me down I was unsure, but as the depression in me grew deeper over the years, it had become a sort of cancer. There was death here, and everyone took their happiness for granted. I would have given anything to feel a smile, to muster out a happy laugh.

I rolled my windows up, closing out this world as I headed north toward the Cascades. As the hills of Seattle whizzed by, each growing less crowded with houses, I felt a sort of liberation. The stern grip I'd had on the steering wheel slowly eased, and soon I was casually driving with one hand. My lonely life had never granted me the experience that was ahead of me, the chance to be with nature as my heart had so longed.

The college brochure had promised a tranquil and secluded experience, and that was just the thing I was hoping my dark heart needed. College had always been a goal for me, and despite my graduation from high school with a bachelor's degree that I had earned taking night courses, it still didn't satisfy my insatiable need to learn.

The sun shone onto the serene valleys of northern Puget Sound, filling the basin with energy and warmth. As I crept further north, the dense forest began to creep ever closer to the road. Like always, I felt a strange pull from the plants that sat there, each bowing toward the concrete as though longing to escape to the other side. The cement was like a wall, much like the invisible wall in my heart that was refusing to allow me happiness. Despite the confines of the

17

road, I still envied their freedom. They had a life of simple happiness, and the ability to adapt and grow. I, on the other hand, had never belonged, and despite how hard I tried, I always stood out in a negative way. The world hopelessly saddened me, as though somewhere in my past life, it had let me down, my soul now darkened by my mere existence. I felt like a mistake, and I felt like God had forgotten me, as though he were too ashamed to grant me a fair life.

I reached into my bag as I drove, retrieving a bottle of medication that seemed like my only lifeline. Keeping one hand on the wheel, I popped a small pill into my mouth, as I habitually did every day for the past twelve years. Each clouded thought was further stifled by the power of Prozac. I allowed myself a brief second to close my eyes as I once again opened my windows, so that the wind could whip through my white-blonde hair. As the sun touched my pale skin, it felt warm and soothing, like a bath of heavenly light. Opening my eyes, I felt discouraged that even a moment like this could not muster a smile.

Even as a baby I had never laughed, never let out even so much as a delighted coo. Smiling was something I did because I had to, in order to fit in. I learned what was funny from my peers, and practiced for hours in front of the mirror, my facial muscles stretching with pain in a way that came so naturally to everyone else. Tears never came, either. Though I knew what I felt was sadness, I never experienced that emotion in the true sense of the feeling. It was as though someone had taken my heart and stashed it away, someplace I could never find it.

I thought about all my adoptive parents and how many times each tried to create a happy life for me, how relentlessly they urged me into activities designed to muster a laugh, though one never came. I was like a poisonous berry, beautiful on the outside, damaged and sick on the inside. It was an inevitable truth that each parent would fail, and so they sent me back to the social workers, apologizing for their failure as parents. After a while, I gave up hoping that I could find a place to fit in, hoping instead that I could just be in one place for longer than a few months. It was that fact that I moved in with Heidi and her other foster kids, and for what I planned to be forever – or at least until I was old enough to strike out on my own.

I exhaled from deep within my charred soul as I finally reached the town of Sedro-Woolly. There, the road split and I turned onto Highway Twenty, heading east into the North Cascades. The small town of Sedro-Woolly was far north, close to the Canadian border and the San Juan Islands. It was just far enough from Seattle to make me feel like I could leave the past behind me and start anew. The town was the gateway to my future, a new life.

As I headed into the wilderness, the trees that edged the roadside seemed to welcome my presence, the branches swaying in the gentle breeze. The air seemed full of magic, and I saw the glimmer of bugs flying between thick rays of light, like fairies in the trees. With my windows opened, the gentle clamoring of water softly whispered in my ear as I passed spring after spring, cascading down the granite rocks and into the roadside reservoirs.

The mountains closed in around me like a blanket, casting deep shadows on the road, but not the same depressing shadows I had grown up around in the city. These shadows revealed a whole other world beyond the dirty streets and sadness, a world full of life. For the first time, I felt a soft warmth flicker in my vacant soul and I gasped, the feeling ripping the breath from my lungs.

Rounding the corner with caution, the trees parted before me like a curtain at the opera. Sun poured into the car, a fresh scent riding on the rays. The river that had followed the road burst open into a large lake that was held back by a small dam. The water sparkled clearer than I'd ever seen in Puget Sound, and the glimmer made my eyes water. The air that blew into the car was crisp and cool from the glacial waters, and I breathed deep, feeling reenergized.

I gazed in awe, wondering how I'd let this whole world hide from me for so long. As I followed the lake, I kept glancing toward it, afraid that it would disappear as fast as it had come, akin to a dream or a fleeting memory.

Like the meandering stream, the road wound to the right and I crossed over the lake on a small bridge. I felt a rush of something cold enter my body as though the water were pulsing through me, becoming a part of my blood and filling every vein. I allowed the feeling to control my thoughts, and I imagined a tidal wave washing through my wounded mind, cooling each burning gash.

Just when I thought I couldn't have seen anything any more stunning, the lake expanded further, revealing an even larger dam before me. The structure was astonishing in its sheer size and power, solid as though the Earth had made it. I took in the complex structure and it amazed me to believe that man could create something so magnificent. As I tore my gaze from the structure, I saw that the college was now before me, nestled into the hillside on the other side of the dam. I was almost there. I was almost free.

As I turned from the main road toward the campus, I slowed my car as it rolled onto the quaint cobblestone roadway atop the dam itself. The gentle vibration was soothing as the cobbles shuddered under my weight. The college had utilized this dam as the crossing to the school, and I allowed myself to imagine that it was a bridge to my fairy-tale castle.

To my left was the lake that I had driven beside on my way up. As I peered over the ledge, I beheld the plunging drop, my head experiencing a gripping vertigo. To my right, the water churned, anxious and foamy in its attempt to escape its confines. The lake itself was crystal blue, and rich with minerals that added a milky consistency. Rocky peaks surrounded the water on all sides, reaching with open arms into an even bluer sky. The unique coloring was unbelievable and I recognized it to be Diablo Lake, upon whose shores the college was situated.

As I neared the other side of the bridge, I noticed a cascading waterfall drop like a graceful veil from a far peak and into the lake on its final decent. Its raw power humbled me, reminding me of my infinitesimal existence on this planet. I watched in silence as the falls misted the air around it, rainbows flashing in its wake. The wind whipped toward me across the water and I enjoyed the untamed beauty.

I tightened my grip on the wheel and held my breath as I heard a gust of wind tickle the small waves of the lake. The wind rushed toward me, unfazed by my position in its path. As it landed on the car, the cool breeze whipped through my long hair, making it dance. My skin prickled and I shivered from the chill, the hairs on my arms now standing on end.

When I reached the other side of the bridge, I released my breath, feeling refreshed and grounded as my car rolled onto the gravel drive, the water no longer flowing below me like a force of energy greater than I could control. I circled Diablo Lake and just a few hundred feet farther east, the road became even rougher. My tires struggled to find their grip so I drove with caution up the hill toward the front of the small cluster of buildings. I tried to stifle the anxiety and fear I now felt toward this unfamiliar place. My mind was cautious, but also roaring with curiosity.

An anonymous donor had created the Cascades College a few years back. Its purpose was to provide a Masters in Environmental Studies through hands-on experience and practice. There were also primary classes but mainly it was a place to get your hands dirty and experience the real world, in its truest sense.

When I had learned about the college, I remembered that it was the first time I'd felt my heart truly beat. Something about its design, location, and description felt more like home than anywhere I had ever been. I needed to be close to the earth, close to the place where life began.

I was never the nature-loving type, yet my choice to come here had been motivated by nature and my desire to heal. Ever since I could remember, I possessed a strange talent for growing plants; a green thumb, you might say. But my talent did not simply involve using the right fertilizers and making sure to water regularly. My talents seemed to involve something much more magical and indescribable; something I was here to figure out.

Turning my car off with a heavy sigh, I sat in front of the main learning center, the large 'Welcome' sign looming over me. I felt something flicker in my chest as it had on the drive up, and for a second time, it stole the breath from my lungs. I was right to come here.

Taking in the small modern buildings, I again wondered if perhaps I was dreaming. I had been trapped by the city for so long, that I had never seen nature first hand. Though I coveted the magazines on every store shelf, I now saw that pictures could not give it justice. Nature was a sensory experience, meant to be enjoyed in its natural environment.

A lanky red-headed man, startled by my abrupt arrival, jumped up from a bench by the office doors and ran toward my parked car with a smile plastered across his face. He couldn't have been much older than I, but his demeanor made him seem years younger. He came bounding down the hill, tripping with inherent clumsiness. He was quick to regain his composure with a small smile of embarrassment. He wore a green plaid short-sleeved shirt with hiking shorts and Columbia boots. I chuckled to myself, finding his outfit a cliché.

The man was breathing hard as he placed both of his hands on the window. He leaned down to my eye level, locking his gaze on mine.

"New arrival?" he asked, in a cheerful voice that was also winded.

I looked at him with nervous eyes as anxiety gripped my stomach.

"Yes," I managed to squeak.

His eyes were a light blue like mine, but unlike mine, his were full of life and happiness.

"Great," he exclaimed, sticking his hand through my window for me to shake. "I'm Scott."

I stared at his hand for a moment, allowing my anxiety to subside. Finally, I deduced that Scott was harmless, and I grabbed his hand between two fingers and gave it a soft shake.

Scott yanked his hand back just as quickly as he had thrust it forward, unfazed by my reluctance.

"Well, it sure is great to meet you. Would you like some help with your things?"

He opened my car door, and I cringed as it shuddered and scraped, rust flakes falling to the ground.

"Um…" I was processing the information as quickly as I could. "Sure. That would be great." I pulled myself out of the seat.

"Thanks," I added, giving him a small, tight smile.

Scott stood there with his hands on his hips, smiling eagerly. He was like a dog, just waiting to be thrown a bone.

"So what's your name?" As soon as I was out of the way, he jumped forward, lunging into my backseat and loading his scrawny arms with my three somewhat small bags, the makings of my whole life.

"I, uh…." I stuttered, grabbing my throat, willing it to stop. "My name is Estella." My medications always caused me to think slowly, as if I were in a cloud. It was an unpleasant but unavoidable side-effect of the medication I needed to make it through my days.

"Hi, Estella." He grabbed a sheet from his pocket, juggling his load as he struggled to bring it to his face. He squinted. "Looks like you got your own cabin." His eyes widened with excitement. "Cool," he crooned.

I nodded in agreement. I had worked a few extra shifts at the fish counter of the local market to make that possible. I wasn't about to bunk up in a group dormitory again, like I had for a good portion of my life at the orphanage.

"Well, then." He smiled with a sweet glow as he urged me forward. "Follow me."

"Thanks." I grabbed my shoulder bag from the passenger seat and rushed to keep up.

"So, Estella…"

"Oh, you can call me Elle," I quickly corrected him.

He looked back at me as I followed behind him. "Okay then, Elle…What brings you here?"

I looked at him sideways. What else would I be here for? "For the Master's course," I said softly.

"Oh, really?" He looked back at me again, this time scrutinizing my face more closely. "Aren't you a bit young for a Masters?"

I shrugged, watching my feet as they struggled to stay on pace, nerves again gathering in my stomach. "I got my undergraduate degree while I was young."

"Really?" He sounded shocked.

"Well…" I felt embarrassed and my cheeks began to flush. "It's just that…it came so naturally." I paused, breathing hard as we passed under a large pine that left a thick bed of needles on the ground. "It wasn't very difficult for me. I had a lot of time on my hands."

The fact that I never had friends made me resort to anything that could pass my time, and mostly that was homework and studying. I was a first class nerd and social reject. Even when I did try to make friends, my awkward personality eventually put them off. I knew that at some point, Scott probably would come to learn this as well. But for now, he seemed to accept this.

His eyes smiled at me when he spoke. "Then I am impressed. I'm in that program, too, but I'm not quite as young as you. I'm twenty-one. I kept pretty much on pace with things through high school." He eyed me with curiosity. "I suppose we'll have the same classes. There aren't many people here."

I nodded, thinking that was how I'd wanted it, quiet and secluded. As we rounded the path, I finally spotted a small cabin nestled on the hill.

"So, that will be yours," he announced. We approached fast, climbing onto the porch with our boots echoing beneath us. He threw down a bag so that he could open the door. I noticed there was no lock.

"I will just set your bags here in the corner. Does that work?"

I nodded again. "Yeah. Thanks, Scott."

He thrust his hand toward me again, still the same energetic spark to his face.

"Well, good to meet you, Elle." He still didn't seem fazed by my standoffish behavior. "I guess I will see you tomorrow in class?"

I shook his hand and tried to give him another smile, though I was never able to succeed in getting it quite right. "Yeah, I guess I will. Thanks again."

I shut the door behind him as he bounded down the hill with the same awkward gait as before. As I looked around the small, square cabin, I was pleased to see there was a lot more than I'd first imagined. I had my own bathroom with a small shower and a tiny kitchenette with a miniature refrigerator. My bed was full-sized, bigger than I'd ever had, and I experienced a small feeling of satisfaction at my turn of luck.

I reached in my bag and pulled out the thick envelope Heidi had given me. I slid it in the crack where the fridge met the cabinet, thinking I'd save it for an emergency. I pulled my boots off, placing my stocking feet on the wood boards of the floor, testing the texture on my toes. I then circled the inside perimeter of the cabin, inspecting every square inch of my new home and opening the blinds as I went to let in the light.

After deciding everything was in order, I sat on my bed and pulled one of my bags toward me. From inside I grabbed a small stack of moleskin journals and placed them on the shelf above my bed. I had began documenting my life the day I was able to write, a craft that soothed me. The simple act of getting my feelings down on paper was cathartic, keeping my soul open for happiness to come in, though it never did.

Deep in the bag, nestled between my clothes, I found the framed note from my real mother. It was the only thing I had from her. I flicked on the bedside lamp so that I could see it more clearly. The beautiful script and rough edges played at my emotions, and every day I read it in anticipation:

> Estella,
> You are beautiful, and it pains me to leave, but some day you will find the beauty you seek living inside your darkest soul. You are safe now.

The poetic words puzzled and saddened me. I had searched for her when I was younger, but found nothing about her or where she'd gone or even if she was dead or alive. And so my soul remained black.

Placing the frame on the wooden side table, I reached back into my bag and pulled a small, tattered brown box from its depths, treating it with extreme care. Opening it with caution, I retrieved a small pot containing a tiny purple plant that was snuggled inside. Grasping it with two hands, I set the purple clover on the sill and touched its butterfly leaves. It reacted to the light and stretched its petals toward the sun like an opening umbrella. I had decided to take just one tubular with me from my vast garden in Seattle, just one child with whom to start my new life.

After unpacking the few clothes I had, leaving some in the bag out of sheer laziness, I finally laid on my bed, letting my platinum hair fan out around me. After a few moments of restful silence, I pulled myself back up and reached into my bag once again, grabbing a book. I leaned back into my pillow and I began to read as the darkness of the night crept in around the cabin. Soon, only the light from the bedside lamp shone dimly across the room, casting eerie shadows against the walls of the unfamiliar place.

I glanced away from the page to the windows and realized that the hours had passed faster than I'd expected. The blackness seemed infinite and my heart began to race anxiously as the world of my book faded away. I lifted my head off the pillow and sat up, sliding my legs to the floor. As I approached the window, I was shocked to see only a few faint lights glimmer from the campus that surrounded me. I had never experienced anything like it in my life: profound darkness and quiet, all at once. I leaned toward my lamp and switched it off, allowing the lights outside to magnify.

After a moment, I walked to my door and opened it, walking quietly onto the small deck, not wanting to disturb nature's slumber. I squeezed my eyes shut and tilted my head to the sky, enjoying the tranquility of the night. When I opened my eyes, I gasped at the tiny diamonds that littered the sky, sparkling greater than I had ever seen and in far greater numbers than I could imagine. I had read about the stars, seen images and studied their matter, but never would I have expected the sight that welcomed me now. The city lights of Seattle and the almost constant thick shroud of clouds made star gazing difficult.

My body and mind felt clear as I stood there connecting with the night. A light breeze swept playfully through my hair, gently caressing my face. I could smell pine and sage, and a feeling I had never experienced before slipped over me: peace.

For a moment I couldn't help but feel I might at last smile, but then the wind subsided and my dark soul remained empty. As the stars twinkled ever brighter, I realized I was getting close. There was something out here I needed to see, something I was meant to do, but what that was, for now, would continue to elude me.

FEAR

The sun streamed through the blinds, waking me to the quiet of the cabin. My restless sleep had left me groggy. I reached to the bedside table for my medication. Putting one hand to my aching head, I felt unsettled and slightly queasy. I hadn't expected the dead silence of the night when I was so used to the hubbub of the city. I knew eventually I would grow to love it, but the transition period was going to be a little rocky.

Urging my lethargic body to sit up, I scanned the cabin, realizing nothing had changed from the night before. I threw a pill in my mouth in one mechanical movement and forced it down my dry throat. Rubbing my eyes, the cloudiness began to fade and I was finally able to haul myself out from under the covers and place my feet on the cold wood floor. For a moment I struggled to gain my balance, placing my hand on the bed frame.

Finally staggering to the bathroom, I grabbed a wrinkled pile of clothes on my way. I locked myself inside and splashed a handful of cool water on my face. Outside the small window, the chirping of birds was deafening, but sweet, and I stood on my toes to peer through the dusty glass. Down the hill I spotted the cafeteria building, and my stomach rumbled at the thought of food. I had not eaten dinner due to my extended reading and dumbfounded amazement with the night sky, and I knew that it would be best to at least attempt something light.

As I slid on my jeans, struggling to force my tired legs through each pant leg, there was a sharp knock at the front door of the cabin. Startled, I jumped in fear, my body going rigid with dismay. I scanned the mess I had made unpacking, half hoping I had just imagined the sound. To my chagrin, there was another sharp knock, this time even louder and more persistent. I quickly threw my shirt over my head, catching the hem on my ears as I ripped it on. I then stumbled through the bathroom door, crawling my way toward the front.

When I wrenched the door open, the sudden burst of light blinded me. I squinted, shielding my eyes with my hand as my gaze finally landed on my visitor. I wasn't really surprised to see Scott standing before me, smiling in the same eccentric fashion he had yesterday.

"Well, hey there, Elle." He paused as he looked at my rumpled clothing. "I didn't wake you, did I?"

I was still stunned from the sudden burst of light, so I just shook my head, my lips pursed in annoyance, but Scott's smile did not falter.

"I was just going to go get some food before class." He pointed down the hill toward the other building. "Just thought since you were new, you'd like to have a guide." He shrugged, suddenly embarrassed.

I swallowed hard, still too tired to attempt an empty smile.

"Sure," I said in a flat voice, cursing myself for my lack of enthusiasm. "I'm starving." Although flattered, I was also perplexed: people usually tended to avoid me, but not Scott.

I pulled my long hair out of my shirt as I grabbed my bag. Giving the cabin one last scan, I pulled the door shut behind me. Grabbing my boots from the deck, I sat on the top step to pull them on while Scott stood on the path, whistling to himself and looking up into the branches of a large evergreen that shaded the path. I couldn't quite understand him. He was so unfazed by my awkwardness, which was something I was not used to.

I finally stood, smoothing my navy thermal shirt over my jeans and collecting my thoughts. Taking a deep breath, I mustered what courage I had and walked off the deck toward Scott.

"Okay." I paused a few feet from him and his attention fell to me. "I'm ready."

Scott smiled again.

"Perfect." He beckoned me forward. "You're going to love the food here, I promise." He attempted a wink, but instead it ended up looking like a twitch. I shook my head, suppressing my thoughts.

As we hiked down the hill, I took in my new surroundings. There were five buildings in my view, and I noted each carefully, eager to find my place here. The structures looked modern and clean, built in such a way that their surroundings had hardly been disturbed. The massive beam frames looked far stronger than necessary and the windows were at least an inch thick. I knew the winters here were long and harsh and the snow pack so great that most of the trees, even now in late summer, were still bowing from the painful weight forced onto their limbs. I guess that was why the buildings were so solid.

Scott noticed the curious look on my face and took it upon himself to elaborate.

"That over there is the bird and wildlife lab." He pointed to the far left toward the bottom of the hill. "That will be our second class today."

"Birds?" I asked, puzzled.

"Yeah," he continued. "They really are an integral part of the ecosystem here." He looked at me with wide, convincing eyes. "And down over there…" He pointed to the right. "That is the greenhouse."

My eyes widened with interest. "That's more like what I'm into."

Scott watched me with an amplified look of interest on his face. He was pleased by the fact I was playing along and asking questions.

"And over in that cluster are the astrology lab, the water lab, and the hatchery," he continued.

I nodded in comprehension. Despite the fact that I was

nervous around people, I was thankful to have Scott, even if I was uncomfortable being this conversational. I had never managed to keep friends, or even really make them to begin with. My personality was too depressing to be around and most people mistook my silence for unfriendliness. I had always thought I was at least reasonably attractive, with my crystal blue eyes and smooth porcelain skin, but looks aren't everything, and people still treated me like I was a pariah.

The gravel below our feet crunched as we approached the cafeteria. The front entrance was flanked on both sides by two large timbers and the walls were mostly glass, allowing the light to shine into the space. My skin glowed milky-white in contrast to the other students and visitors filling the hall. They had obviously spent most of their lives outdoors whereas I was always shielded in the city shade.

We walked to the counter and I grabbed a plate. There were droves of fresh berries and grainy breads, and what I deduced to be tubs and tubs of granola. I cringed at the sight. I hated granola more than anything, the needless chewing and tasteless texture repulsed me. Settling for a soft bran muffin, I placed it on my plate and then watched wide-eyed as Scott piled his plate high with berries and tofu-scrambled eggs.

"I can't get enough of this stuff."

Scott mounded another scoop of eggs on an already dangerously teetering stack and then grabbed some silverware. I followed him to a table in the far corner where the sun warmed my back as I sat.

"So what made you come here?" I asked, eyeing him

with acute curiosity as I tried my best to be social. Scott looked at me over his glasses as he chewed on a mouth full of blueberries.

He smiled, revealing his berry stained teeth. "My mother is an environmental researcher." He paused, wiping juice from the corner of his mouth. "She's out in the woods of Alaska right now, but she will be back in about six months. She was always my source of inspiration."

I nodded as I picked at my muffin, my appetite somewhat diminished. "That's nice." I was saddened at the thought of what I had missed by not having a mother. It sounded like Scott was close to his, and I wished, not for the first time, that I had known my own mother, even briefly. It seemed that most of the orphans had had at least some memory, even if it was the memory of their parents leaving; but I had nothing.

Scott swallowed a mouthful of eggs. "So what's your story? What brings you here?" He was analyzing my sadness like a Petri dish. I understood, people usually found me interesting, at least at first. Once I told my story, though, that was when people usually lost interest in me.

I thought for a moment, finding the right words to say that wouldn't cause him to turn and run.

"Well…" I flicked a sugar crystal off the table. "I was an orphan." I watched his face for some sort of reaction, but one never came. So far so good. No unnecessary pity or scorn. "And I've always had this thing with plants, with nature," I blurted.

He looked at me surprised, only a slight trace of confusion on his face. "Like what?" He laughed. "You make it sound forbidden, like a fairy tale." He smiled at me encouragingly. "Or do you mean, like a green thumb?"

I gave him a small smile, finding his imagination refreshing.

"No, not like fairy tales." I tore at my napkin as I struggled to explain. "More like a mother thing. The plants...." I paused, trying to see how I could explain without sounding like a complete nutcase. "...they love me. They react to me even when I don't take care of them at all. No matter what, they still flourish under my care, just by being near me." I held my breath after I said it. It had always been a strange talent of mine and certainly not something a normal girl could do.

He looked at me and I could see he hadn't really gotten it. "Mother Nature then, right?" He let out a small chuckle.

I rolled my eyes and breathed a sigh of relief. He had gotten it, and he hadn't run away in the process.

He continued. "So then, you're a tree hugger," he said matter-of-factly, looking at me as though it were a typical occurrence. "We've got two types here: animal activists and tree huggers." He chewed as he pointed at me with his fork. "And you are a tree hugger."

I lowered my gaze, feeling somewhat hurt and very annoyed. I was no hippy, that was for sure. I had never been an obsessed recycler or taken to eating granola, yogurt, and tofu. I knew that what I had was a different passion, a real passion, not a means to fit in. Scott noticed my pained expression.

"Oh, sorry." He looked concerned, "I didn't mean to offend you." He let out a nervous laugh in his attempt to erase his prior remark. I looked up at him.

37

"Don't worry, you didn't." I felt bad for him. He was trying hard to be my friend. "I don't really have feelings. Well, at least no feelings other than pain, so don't feel bad."

Again, he gave me the same confused stare, and I could see that he and I were going to become great friends. He didn't seem to understand me but accepted me nonetheless, and that was good.

"Well, good." A bubbly smile was again plastered to his freckled face, his glasses smeared with blueberry juice where he had grabbed the rim to readjust them.

He finished his whole plate while I stuffed the muffin in my bag for later, feeling an acute loss of appetite after the depressing conversation and having to watch him eat. Scott grabbed our plates, throwing them with expert aim into a nearby tub as we left the building.

"So, we're off to the hatchery." He looked at me with excitement in his eyes. "That's my favorite class," he whispered, as though there were anyone around to even hear or care.

It was a sunny day, the weather of summer giving way to fall, yet still somewhat warm. I followed him down the hill toward the crystal blue lake, watching as he hopped ahead of me. The hatchery building was old and water stained like an antique boathouse, and it was the full length of the dock, about eighty feet long. Once inside, I noticed how its shape reflected its function. To the front was a long, segmented tank that spread down the side of half the room, each filled with a dozen fish, divided based on their age and relative size.

Scott ran like a child to the edge of the tank and looked

deep within.

"Hey, Elle, come see!"

I approached the tank with wary footsteps. I'd never really cared for fish, especially live ones. Anytime I got in any lakes or oceans, they would nibble at my feet as though I where I giant chunk of floating Wonder bread.

I peered deep into the turquoise water, the pearly green scales of the fish glittering like dark clouds as they twisted their way around their bleak confines. They were beautiful and silent, like clouds.

"Hey, look!" Scott pointed to the fish now circling in anxious rings in front of me. "He likes you."

I sighed, looking down at the struggling fish as it tried with all of its might to get closer to me. I felt sorry for the poor thing, a runt, stuck in a glass box for the rest of its life. With reluctance, I raised my trembling hand to hover above the water of my rippled reflection. I watched as the trout swam toward the shadow, following the shelter my hand was creating for it. I felt his warmth enter my palm, his rapid heartbeat pulsing in my fingers.

Scott watched in amazement, and I noticed his shocked expression out of the corner of my eye. Ashamed that he had seen what I'd done, I jammed my hand back into my pocket, feeling my pale skin blush to a dramatic red. The fish's heartbeat left me and I no longer felt his warmth. I had let him go.

"How did you do that?" Scott came to my side, watching the once-anxious fish now swimming tranquilly, still as close to me as possible. "He was like, following you."

I shrugged. "That's what I was saying. They love me." I felt like a freak and I was waiting for him to blow me off, call me a weirdo, and never talk to me again.

"Well," he gave me a stupid grin. "Then I guess they do."

I narrowed my eyes and stared at him in disbelief. How Scott had made it this far in life amazed me. With his unassuming demeanor and oblivious personality, he would never survive in the city; he'd be eaten alive. As I tried to calm my nerves, the room filled with students, each eyeing me with curiosity and wariness. I shrank to the back and stared at the ground. A few minutes later, a frumpy, frizzle-haired professor entered the room and began to preach before everyone was even settled, her lisp making her voice hard to listen to.

"The fith are our friendth," she droned with passionate respect, and I could tell this was going to be a long hour.

I watched Scott as he stared in obedience toward the front, alert in his love for marine life. Soon, my eyes wandered to the other students. People of all ages filled the room, each as unremarkable as the next. I felt like I had a giant, flashing arrow pointing directly at me saying, "Which one of these things does not belong?" But then again, when had I ever belonged? My blonde hair was striking against the muted colors of the people around me. At one point, I noticed the teacher could barely stop staring at me, an almost entranced look on her face.

At the end of class, Scott turned to me with elated eyes.

"That was amazing," he gasped, throwing his bag over

his shoulder. His happiness radiated from him and I longed to know how that felt.

I gazed at him as a lump grew in my throat, but I didn't want to ruin the moment for him.

"Yeah, sure was." My tone was edged with sarcasm but there was nothing I could do to help it. I hoped he hadn't noticed my unconvincing attitude. Luckily, he hadn't.

"Well, Elle, time for the birds," he said, giving me a playful nudge. "We'll get to plants soon though, don't worry." He winked at me and grabbed my arm as he led me out the door and back to the gravel path.

As we walked in silence to the bird and wildlife lab, I began to doubt my presence here. Surely no one would take me seriously. Scott wasn't absorbing the fact that my strange abilities weren't just with plants, but with everything in nature. I just favored plants because the extraordinary pull I had for them was safe. With animals, you never knew what was going to come at you. Bulldogs were the worst; not that they wanted to hurt me, but the drool was gross.

Scott pulled the heavy door of the lab open and we walked into the stark classroom. Students were socializing in small groups, roaming from table to table. They mimicked the same roaming movements the fish had, circling in endless waves. I followed Scott to a station toward the back and we settled onto the tall stools. I scrutinized his face as he sat poised on the stool like a kid fresh from etiquette school, and I wondered why he didn't have more friends.

Looking around the room, I noticed that all the windows were covered with grids and I assumed it was to prevent the birds from flying into them. To the far left was a large aquarium-like enclosure that stretched from the floor to the ceiling. Inside I saw a squirrel scampering amongst the branches of its confined habitat. There were six rows of desk stations, all big enough to hold two to four students. The room felt sterile, like a doctor's office, but I liked it.

Even though the overall space was bright and refreshing, it still did nothing to boost my sullen mood. After a few moments of idle chatter, the students began to settle, taking their seats in a routine manner. A door toward the front of the room swung open, the handle slamming against the wall before bouncing back.

A hush descended over the room, the students sitting up straighter in their chairs, suddenly alert. I looked to Scott for an explanation as fear and confusion began to fill my mind. He shot me a nervous look, his hands folded neatly before him.

"Professor Edgar is very strict," he hissed between clenched teeth. "You've got to remain as still as possible, as alert as you can be, or…" He cut off abruptly as the sound of heavy footfalls filled the room.

My eyes widened in alarm as a tall figure took the stage with a large hawk poised on his strong arm. What shocked me most was the professor's apparent youth. I deduced that he must not be any older than twenty, possibly even younger. His face and eyes were like ice behind his tinted glasses, his imposing body encased in a lab coat. I shook my head as a sudden fog filled my mind, and I felt a flurry of anxiety grip my chest. My heart rate quickened and I struggled to remain calm, focusing on his face. That proved to be a mistake.

The professor's youthful skin was radiant and unflawed. He had a prominent chin and thick eyebrows that framed his strong face well. The glasses he wore shielded his eyes, making it hard to tell the exact spot at which he was looking. The pitch black of his hair created a striking contrast with his pale skin. For the first time, I felt I wasn't the only one that stood out.

My heart rate remained elevated and the flutter in my chest became a sharp pang. I winced as I struggled to control the pain, my head now ripping open in agony. It felt as though something was attacking me and drawing the very life from my bones. I found myself struggling to remain calm.

Scott noticed my trembling and he eyed me with a worried look, hoping I wouldn't attract any attention to us. I shot him a tense glance. My cheeks were flushed and my breathing was becoming erratic. I was in dire need of help. My panic attacks were not a pretty sight.

"Class," the professor boomed. I wasn't sure if he had even noticed me, but I prayed he wouldn't. "The red hawk is a fierce predator."

I noticed the squirrel in the tank leap from its branch and scurry into a small house in the far corner. I understood its fear, as beads of sweat gathered on my forehead.

The professor suddenly froze, scanning the class with sharp eyes. His mouth was pursed into an angry line and his nostrils were flared. The hawk sat steady on his arm, unfazed by his carrier's abrupt mood change. As his eyes landed on each student, I saw them squirm on their stools, each praying the following words were not directed toward them.

I was stifling my heavy breaths when his eyes met mine and halted, remaining locked on me. He took a single step forward and then stopped. My whole body went weak. Placing my hands on the table to keep myself upright, the world around me seemed to slowly dissipate. I felt something inside him pulling me closer.

His eyes were burning in their intensity, paralyzing me with fear. I prayed that it would stop, begged for anything to interrupt this painful and silent attack. No matter how hard I tried, I couldn't look away from his perfect face. It felt like an eternity had passed as we stared at each other, but in reality it had only been a few seconds. His brows furrowed even deeper, the lines on his face now creasing his skin, making him seem years older. A student bravely shifted on his stool. As it scraped across the floor, the professor's stare was broken, leaving him looking bereft. I inhaled sharply and the world around me returned in a rush of warmth. I ran a hand over my face to steady my churning emotions.

"Elle," Scott whispered, his voice frantic and scared. "Are you okay?" His throat sounded dry and his voice was cracking.

"Yeah." I took a few heavy breaths, regaining what composure I could and summoning my courage.

The professor staggered to his desk, swaying a little and looking away from the curious stares to hide his faltering expression. He appeared, like me, to be having trouble regaining his composure. I watched with observance as he leaned one strong arm against the mahogany desk where the hawk still sat, steady and unfazed. After a brief moment, the professor turned back and I noticed that his eyes were now serene, devoid of the murderous black of before.

"Class," he started again, wiping a sheen of sweat from his brow, "This hawk has been injured." He motioned one shaking hand toward the hawk, clearing his throat.

I struggled to understand what had just happened as everyone else focused on the professor, somewhat confused but eager to move on. Why had we both reacted so strongly toward each other?

"Our lesson today," he continued, "will be in the preservation and health of this creature."

The professor began making his way down the aisle, his gait easy and graceful, reminiscent of another time. In fact, he exuded a certain elegance that could only be achieved after a lifetime of confidence and practice, both clearly impossible given his youthful appearance.

"He has a broken wing," he continued, his eyes focused on me as he spoke, full of emotions I couldn't name.

As he approached our table, my heart rate quickened.

"And your name is?" He finally halted in front of me.

I pressed my palms onto the table in an attempt to steady myself, to remain calm. His eyes held mine prisoner, and even behind the tinted lenses, they seemed to glow.

I stuttered nervously. "El…." My voice was hoarse and low. "Estella."

I saw his eyes react to my name, flashing a bright blue. He stood there quite still for a moment, and I noticed the students around me staring with looks ranging from pity to

45

spite, all relieved to not be where I sat.

"Estella," he repeated. A smile spread across his face and his voice was like honey as he breathed my name.

A strange part of me still felt a pull toward him, his almost floral scent wafting toward me and tickling my nose. Despite the fact that he was the most intimidating person I had ever encountered, I also felt a small amount of intrigue and admiration.

"Can you help heal this hawk?" His eyes were now a calmer grey as he looked at me, head tilted in contemplation.

I looked at him, horrified. If I even so much as touched the bird, people would immediately notice there was something different about me. I knew that my abilities to heal were not normal and far too obvious in a situation like this. The hawk stirred on his arm, its gaze piercing me in a way that unsettled me.

"I...uh..." I tried to gather my thoughts. "Wh – what should I do?" Fear filled my eyes and I felt the hairs on the back of my neck rise as the tension in the room filled me with terror.

The hawk tilted his elegant head at me as though he understood my words, mimicking his handler as his talons twitched on the sleeve of the professor's dark shirt. Without warning, the bird turned its gaze from me to the professor, as the professor also looked toward the bird. They appeared to be engaging in a silent conversation over the matter.

I blinked once and they both turned back toward me, causing my chest to begin stinging once again. I leaned back on my stool in an attempt to resist the professor's pull, to get

46

as far away from him as possible. The hawk jumped from his arm to the table and the whole class gasped. I took a few calming breaths, knowing the bird wouldn't hurt me but my heart still pounded hard in my chest.

The hawk hopped toward me, its poise never faltering despite its broken wing and assured pain. I felt the bird's discomfort sting my chest, and I winced. As he approached, I could almost hear his thoughts, filling my dark soul with a faint haze.

"Grab its wing," the professor boomed as he looked down on me, startling me. "Feel the bone so you can share your findings with the class," he demanded, a crooked smile crossing his smooth, young face.

I looked away from him as my throat grew tight, my gaze now locked on the warm, amber eyes of the hawk. Little by little, I released my grip on the table and raised my trembling hand toward the injured wing. The hawk watched me with confidence, never shying away from my advancing touch. His amber eyes glittered like coins as he looked into mine, finding calm there.

With extreme caution, I lowered my hand onto its powerful wing, stroking over the ridge of his elbow and down the length of his feathers. His warmth transferred to my hand, his heartbeat more prominent than that of the fish. The bird opened his beak, breathing deep as it relaxed its wing into full span. The students toward the front of the room rose from their chairs, anxious to get a better view. With slow movements, I again grabbed the bird's wing, bringing my other hand up to cradle its chest as I felt the bone, finally finding the protrusion halfway down its bicep. Closing my eyes in regret at the reaction my performance was surely going to evoke, I felt the bone molding beneath my touch as it healed with shocking speed. My stomach churned with anxiety. I had never been confronted like this before and I was certain that this unfortunate incident would grant me a one-way ticket back home.

I looked to the professor with distressed eyes, begging him not to expose me further. He nodded in approval, his hungry stare locked on my hand as I continued to massage the hawk's wing, now nearly healed. I jumped when the satisfied hawk clicked its tongue, ruffling the feathers on his back. He leapt away from me and repositioned his wing against his smooth brown body as though no harm had ever been inflicted.

The professor continued to stare at me, his face a solemn mask. He stood there for a brief moment while the hawk returned to its perch on his arm with its feathers puffed in happiness, both eyes glinting with a playful light.

Just as quickly as he had come, the professor spun on his heel and marched back up the aisle.

"That will be all today," he boomed with a dismissive tone as he exited with haste through the same door he had entered, not another word or explanation offered.

My breathing returned to normal and the fog in my mind cleared. It was all a blur, the way he'd looked at me, the way the hawk had known something about me.

Scott put one hand on my back to support me. "Are you alright?"

His words came as though from afar, a buzzing rang in my ears, and my eyes rolled back into my head, the room fading to dark.

EDGAR

When I woke, I noticed I was in a different room. The ceiling was lined with timbers and the place was cool and dim.

"Oh, there you are, miss!" A voice with a slight British accent coaxed me awake. "You'll be alright. Just a bit of an anxiety attack, I am afraid." The owner of the voice pressed a cold, damp towel to my head as I lay on my back, my head throbbing.

"What happened? Where am I?" I stammered, my memories of the hawk and the professor swimming in my head like an anxious dream.

"Oh, don't you fret, dear," she urged. "This happens more than I'd like in Edgar's lessons." She chuckled merrily. Her voice was high like a bell, but soft. The smell of tea lingered in the room, the air humid.

As my vision cleared, my gaze fell on Scott, who smiled and gave a little awkward wave from a stool in the corner, his face etched with relief upon seeing me back in the land of the living.

My gaze flickered to the nurse. Her chubby face was squeezed into a helpless smile. "Scott here brought you in. He was rather frantic at first, said you'd had quite the first experience with Edgar." Her sweet smile never faltered and it somehow reminded me of cupcakes and ponies.

I sat up, pulling the towel from my head and running my fingers through my hair. I glanced around the room, seeing that every shelf was filled with empty bottles of all shapes and sizes. There were no labels to indicate what they had previously held, but her strange collection left me suspended in curiosity.

"Oh," I stammered. "Yeah."

"Will you be alright then, miss?" She put a hand on my back, rubbing it in a gentle circular motion.

I gave her a look that I hoped seemed reassuring. "Thank you, Miss...?"

"Miss Dee." She supplied politely.

"Thanks, Miss Dee. I'll be fine." I swung my legs to the floor very gingerly, still feeling somewhat dizzy but willing to walk it off.

Scott hurried to my side, grabbing one arm and propping me against him. I could see the look in his eyes as I leaned into him, and I cringed at the thought of falsely leading him on. I knew there was a reason he was putting up with me: he thought I was cute.

We made our way outside into the sun and Scott turned to lead me to my cabin.

"Oh, wait!" I shook my head, coming to an abrupt halt on the path. "Scott, we should get to class." I looked at him, alarmed that I'd miss any part of my first day.

Scott gave me a sympathetic look.

"You've been out for a while. Classes are already over." He looked at me sideways, questioning my ability to walk. "I'm just going to take you to your room, maybe go get you some food."

I sighed, angry that I'd let myself be so vulnerable. It was bad enough that I was the youngest in my program, now I looked like the weakest, too. Halfway up the hill, I strategically shrugged Scott away, letting him know he didn't have to hold onto me like a child.

"So…" I looked at him as I took a few faltering steps on my own. "What's the deal with Professor Edgar?"

Scott laughed as he looked at me. "He's a creep, that's for sure." His eyebrows were raised and his voice full of contempt.

I thought about how Edgar's stare had seemed to burn straight into my soul, and how fast my heart had raced, as though I were in grave danger. It was strange that though my body reacted as it had, my mind wasn't as scared as I would have thought. It was like he'd bewitched me into a false sense of security, like a predator does with its prey.

"He's been here a while, I suppose," he continued. "But it's hard to tell just how long. I don't think people ever really notice him. He's sort of…."

"Young?" I cut in, my voice sounding somewhat sarcastic.

"Well, yeah. He is pretty young." Scott shrugged, probably doing the mental math and becoming further perplexed. "But like I said, he's a very odd character."

"He can't be any older than twenty." I tried to rationalize this fact, but came up empty-handed. I still couldn't get over his beautifully youthful face.

"I mean, I guess I'm just eighteen and here to earn my Master's degree, so maybe he became a professor at eighteen, too?" I ventured.

"Well, that's the thing. He's been here longer than that, and at any rate...." Scott paused as we reached the large evergreen outside my cabin. "I wouldn't try to dig up too much about him. You saw what happens." He looked at me as though he somehow knew I wouldn't let this go so easily.

I nodded gravely, professor Edgar's eyes still floating in my memory.

"So what was it like?" He dropped his gaze to the path. "I mean, what happened? It was so weird." He looked at me with wide eyes, his body trembling in anticipation. "Everyone is sort of curious."

I crinkled my nose as I thought.

"Well...." I tried to fish through my memory but the more I tried to remember, the more I seemed to forget exactly what had transpired. "I guess I'm not sure."

I wanted to keep it all under wraps, at least until I could understand it myself. "I suppose it was an anxiety attack, like Miss Dee said." I paused to come up with a more believable excuse. "I mean, it's not like I'm the most socially outgoing of the bunch. It doesn't surprise me that I fainted."

Scott shot me a bemused expression, but thankfully seemed to buy my theory. He shrugged.

"Well," he said, giving me an awkward pat on the shoulder. "You go lie down. I'll go get you some food."

I nodded and he took off down the hill. I turned and made my way to the porch, taking my boots off and leaving them outside. Entering my cabin, I noticed nothing had changed; the fact that there were no locks on the doors sort of irked me. Exhausted, I went to my bed and snuggled under the covers, pulling them up to my chin and hiding myself away from the world.

My eyes were heavy and the throbbing in my head was excruciating. I closed my eyes to the pain and before I knew it, I was fast asleep and I immediately began to dream.

I was in Edgar's classroom, but it was dim and somewhat hazy. Confused by my surroundings, I looked around for someone to talk to, but there were no students. I was alone in the empty classroom, my brow beaded in a cold sweat.

A feeling of calm engulfed my empty heart, and I took a few deep breaths. As I exhaled one last breath, something pitch black caught my eye as it hopped between the stark white counters. I jerked back, lowering my gaze to floor, my heart hammering in my chest.

I rose from the stool and crouched to the ground, assuming a defensive pose, though curious to see what it was. As I made my way between the rows, carefully scanning each aisle, my heart pounded harder as I got closer to whatever was there. When I rounded the corner toward the front, a shrill "caw!" caught me off guard and my eyes flew to the table at the far right of the room; my body falling hard onto the floor, going rigid with horror.

There, standing above me on the counter was a large black raven, its eyes glowing brightly despite the dimness in the room. It stared at me for a long time, its sleek body like stone. I winced as my chest began to sting and I clutched it in agony, no longer trying to hide the pain. The menacing black raven spread its wings and let out another shrill "caw!" as it lunged from the table straight toward my face. As fast as I could manage through the pain, I struggled to shelter my eyes, trying to scream.

Still screaming, I woke as Scott ran in the door, dropping a plate of food to the ground and rushing to my side.

"Elle?" His frantic breath fell across my face, his hands shaking my shoulders, willing me to calm down. "Elle, you're all right." His eyes were wide with concern as I finally looked into them.

I was breathing as though I had just run a marathon, sweat coating my brow and my throat painfully dry.

"Elle, it's okay. You're fine. I think you were just dreaming." He stared at me for a moment as my breathing slowed, my blankets tangled around me from my vicious thrashing.

"Sorry," I muttered. "It was just a nightmare." The raven's eyes were still seared in my memory, glowing with power.

"I think you bumped your head pretty hard when you

fell from that stool." Scott knelt to the floor to pick up the plate and salvage what food he could before bringing it to me.

"Here you go." He placed it on my lap. "Sorry about that."

I sat up against the headboard and tried to smile, looking at his feeble grin as he eyed me carefully.

"Do you want me to stay with you?" he asked. His voice was full of hope and I saw the eagerness in his eyes.

Guilt washed over me, I didn't like him like that, not even a little. If anything, I pitied him for wanting to be my friend and how depressing that must be for him.

"No." I chewed on a piece of dry tofu. "I'll be fine. You don't have to take care of me."

"Are you sure?" I could see he was disappointed. "I wouldn't mind." I thought about his mother and how much he'd probably missed having her around to dote upon.

I forced another empty smile.

"Yeah I'm sure. I'll be fine." I wasn't scared by my dream; if anything, just further perplexed and intrigued.

"Okay, well I guess I should go. We have rock club tonight. I'd invite you but, considering your condition, I think it's better if you rest. I'll fill you in later." He looked satisfied enough with the task, and I nodded in compliance. He stood and walked back through the open door, closing it behind him with a gentle click.

As I picked at the ruined dinner, I thought about the raven in the dream. It didn't make sense for him to attack me. Animals never attacked me, even the most dangerous. Something about it was frightening, but also familiar.

Professor Edgar's face still stood out in my memories as well: the fair complexion and beautiful eyes that had enchanted me. He was so dark and so utterly mysterious, and then there was the question of his unjustifiable youth. It didn't make sense that he should be so young. Besides his unearthly appearance, there was also something about him that drew me in and beckoned at my heart; a feeling I did not recognize.

I put the plate on the bedside table as I stood and walked to the window. It was dusk and soon the stars would return. I looked toward the bird lab, filled with curiosity, but to my disappointment, everything was dark.

I placed my hand on the handle of the door, my sweaty palms welcoming the cool touch as I twisted it open and stepped out on the porch. My nerves jangled as I glanced around and into the darkness before finally sitting on the railing. I sighed, looking to the navy sky and picking out the few first stars. Despite my fears, I was secretly thrilled by today's events; it was finally something worth feeling, something worth discovering.

My gaze was drawn back to the dark lab like a magnet. I furrowed my brow in frustration at the mix of emotions swimming in my mind: fear, calm, and confusion. I put my hand to my chest as I tried to feel for my soul, but still, there was nothing. The only thing that I could deduce was that my soul had been taken from me somehow. I knew it sounded absurd, but I knew what I felt, and that was nothing.

The unfolding events of the day were drama enough, and I was certain that at least the hawk was grateful for my presence here. The animals, they knew what I felt, and to feel them was like spying in on a real life. It was worth staying, the thought of returning home making my stomach ache.

I puzzled over what Professor Edgar had thought of the phenomenon. He had almost seemed to orchestrate the situation, but then he had left the room so fast, as though the task he had forced me to do had enraged him somehow, that I couldn't be sure. The air of danger that emanated from Edgar seemed to pierce into the soul of every student, including me. Yet my feelings were much more than just fear. I attributed the reason for my sudden sense of calm to my lack of a human soul, something I so genuinely longed for. Perhaps my attitude of having nothing to lose appealed to the professor. I felt nothing but sadness as it was. There was barely anything left that he could damage, nothing he could hurt.

Night finally set in and I moved back into the cabin to lie down. A rush of suppressed fear washed over me as I wondered if the raven would again visit my dreams. A part of me wished it would, longed to know what it would do. It was just a dream after all, and though it was terrifying, I was curious to get closer and peer deeper into those beautiful eyes once again.

A GIFT

In the morning, I awoke to the deafening sound of sparrows and robins in the trees outside the cabin. I glanced at my alarm clock, determining I had more time today than yesterday to get ready before Scott would inevitably come knocking. I flopped back on my pillow in annoyance. To my disappointment, my dreams had remained blank all night and the raven had not returned.

I crawled out of bed and grabbed the same jeans I'd worn the day before, wrinkled but otherwise clean. Digging deep in a nearby bag, I also grabbed a dark blue long-sleeved tee, which thankfully, was fresh and clean. I knew eventually I would need to do some laundry.

Walking to the bathroom, I slid the pocket door shut behind me and snapped the small lock out of habit. I grabbed some soap from the holder in the shower and briskly washed my face, slightly spooked that when I opened my eyes, a raven would be standing there. After I washed my face, I absently brushed my hair, thinking about Edgar's powerful physique and amazing strength. He was like a Greek god and a far cry from all the boys I'd seen back in high school. I couldn't help but acknowledge the fact that he was exceptionally attractive.

Staring in the mirror, I became lost in my clear blue eyes. I forgot the professor and instead began wondering what essential part of me was missing that kept me from fitting in and finding happiness. I had seen the life in Scott's eyes, the depth of emotion, whereas mine were completely stripped of that spark, reflecting utter emptiness. I finally pulled my gaze away, sighing in frustration.

I walked back into the main space and approached the window, sunlight brightening the room. The purple flower on the sill had begun to bloom and spread. I gently touched one leaf and it opened toward me. I sighed at the simple bond I had with nature, wishing it were so easy with humans.

As I glanced up from the plant and out the window, I saw Scott making his way up the hill toward my cabin. Rolling my eyes, I opened my door and gave him a wave, figuring I'd meet him half way. I knelt down for my boots, jumping back in horror as I saw what lay beside them. Discarded near the heel of one boot, was a single black feather. The feather was coaxed by the breeze as it fluttered slightly. After a moment's hesitation, I bent down and picked up the quill with a shaking hand. I brought it to my face so that I could examine it.

"What's that?" Scott huffed as he approached me.

I continued my inspection of the feather, at first unfazed by his interruption. After a moment, I spoke.

"It's a feather," I said incredulously, my mind awash with recognition. I twirled it in my fingers, marveling at its opalescent glow. Scott snatched it from my hand.

"A crow feather," he pronounced, after inspecting it briefly.

I slowly knelt down and grabbed my boots, my eyes still wide as I pulled them on.

"I think it's a raven feather, actually," I corrected him absently. Scott gave me a confounded look.

"Raven, crow. What's the difference?"

I discreetly rolled my eyes, snapping out of my trance, unwilling to correct his inaccurate statement a second time.

"Sure, maybe you're right," I agreed half-heartedly.

Scott handed the feather back to me and I ran inside to place it on my bed stand. It was breathtakingly beautiful, and the way it sat on the table made it seem like it was unearthly. I heard Scott whistle with impatience outside so I quickly grabbed the framed note from my mother and touched my hands to the words.

"I love you mother," I whispered before placing it back on the stand next to the feather.

I grabbed my bag and rushed out the door. Scott stood tapping his foot with his hands in his pockets.

"Sorry," I breathed as I reached his side. "I know we're late."

His sweet smile and careless shrug suggested he didn't mind, but I knew he was just being polite.

61

As we hurried down the hill in silence, I considered the appearance of the feather and how it could be linked to the nightmare from yesterday. It had all seemed surreal in the light of a new day, and as we approached the cafeteria, I was anxious to get to the bird lab. There was so much I needed to find out.

Today, Scott piled his plate high with what appeared to be country hash browns and tofu gravy. Looking at his massive portion made my stomach lurch, so I quickly glanced away. I again opted for a bran muffin, figuring it would be the easiest on my stomach. At this rate, I would be losing weight rather than gaining the infamous freshman fifteen.

As we sat at the same table from yesterday, I watched Scott shovel spoonful after spoonful of the unappealing fare into his mouth. I urged myself to eat, despite the unsettled feeling in my stomach.

"So," Scott looked up at me as he at last began to get full. "You think you'll make it through all your classes today?"

I shrugged. "I hope so." I took a moment to swallow my last bite of muffin. "Depends on what Professor Edgar has me do today, I suppose."

Scott chuckled. Thankfully he didn't spit any food in the process. "You've got to figure the worst is over. He never picks on the same person twice."

I looked at him sideways.

"Is it normal for people to react the way I did? For him to react the way he had?" I was searching to see if it had just been me or if I was imagining that there was some connection.

Scott snorted under his breath and raised his

eyebrows.

"I don't know. That sure was weird, but seeing as he's weird all around, I wouldn't really worry about it." He waved his hand to indicate I should just brush it off, but I couldn't.

I was eager to get through hatchery class, anxious to see those eyes again. We took our plates to the cleaning tubs and left the cafeteria a little early, our pace brisk. We arrived at the hatchery, and again, the room was empty. Scott shuffled to the tanks and peered in. I hung back, fearing that if there was a repeat of yesterday, eventually Scott would notice something about me really was strange.

"Hey, look!" Scott pointed to the same tank as yesterday, the one where I had made the mistake of interacting with the fish. "This tank has one fish that's much bigger than the rest." His voice was shrill with excitement.

My body tensed, knowing it was the fish I'd helped yesterday. He had grown overnight, as I'd feared he might.

"He must have jumped from one of the adjoining tanks," he said in bewilderment, trying to rationalize the occurrence. Scott's theory was deeply flawed considering both adjacent tanks were filled with smaller fish, but I wasn't about to point that out.

I nodded, "Hmm... Must be."

He looked at me with a proud grin, as though he had accomplished some grand feat.

To my relief, the rest of the class began trickling in, and I again sunk to the back of the room, as far away from the tanks as possible. The professor showed the class several vials containing different breeds of fertilized fish eggs. From far away they looked like miniscule dots and I didn't really see the point, so I tuned the lesson out.

I glanced out the high, narrow windows of the hatchery toward the glacial peak across the lake. Since I had spent most of my life in Seattle, I still hadn't really seen snow, at least, not in the way I would hope. The slushy mess in the city was more of a wet inconvenience rather than a beautiful occurrence. My eyes scanned the ominous clouds, hoping they might produce some of the fluffy white stuff for me to enjoy. For a while, I let the tranquility of the scene sweep over me, letting the world around me fall away. I closed my eyes, imagining the feeling of being up on that peak, imagining what it was like to be the cloud, floating above the world. When I opened my eyes a few minutes later, I fell back to my sad reality. There was no soaring in the clouds in my near future. I shook my head at my silly daydreaming, forcing myself to pay attention to the lesson.

The students were now passing the vials around the room. I watched with fear as they made their way toward me. I jammed my hands deep into the pockets of my jeans as Scott thrust one vial toward me. I pursed my lips in my best imitation of disgust and shook my head vehemently. Scott shrugged and passed them back forward. I wasn't about to touch the eggs, dead or alive. The outcome would prove difficult to conceal or explain.

After the vials were returned to the front, the professor dumped each into a separate tank that sat on her desk. My guess, since I hadn't been listening, was so that we could watch the hatching process throughout the week. I took a deep breath before exhaling, realizing I had narrowly escaped this one.

The class was dismissed and the room broke out into the low hum of quiet conversation. One group of students gathered in the corner where it was no secret whom they were talking about as their eyes shot back and forth between Scott and me, their voices reverberating in hushed tones against the walls. I swallowed hard, uncomfortable with their scrutiny. I hurried toward the exit, Scott at my heels. He took no notice of them as we made our way to the door, though my eyes were fixed on their cold expressions.

A sudden snort of laughter erupted from Scott, causing me to break the gaze to look askance at him.

"Well, off to see Professor Doom now," he said, by way of explanation.

I gave him an annoyed punch on the arm, making him laugh and jump away from me. The tense moment had passed, and I suspected that had been Scott's intention. I was grateful for his thoughtfulness. He was proving to be a great friend.

As we walked to the lab down the gravel path, I let the crunching sound of our footfalls calm the erratic beating of my heart. I couldn't tell if I was scared or just anxious, but there was a feeling inside me that I had never really felt before. As Scott opened the large door to the lab, my eyes fell on the familiar scene from my dream, and the feeling intensified. What was it?

We took our same stools in the back row and I sat there anxiously tapping my fingers on the table, scowling at the scuffed surface of the Formica counter, letting my hair fall forward to conceal my expression. I felt Scott's eyes on me and I knew he was worried. He gave me a characteristically awkward pat on the back, and I squeezed my eyes shut, wishing he'd just leave me alone.

Like yesterday, the door to the front again flew open and the room fell immediately silent. Professor Edgar entered the room, a small owl perched on his shoulder, but this time, my chest didn't sting, and I was surprised. Though nothing hurt like before, the unidentifiable feeling I had experienced earlier grew in intensity. I watched the professor intently as he strode with confidence to the front.

The grey eyes behind his tinted lenses no longer possessed the same intensity they had before, and there was something that felt different about him, more guarded. His porcelain face and dark hair were perfect, and I once again marveled at his ethereal beauty.

"Alright, class," he boomed, scanning each student, but this time avoiding my gaze. "This is a Northern Spotted Owl," he continued, lifting the small bird in the air for everyone to see. The bird blinked slowly, confident and comfortable in Edgar's grasp.

There was no sign of the same heated intensity from yesterday but I could still feel the pull toward him, along with the new, unrecognizable emotion. I sat on the edge of my stool, my eyes fixed on his countenance, mentally urging him to look at me.

"He is from the Strigidae family and classified as vulnerable under our conservation status." The owl turned its head as though it were unattached to its body, his yellow

66

eyes flashing and its beak barely peeking below its feathers.

"Because they live in old growth forests, we must learn to care for them respectively." He paced with long strides at the front of the room as he spoke.

I was frustrated by his sudden change of attitude toward me. He was pointedly ignoring me, and I hated it. I squirmed on my stool with the intention of gaining his attention.

Scott whispered from the corner of his mouth. "You okay, Elle?"

I nodded quickly, irritated that I managed to attract his attention, but not Edgar's. Scott eyed me nervously for a moment longer before turning his concentration back to the lecture. I noticed Edgar's face held a trace of a smile but he still did not look at me.

Time passed as professor Edgar droned on about the owl and I eventually gave up my attempts, settling back on my stool. My initial excitement about the professor, and also the condition of the hawk, subsided. I began to wonder if yesterday had really happened, or if I had just imagined it. If he knew anything, Edgar wasn't going to reveal it to the class, but still, his eyes mesmerized me and the strange pull toward him remained.

"And that will be all," he finally boomed.

I snapped out of my transfixed state in time to see Edgar heading for the door. He strode elegantly out of the room with a speed that surprised me. I sat there dazed for a moment as my chest relaxed and the pull I felt toward him began to subside. Scott rose from his stool eyeing me carefully, poised to catch me should I faint yet again.

"You okay there, Elle?" he stammered, probably not sure if he could handle another trip to the nurse.

The hint of concern in his voice only irritated me further. Why hadn't Edgar approached me? Why hadn't he questioned me about what had happened the previous day? I released the tight grip I had on the table. I grabbed my bag, storming past Scott and pushing through the doors.

Scott followed me timidly, unsure why I was suddenly so angry.

I took a deep breath.

"What is that guy's problem!" I demanded angrily, my voice ringing across the courtyard. I regretted my outburst when some students turned to stare at me with curiosity.

Scott looked at me with a startled expression, and for a moment, I felt guilty for snapping at him. His eyes were wide and his lips were set in a grim line as he shrugged, finding himself at a loss for words.

"I'm sorry, Scott." I let down my guard and walked back toward him, giving him a reassuring pat on the arm. "I didn't mean to snap at you, it's just…." I quickly thought of what to use as an excuse. "It's just that he didn't even apologize to me for what he did."

A look of relieved understanding crossed his face.

"Yeah," he paused as his demeanor now changed back to his usual bubbly self. "He's just a weird guy."

I faked a laugh, figuring it would help to put the whole incident behind us. We began making our way to the greenhouses and what I would hope to be my favorite class. I needed something to calm me, something to distract me from

68

my obsession with Edgar.

The greenhouses were past the cafeteria, down a long outdoor hallway created by the eaves of the adjacent buildings. As we entered onto the trail that passed through a large field, the tall grasses bowed toward me as though drawn by an unseen force. Scott looked around him curiously, but the bending grass was so slight, he couldn't be sure of exactly what he was seeing.

"So, how was this class yesterday?" I asked, making a concerted effort to distract him.

He dragged his gaze away from the grasses.

"Good. We, uh…" He was still looking around uneasily. "Well, I mean, after I took you to the infirmary, we planted some sunflower seeds and learned about edible plants."

My eyebrows rose, feigning interest. "Edible plants, huh?"

"Yeah." His voice sounded far off and dazed.

I cleared my throat in an attempt to break his trance. He jumped and turned to look at me.

"So, if we're ever out hiking or get lost, we know what we can and can't eat," he continued, more confidently.

To my relief, he had lost interest in the grass phenomenon, and I mentally applauded myself for successfully distracting him. The wind blew across the field, filling my ears with a rustling sound.

"Well, that's always a useful tool isn't it? Knowing what won't poison us?" I ventured.

He nodded gravely, now completely distracted. As we finally reached the door to the green house, I had the notion that if he thought the grasses were odd, he should wait until he saw what would happen inside. I only hoped they had wide enough aisles so I could distance myself from the plants enough so as not to create a scene.

Scott grabbed the handle and held the door open for me to enter. To my relief, my wish had been granted: spacious and wide aisles ran the whole length of the room. Everything was cast in a warm green tone from the glass, and the humid air of the greenhouse was welcoming. Any environment where plants could thrive always made me feel exceedingly more comfortable, and soon, as my tension eased, the effect I had on the plants started to become obvious.

"So, here we are…" Scott's voice trailed off. He stared at me in amazement as I stood beside a long bench of planted lilies.

Each lily slowly turned its petals toward me, so slowly that it was hardly discernable, but clearly Scott had noticed.

He tilted his head, blinking as though trying to wash the image away. "How did you…." He stammered.

I met his gaze head-on, keeping my expression neutral. I backed away from the table, bumping into one behind me instead. I jumped, turning to see that the plants there were also beginning to react. Skipping away and closer to Scott, however, I managed to narrowly escape a full infection of my talents. The plants slowly resumed their natural pose.

"How did I what?" I questioned with feigned innocence, figuring like always, it was easier to convince people they'd just imagined it than to admit that there was something awry.

"Never mind," Scott said, shaking his head in disbelief,

internally fighting with what he had, or rather, hadn't seen.

The rest of the class filled the room, bringing a welcome distraction and I was filled with an acute sense of relief. Amongst all the students, it would be easier to keep my secret. I stood perfectly still, breathing as shallowly as possible.

The rest of the day Scott eyed me perplexedly. I kept up a constant stream of chatter that was meant to keep his mind off what he had witnessed. My ploy seemed to work well enough, so that when he eventually thought of the incident, he probably wasn't very sure about what he had seen. After our last class, he walked me toward my cabin, but his new found silence was a worrisome addition and I began to fear that he was shying away from our friendship.

"So..." his brow was furrowed, as it had been all day. "You want to go get dinner or something?" He didn't sound very enthused by the idea.

I shot him a sour look. I might have finally managed to scare Scott away, even though I didn't want to anymore. Sighing, I tried to shrug off my disappointment. I desperately wanted to rush back to my room to examine the raven feather more closely anyway, so I came up with an excuse not to join him.

"No..." I pushed my hands in my pockets. "I'm still tired from yesterday. I may just go lie down."

Scott's gaze was fixed on the ground.

"Oh..." I could tell he was still mildly perplexed but didn't want to hurt my feelings. "Yeah, that's totally cool."

We stopped on the path and he finally looked at me.

71

"Well, guess I'll catch you tomorrow?" He gave me a crooked smile and I felt a surge of hope. Maybe we would still be friends after all.

"Sounds good." I smiled up at him shyly. "Just come get me in the morning." He was a resilient friend.

He turned toward the cafeteria with a wave.

"Bye!" I waved back but he didn't see me, so I turned toward the cabin, picking up my pace in sudden excitement as I thought of the feather.

A PLACE LIKE HOME

I rushed through the door, slamming it hard behind me in my haste to get to the bedside table. I regarded the feather with eager eyes as I raced across the room, discarding my bag on the floor in my wake. Sitting on the edge of the mattress, I leaned over to switch on the lamp. As the light came to life, it caused the feather to glimmer like brilliant steel. I reached cautiously for it, not wanting to harm the plume yet longing to hold it once again.

I spun the feather under the lamp, examining its color and texture. Never before had I seen something so radiant, so mysterious.

"Ouch!" I yelped, looking at my finger in dismay. The quill had sliced through my skin as a deep red bead of blood now seeped from my finger tip. I watched the blood as it gathered and ran down my pale finger, not bothering to wipe it away. I then examined the bloodied end of the feather, noting that it was sharp as a razor. With greater caution, I held it like a pen and scraped it along the wood table. A bloodied sliver of maple curled up toward me in its wake. The feather was not only sharp, but also extremely strong. I gasped in disbelief, finally bringing my cut finger to my mouth and sucking the blood from the now clotting wound. This was no ordinary feather, I finally deduced: it was armor.

Once my finger stopped bleeding, I brushed the tip over the vane of the feather, careful to avoid the sharp edge. As I tried to flatten the black barbs into the center, they instantly sprayed back out into a perfect fan. I held it close to my face to examine the weave and found it completely unaltered, as though it had never even been touched. No matter how much pressure I applied, I couldn't hurt it or unravel its secrets.

I lay back on my bed, questioning if the quill really could have come from the raven in my dream. A wave of anxiety washed over me so I placed the feather back on the table. I shut my eyes as I lay back once more, going over the possibilities in my head.

Suddenly needing to get out of the cabin to clear my head, I leapt up and grabbed a coat from my bag that still sat unpacked on the floor. Slipping my arms through the sleeves, I headed back outside. It was late afternoon and though the temperature had dropped somewhat, I longed for some sort of release and exercise. Looking around, I noticed there was a path that advanced further up the hill and into the woods, so I took off at a brisk pace past my cabin.

Before long, I came across a small bench and decided to take a moment to rest after the steep uphill hike. The air was cool and the sun streamed through the branches in misty bands. The forest was alive with vivid colors and I felt at peace here among nature. As I sat there looking around, I was suddenly filled with the uneasy sense that I was being watched. There was no one there but me and I shook my head, blaming my overactive imagination. Nonetheless, I rose to my feet and took off further down the path, leaving that spot behind.

My gaze was fixed toward the sky and the massive canopy above me as I tramped along past droves of berries and moss, my feet sinking into the saturated ground. I slowed my pace as ground beneath me gave even further, making it hard to find a good footing. I struggled along for what seemed an hour. Finally, the trees began to thin ahead. I squinted toward the light, and as I approached, the forest opened up to a large, pristine field of grass and flowers. I gingerly stepped into the clearing. The sun beamed down on me, warming my face. Pulling my hands from my pockets, I held them out to my sides, allowing my fingers to trail through the tall grass as it leaned toward me. In my wake, the grasses bloomed from my touch, leaving a trail of small white flowers and a burst of fragrance that tickled my nose.

I made my way to the center of the field where I found a spot of grasses that seemed suitable to rest in. Easing my tired body to the ground, the earth cradled me like a bed, the roots gradually growing into a sort of frame beneath my weight. Looking toward the blue sky, scattered with puffs of clouds, I eventually closed my eyes and cleared my mind of all thoughts until there was nothing but the sounds of nature. A gentle breeze blew over me and I could feel the way my peculiar abilities had delightfully aggravated the plants in my radius.

I opened my eyes one at a time, seeing that a perfect circle of blooming wildflowers now surrounded the spot where I lay. The sun made me warm so I shrugged out of my jacket. Bugs began to flock toward the fragrant scent of the flowers and a few landed on my pale skin. Before I knew it, no less than five ladybugs were crawling on me, their red wings deepening in color as they drew in my cocktail of life and energy.

In the far distance, I heard the song of a bird. A strange calm fell over me and all I could hear was my shallow breathing and the breeze blowing through the grasses. I concentrated on the subtle sounds, finding them somehow familiar despite the fact I had never experienced this type of peace before. My arms were sprawled to each side of my body and my fingers were spread as the grasses intertwined them like rings.

As I rested there, the sounds of the forest abruptly ceased, an eerie silence descending upon the field. For a moment, I didn't move. My breathing quickened and the tight feeling in my chest returned. I twisted my head to look around me. I saw nothing, yet something made me sit up straight as an arrow.

The sound of my ragged breathing echoed through my head. I looked around fearfully and my eyes instantly shot to a dark object now straight in front of me. There, at the edge of the flowers, sat a large black raven. Terror struck my heart as I stared, motionless, contemplating my next move. Clutching my chest in pain, we locked gazes.

The raven's stare did not falter. His gaze was questioning, piercing my head as he searched my thoughts for answers. Its eyes and feathers were not like the one in my dream. They were dull and flat, like you would expect from a regular raven. Something about the bird seemed far more sinister as it stood there, very still, its head turned to the side with his mouth open, breathing through its beak.

Anxiety filled my limbs as I tried hard to push through the fog in my head. Without warning, the raven made an abrupt hop closer to my shielding flowers and let out a shrill "caw!" as though angry I had tried to block his invasion into my head. I jumped, feeling the adrenaline pulsing painfully through my body. From behind me came another piercing "caw!" and I snapped my head around at the same time as the raven released his stare to look to the sky. The terror in me grew stronger at the sight of another raven diving down at me, talons curled and eyes blazing a deep blue-grey, just like the raven of my nightmare.

As fast as my limbs could manage, I summoned them to move, staggering to a standing position before breaking into a panicked run. The large raven flew down over my head, and I ducked, feeling the wind from its wings as it fluttered through my hair before it dove violently down onto the other raven. I stumbled in shock, falling onto my arm and feeling my skin rip.

As I struggled to get back up, my eyes shot to where

the two ravens were now fighting, horrifying screams coming from both. The raven that had seemingly come to my rescue glittered like a black pearl in the sun, and I gasped as I saw the fury in his glowing eyes. As the glowing raven struck with fierce blows at the matte raven, my chest began to seize with so much pain I could barely remain conscious. I averted my gaze as the agony buckled me back onto the ground, hampered in my attempt to get away.

I squeezed my eyes shut as everything around me began to fade to fog and darkness. I crawled along the ground blindly, half dragging myself. In the far distance, the sharp screams of the ravens ceased abruptly, and for a moment the silence of the field returned.

I breathed hard as I struggled to see through the blackness. Without warning, I heard footsteps approach where I lay, unmoving. Strong arms lifted me from the ground, cradling me with surprising gentleness. There was nothing I could do to get away, even if I wanted to, so I didn't bother to try. Something in my chest tried to surface beneath the clenching pain, but I couldn't discern the feeling. I did my best to see who had grabbed me, but there was only darkness clouding my vision. I groaned in pain, sensing that we were now moving swiftly away from the flowering field, the sound of breaking branches and ferns brushing past us, marking our progress.

I heard the familiar crunching of the gravel path sooner than I'd expected. I had been fading in and out of consciousness, but now I recognized that we were back at the college. The footsteps were slower now, calmer than they had been. The clouds in my mind began to dissipate. I heard a door opening and felt my body being placed on a soft bed. As I was released, I heard a curious scratching sound. A gentle wind blew over my face and I struggled harder then ever to see. Forcing my eyes to open, I caught nothing more than a dark flashing silhouette of something I couldn't recognize. A familiar voice came from another room then.

"Oh, Miss!" I saw the nurse bustling toward me. "What happened?"

I moaned in pain. The burning in my arm increased as a warm, thick substance oozed from it. As the fog lifted from me, I became aware of various aches and pains.

"Miss, who brought you here?" Miss Dee asked, as she gently gripped my arm.

I attempted to get up, but she eased me back down on the bed. Memories whirled through my head as I worked to put the events that had led me here together. The ravens, I thought, and those eyes. There was no reply to give her, no hint of who saved me, so I remained silent.

"Just rest, then," she said, realizing I was in no condition to answer her. She put a cold towel to my head, and she began to hum.

Through my pain and exhaustion, I noticed it was dark outside. I struggled to put the events of the past few hours together. Why had the matte raven tried to read my thoughts? It had tried to take something from me, something I hadn't even known I had. I searched my mind, but I kept coming up empty, remaining as baffled as when it had happened.

I winced as the nurse poked me with a needle and

the stinging subsided to a numbing relief. I listened as she continued to hum, the song soothing my mind and encouraging my body to relax. I heard the plinking and felt a gentle tug at my skin as she stitched a large gash close to my elbow.

"There you are now." I heard her snip the string.

I turned my head, opening my eyes to look at her. She had a small smile on her plump face. The single light in the room was aimed on my blood stained arm as she pressed a warm rag to the wound. After she washed it, she reached for some gauze and wrapped it snuggly around my arm, the pressure relieving some of the deep, aching pain.

She patted me on the shoulder and pulled a blanket over me. "Sleep," she whispered in my ear.

I closed my eyes as she flicked off the lamp, and I heard her walk quietly from the room, closing the door behind her.

As I lay there falling asleep, I thought of my mother. She had lied to me when she told me I was safe, lied that I'd find my soul and happiness. There was something she had known, something I longed to remember about her. I squeezed my eyes shut as the same depressing numbness of old filled my heart, and I tried harder than ever to cry.

SPY

I woke the next morning to the sharp feeling of pain as I opened my eyes to find the nurse re-wrapping my arm. She was humming again, but this time the stinging was too great for it to calm me.

"Well, now," Miss Dee said when she saw that I was alert. "Are you able to remember how this happened?"

I glanced at my exposed stitches, my arm bruised a deep purple that stood out starkly against the rest of my milky skin. The gash was about six inches long, and from the look of it, very deep.

I worked to form the words. "My…" I paused, clearing my throat. "I fell."

She blinked at me in a way that suggested she didn't quite believe me, but would accept my lame excuse.

"I fell out in the woods while I was hiking." I tried my best to lie, my voice full of persuasion.

She smiled at me. "We all do." She let out a small sigh as she looked at me with pity as she tightened a new bandage around my arm. A silhouette filled the door. Scott entered, a dorky smile plastered on his face. My heart sank and I realized a strange part of me hoped to see Edgar. I had to stop myself from thinking of him so often!

"I guess I've really got to keep my eye on you," he joked, his hands clasped at his waist.

The nurse watched his nervous and caring manner toward me, and she smiled in delight to herself.

I gave him a blank stare, mortified that she'd assume he was my boyfriend.

"Yeah, I guess so."

"You up for going to class?" he asked eagerly.

I was quick to sit up, a surge of excitement filling my limbs at the thought of seeing Edgar again.

"Definitely." I looked to the nurse for permission, "I feel fine."

She gave me a solemn look.

"Are you sure, miss?" She then looked at Scott and another smile crossed her face.

Rolling my eyes, I nodded. My arm stung when I moved but I was determined to go. Miss Dee helped me up as I worked hard to stifle a wince. Scott handed me my bag, which he must have retrieved from my cabin before he came to fetch me. I grabbed it with my good arm, sliding it up to my shoulder.

"There's a muffin in there for you, too, since you missed breakfast." The sheepish look on his face made me smile despite the face that I was getting really sick of muffins.

I gave him a brief nod as I walked toward the door on weak legs.

"Thanks, Scott." I took a deep breath as we exited, willing my body to work like normal.

We took our time getting to the hatchery, though I noticed we were very late. As we entered, everyone stared at my arm with intense curiosity. The last thing I needed was more attention and more reasons for them to start rumors. The professor stood silently as we walked to the back of class and stood.

"Glad you could make it." She gave me a warm and encouraging smile, and I figured she must have heard I'd been injured. It was a small school, after all.

She continued her lecture. After a moment, Scott turned to me.

"So what did you do this time?" His voice was laced with humor.

I kept my gaze forward, to hide the lies.

"I fell while I was taking a short hike."

He let out a quiet snort. "So then who brought you in?" His expression became doubtful.

I stood still, breathing for a moment, struggling to remember who it was.

"I'm not really sure." I crinkled my brow in irritation.

"Strange." I could feel his stare boring into me.

I looked at him, a cheerful smile pasted on my face,

"I'm sure it was just another hiker."

He nodded in agreement, willing to accept the explanation.

"Yeah, you're probably right. Too bad they didn't stick around." He shrugged.

"Yeah." I thought about the obscure figure as it had left the infirmary. I didn't want to believe the raven had taken me down the hill. So who had it been? Had Edgar been there? And if so, why had he saved me when he didn't even seem to like me. I was anxious to get to his class, motivated to find out the truth.

The professor pointed to the other tank of fish eggs as we gathered around. Two had hatched and were huddled into the rocks at the bottom while the other eggs still sat idle. Scott looked enthralled.

The professor motioned us to the tanks, but I hung back.

"So. Do you think Professor Edgar is hiding something?" I asked, curious to get Scott's take as I leaned toward him.

"I'm not sure," he hissed. There was a strange hostility now lacing his voice, and I realized he was probably angry because he was thinking my obsession with the professor meant I liked him, which was absurd. Or was it?

I leaned back, realizing Scott was in no mood for chitchat. Finally, the professor excused us, so I grabbed Scott's arm and dragged him outside before he could ask the professor a million stupid questions and make us late.

"Ouch! Gosh!" He looked at me confused, his face still a little angry.

"Oh, just hurry," I hissed back.

A sly smile spread across his face, mixed with a subtle hint of disappointment. "You like Professor Edgar, don't you?"

I snorted. "Yeah, right." I gave him a menacing glare, my blue eyes blazing at him with anger. "He's just..." I paused, trying to think of the right word. "Interesting," I ended lamely.

Scott rolled his eyes at me as I dragged him by the arm down the path.

"Sure. Whatever." I saw a wounded glimmer in his eyes, but he forced himself to hide it. I felt somewhat guilty, but at the same time, I had too much to worry about already.

"I just don't know, Elle," he paused, the concern in his voice irritating me. "He seems dangerous somehow. Just weird."

We blazed into the lab and I practically threw him down in his stool.

"Just watch him. Tell me what you think he's got on his mind," I snapped.

He blinked at me, nodding in obedience. We were early, I knew, but I was anxious. The rest of the class trickled in as my nerves mounted. My injured arm pulsed in pain from the rush of blood through my veins. I kept my eyes locked on the door where he usually entered, thinking that at any moment he could burst in.

Everyone had arrived, each still eyeing me with interest and mild distaste. I had never had so many people stare at me with such regularity. I was really making a spectacle of myself in a short amount of time. In the city, there was always someone that looked more like a freak than me. Out here, though, my uniqueness, shall we say, stood out like a sore thumb.

The door finally swung open and Professor Edgar entered the room. My heart nearly stopped when I noticed the vicious scratches on his neck and hands. He wore the collar of his lab coat turned up in an attempt to conceal the wounds, but I saw them because, deep down, I knew they would be there. I knew exactly where they came from and it finally all began to make sense. He was the person that carried me from the field, and he was somehow involved in the fight between the ravens. He scanned the class, his gaze behind the glasses a calm and familiar blue-grey.

My eyes widened when his gaze suddenly met mine, taking me by surprise. In the split second he allowed it to linger, Edgar's expression told me two things. The first was that he was concerned about me. The second was a silent plea to remain calm, as though something horrid was about to happen.

Satisfied that I would finally get some answers, I took a deep breath and then slowly released it. I caught Scott glancing at me from the corner of my eye. I brought my hands to my face and tucked my hair behind my ears in a casual manner. My movement drew Edgar's gaze to my arm as he knelt to lift a large wooden box to the table in front of him.

"Today, we will discuss the environmental impact humans have on the country, how this is causing non-native species to flock to the area, and how this changes our ecosystem." His eyebrows were furrowed as he opened the box before him.

Something about the box made my heart race, and I worked to stifle the urge to flee, telling myself to be brave.

Edgar pulled on a pair of rubber examination gloves, his youthful face tense as he concentrated on the box. He hesitated before reaching in, his hands fumbling with the contents. I gasped as he pulled out the lifeless mass, and he shot a quick glance at me over his glasses, his eyes calm and glowing.

My hand flew to my mouth, silencing my disruption as a few students shot me curious looks. There in his hands was the motionless and shattered body of the matte raven. The creature's eyes were dead and blank, no longer sinister in their bottomless draw.

Some of the class squirmed as Edgar placed it on the stark white table, blood smearing across the Formica.

"This is a raven," he boomed, his gaze on me strangely protective.

Scott nudged me and I glanced at him sharply.

"Or a crow," he ventured with a joking smile on his face.

I glared at him before I turned back toward the front.

Edgar seemed to hear exactly what Scott had said because his stern gaze fell on him.

"Not to be mistaken for a crow, though they are from the same Genus, the Corvus group," he added acerbically.

Scott's back went rigid at the comment, the blood draining from his face.

A brave girl toward the front raised her hand. Professor Edgar glanced toward her, nodding in acknowledgement, granting her permission to speak.

"But that's not non-native," she stammered, an obvious shake to her voice. "Northern Ravens are common in Washington and Canada."

Edgar gave her a speculative look.

"This is true, but unless you are as well-trained as I, you might not notice that, in fact, this is a large English raven."

The girl leaned forward, examining it more closely, swallowing hard and nodding as she acknowledged her mistake. I watched as she looked around the room, her cheeks flushed with embarrassment.

"So then," Edgar paused dramatically before addressing the whole class. "How did this bird manage to cross the Atlantic and the entire country to end up here?" His voice held a hint of amusement.

The class looked at him in bewilderment. Our gazes locked once again, and in that instant I knew that this bird was more than just a simple English raven.

"One may think this is impossible," Edgar boomed. "But it is amazing what can happen in nature when one finds its life threatened." He paused, eyes glinting. "Or hungry."

I shuddered at his comment, thinking how threatening the matte raven had been and how viciously he'd attacked my mind. There was something he wanted from me, but fortunately, he didn't get it.

The professor motioned for the class to come take a closer look and everyone gathered around with caution. I rose from my stool, keeping the professor in my peripheral view as I approached the dead carcass with a guarded expression. Scott looked at the bird in dumbfounded amazement as Professor Edgar made his way around the crowd of students toward me. I watched him approach, my lips parted in breathless anticipation, my heart racing. His coat grazed my calf, sending a small thrill through my system. His scent triggered my memory. It was the same sweet smell I had remembered from last night in the woods, something resembling honey and lilac. My suspicions were confirmed at that moment, and my accusing gaze met his. He returned my gaze calmly, acknowledging my realization with a small nod.

Startled by our bizarre exchange, I turned away and rushed back to the safety of my seat, my back rigid with surprise and fear as the rest of the class also returned to their stations. Edgar recaptured their attention as he removed the gloves from his perfect hands, discarding them in the trash.

"So…." he began, pausing as a few stragglers hurried to get to their seats. "Your job is to research the area, develop a theory on what made him come here, and write me an essay."

The class groaned in objection but he quelled them with a look, his blue-grey eyes flashing.

"You are excused to begin your work," he boomed dismissively, his eyes falling to me. "Estella." He said my name in a way that made my heart stop and my face flush. "A moment please?"

Everyone glanced at me as they gathered their belongings, most with amusement and spite, but a few with grave compassion.

Scott looked at me, a pitiful look on his face.

"Good luck, Elle," he squeaked under his breath. "Catch up with me later. We can work on this together."

I nodded, realizing I probably had the best theory of everyone, but of course, who would believe me, let alone resist the urge to pack me off to the psych ward? Again.

When I had tried to explain my ability to someone for the first time, that was exactly what they had done. A psych ward is no place for a twelve year old. No place for anyone, really.

I stood on shaky legs and walked toward Edgar as the last person left the room. I was fidgeting with my hands, nervous about what he might say. His eyes had faded back to their usual calm grey, and though I tried to look away from them, I couldn't. He leaned against his desk, facing me, with his arms and ankles crossed. As I grew closer, I became acutely aware of how beautiful he was, running my hand self-consciously through my hair, worried that I'd pale in comparison.

Under his lab coat, he was wearing a cream-colored cable knit sweater that hugged his muscular torso just right. His jeans were tailored to his body, and it was apparent that they were much more expensive than my entire outfit. He was like a model from an Abercrombie ad, perfectly proportioned and toned.

Edgar looked at me for a moment and I could almost see the thoughts forming in his head. I stood awkwardly a few paces away like an embarrassed idiot, forcing myself to continue to look into his electric eyes while still keeping a safe distance. He broke our stare, removing his tinted glasses and folding them in his hands.

"Estella," he whispered in a tone I hadn't heard him use before, his gaze fixed on his lap. His change of attitude toward me from the first day to now was astounding.

"Professor?" My voice sounded weak.

"Please, call me Edgar," he breathed, his tone silky.

Edgar slowly lifted his gaze back to me, and it took all my strength to resist the urge to step back. His pearl eyes glowed in a way that was so unnatural and strange. He took a steadying breath, releasing it as it fell across my face in sweet waves. He did not speak further.

"That was you," I breathed, jumping right in. "You brought me back here from the field." My eyes were wide. I had no desire to assume it was anyone but Edgar. What he had showed me today, was proof enough. "How did you do that?" My memory flashed back to when he'd picked me up, as though I were a child. "You were so… strong." My voice caught in my throat. "Why did you? How…"

He was quick to interrupt me.

"You're…" he paused, scanning my face with a look of longing. "You're imagining things, Estella. I merely found you while I was hiking, lying helpless in a field. I want to make sure we get that straight."

I looked at him in confusion, my thoughts a tangled mess.

He pushed himself away from his desk with ease, coming to stand before me, close enough for me to feel the heat from his body.

"And besides, it was nothing to write home about. You're light and easy to carry," he whispered, a crooked smile brightening his face.

I shook my head, trying to clear my thoughts.

"No, I..." I paused, struggling again to find the right words. It still didn't make sense. I was missing something, something big.

"Then what do you think happened?" he demanded softly, his gorgeous face now close to mine. "You obviously know something. I can see that you are perplexed." He scanned my face intently.

I shook my head, refusing to accept his easy explanation, my brow creased in frustration. He was hiding something, and I was determined to find out what.

Edgar smoothly shifted the focus to me, distracting me. "I know that you possess certain..." His voice trailed off as he narrowed his eyes thoughtfully. "...talents." He watched me as I absorbed his words. "You think I didn't notice what you did to my hawk? You healed him."

I opened my mouth to protest, but no sound came out. I tried to think of an explanation, a lie, anything, but nothing believable came to mind. I could not tell him. I didn't want him to know.

He closed his brilliant eyes and leaned toward me, inhaling deeply, obviously taking in my scent. When he opened his eyes again, an extraordinary realization washed over me. He looked invigorated, as though I was the perfume of life - which I was, but how could he tell?

"Don't be afraid, though. What you did comes as no surprise to me. It was more of a positive affirmation of who you are." He looked at me with knowing eyes.

I felt the familiar pull toward him.

"What do you mean?" I asked. How did he know about me? He couldn't. I felt dazed, hypnotized almost. The affect he had on me was all so profound. I had trouble thinking with him so near. "This makes no sense. I don't even know you, but you act as though you know me."

The way he was leaning in my direction was somewhat unnerving. It was clear that he was attracted to me, but I was still so confused about how I felt toward him. It wasn't hard to see the way the other girls in class watched him, their eyes dreamy but their wits frightened. Like them, I also could not help but succumb to his beauty, but at the same time, I found him terrifying as well. I had so many questions, so many things I needed to know.

A slow smile spread across his face, my heart racing along with his as I began to feel his warmth, like that of the fish and the hawk. "Would you like to know me?"

I stared for a moment before nodding, so desperate for answers, that I didn't care about the threat.

I jumped as he let out a sudden laugh. "Well, then," he breathed, "You will."

I felt my knees nearly give as he pulled back and away from me. I experienced a sudden release, the beat of his heart fading from mine. I had never felt this way toward anyone. Never before had I felt a human heart like that. I heard it calling to me, echoing every beat throughout the empty place

93

inside my chest. I licked my lips, forcing air in and out of my lungs in order to stay conscious.

"But the raven…" I forced the words out as I looked toward the dead carcass. "The other one. The one that lived. What happened to it?" My body felt warm and weak. My assumptions, based on the scratches on his throat, were that he'd been attacked also. He must have seen what had happened to the other bird.

He smiled, his eyes blazing. I waited for his reply, but he gave me no answer. He chuckled, the sound reverberating off the walls of the room. "You don't have to fear me, Estella. I won't hurt you." He paused. "I know that since you've met me, I've been a bit, odd. It's just, I hadn't expected to ever see you again, and it's a little shocking."

My face was twisted in confusion. "See me again? Professor, I think you have me mistaken for someone else." This was all so weird. "I'm sorry, it's just…" I gave him a fake smile, not knowing exactly what to say. There was no other explanation: he must be confused.

He let out another abrupt snort as he rolled his eyes away from me. "You don't have to do that."

I looked at him with a sour glare. "Do what?" I snapped defensively as I wiped the smile from my face. By now I no longer feared him. If he wanted to hurt me, he would have.

His gaze met mine once more. "Fake a smile. Though, it is beautiful." His eyes glinted. "Very convincing, too." He winked.

I blushed. How did he know I was faking it? Surely eighteen years of practice had produced a convincing act? I looked at him with renewed intensity. "How do you know I'm faking it?" I stammered.

He laughed. "Because, you're not happy. Not even close. You're too empty." He said it as though he pitied me.

I hated to be pitied. My eyes searched his, "How..."

He cut me off. "Like I said, you've met me before. You just have to trust me." His smile never faltered and his eyes were still radiant. "How do I say this so you understand?" He raised his eyebrow thoughtfully. "Let's just say, you met me in another life."

"I..." I was mystified, putting my hand to my chest and feeling the emptiness that he somehow knew was there. He met me in another life? That was impossible.

He looked at my scarred wrist, his face changing from pity to sadness. Glancing away, he shifted to remove his coat. As he pushed the jacket from his biceps, I stared at his neck in amazement. His skin was like a pearl, shiny and smooth, and something inside me suddenly clicked. I laughed to myself, finding the thoughts absurd. That could not be, there was no way. My eyes darted to his, and they affirmed my notions. It had to be. He *was* the other raven!

His gaze lingered on mine, amused at the way I was gawking at him.

Without a second thought, I reached out to touch his skin, but he jerked back and out of my reach.

"Estella, no!" His eyes became a deep black and I stepped back in horror. My hand was now trembling, the sound of his voice shaking me to the core. "Don't do that," he snapped.

I looked at him with wide eyes, crossing my arms against my chest, now shunned.

He calmed himself and his eyes changed back to grey. "You can't touch me," he sighed. "I wish I could explain to you why, but not yet." He looked at my face, now angry with himself for getting out of control. His jaw was clenched. "I have to be prepared for something like that." His eyes began to lighten as he drew in a heavy breath.

"Sorry, I…" stammering, I pulled my arms tighter to my chest. "I couldn't help it."

His jaw relaxed and a smile returned to his face. "Don't apologize. It's not your fault. I should have anticipated that you would do that. It's just that I need to learn better control of my mind. If I touch you, as strange as this may sound, it could really hurt you." His gaze was drawn to my arm again, and he abruptly changed the subject.

"Are you okay? You were bleeding pretty profusely."

I looked at him, my head swimming with questions. "Yes, I'm fine. It's just a cut."

He nodded.

My eyes were fixed on him. "I heal quickly anyway." I looked toward the table where the dead bird lay, unable to handle looking at Edgar anymore. What was Edgar? Why couldn't he touch me, and worse yet, what would it do?

He still watched my arm. "Yes, I figured you would." He followed my gaze and a grave look crossed his face.

I stared at the carcass for a long moment before speaking. I swallowed a lump down my throat. "What is it?" I asked, somewhat disgusted by the small drops of dried blood on the white table, wondering if he knew more than what he was letting on.

He sighed. "The raven is a spy, of sorts." His voice was vague. "You have no need to be afraid, though. It won't happen again. I'll personally make sure of that."

I finally mustered the courage to ask what I was now dying to know.

"It was you, wasn't it?" My tone was accusing and my eyes narrowed. "You were the raven, the one that was glowing in the sun and the one that killed this one. You can..." It was inconceivable, but suddenly so logical. I had a talent of my own, and being gifted as I was, I knew that there had to be others. "You can change into that thing, can't you?" I was certain I was right.

He dropped his gaze to his lap, smiling to himself as he unfolded the tinted glasses in his hands and slid them casually back over his eyes. He changed the subject again. "You should probably get going. You're going to be late for your next class."

I refused to be ignored. "That's it, isn't it? I'm right." His avoidance had said it all.

His eyes narrowed behind the lenses. "I'd love to talk more, but..." he exhaled. "I think we've said enough." He leaned toward me, his eyes now very dark behind the lenses.

My instinct was to lean away from him, but I held my ground.

"You are utterly beautiful, if you don't mind me saying." He smirked.

I wanted to gasp, I wanted to pretend I was offended

97

by his abrupt comment, but I wasn't. Instead I just stared, speechless. Taking advantage of my silence, he stood and walked toward the door to his adjoined office.

"I will see you later, Estella," his voice echoed over his shoulder. "And try not to let people notice what you are doing to the plants."

I further gaped. How did he know about the plants? I knew he had seen what I'd done to the hawk, but he wasn't there in botany. He couldn't know.

Edgar laughed as he glanced back at me one more time before gracefully exiting the room.

As he closed the door behind him, my gaze fell on the black raven, still dead on the table. Fear washed over me, and I walked toward the door, keeping my eye on the carcass, as though it would jump back to life. My limbs were tingling with the urgency to get away.

As I burst through the lab doors, the sun blinded me. I looked to the sky and drew in a deep breath. I was trying to process what had just happened as Scott came running from the building across the path, panting as though he'd just been chased.

"Are you okay?" He looked exceedingly concerned.

"Yeah," I paused as he grabbed my arm. "Yeah, I'm fine. He just…" I thought of another lie. "…wanted to tell me about the hawk. He's healing very well." I was in a daze.

"Oh good," he said with a laugh in his voice. "Because if any more time had passed, I was going to burst in there and make sure you weren't dead on the floor." He chuckled to himself.

We walked to the greenhouses in silence. I was too lost in my thoughts to make inane conversation with Scott. I put my hand to my chest as we walked into the field, Scott still eyeing the grasses with caution. Edgar knew what was in me, but how? And how had he known me? There were so many questions I needed answers to. I needed to see him again.

In class, my mind was useless. Though the sunflower seed I'd planted a little later than everyone else was already a foot taller than the rest, I didn't care. When the teacher questioned me, I just shrugged it off as though I myself was truly amazed at the strange occurrence.

I was frustrated that Edgar had somehow left me with so many more unanswered questions that I originally had. He had been the one to save me in the field, but how? How was he also the raven, and why had he killed the raven that was threatening me? This whole situation was unbelievable: the ravens, my attraction, Edgar's outrageous claims. I needed answers, not more questions.

After classes were over, I ditched Scott at the cafeteria and went back to Edgar's lab, but it was already locked. My hopes to find my answers today quickly faded. Despite my fear to be around him, I couldn't resist. I had never been attracted to the guys back home, never tried to have any sort of relationship figuring they would eventually see my freakish nature and leave. But Edgar, he was different, something about him felt so appealing, so deeply attractive, and besides, he already knew I was weird.

I walked in disappointment back to my cabin and lay down to think. After a moment of thought, I got out my newest journal and drew the field from my foggy memory. I added the dead bird as I tried to remember the events. There were three things I listed about the scene.

The first was that the spying raven did not enter the field of life that had grown around me. It was like the flowers were protecting me.

Second, as I had become paralyzed on the ground, the grass around me had actually died. It had seemed really odd, especially since that had never happened before.

And third, that it had been Edgar that saved me, that Edgar was somehow the armored raven. The fact that he didn't want to tell me affirmed that. It was the only explanation. If I were wrong, surely he would have said so.

I mulled over what I had written and found that it still made no sense to me. Frustrated, I threw the journal across the room, hitting the log wall with a loud thump. I flopped onto my pillow, depressed that I had gotten nowhere today.

Eventually, I fell asleep. Once again, I found myself in the field, but to my horror, everything was lifeless. All the grasses and wildflowers had wilted and the trees were no more than torched sticks spearing from the ground. I was dismayed, the whole world seemed to be dying and I was helpless to save it.

As I looked to the edge of the clearing, I saw Edgar standing there. His eyes were dark ebony and there was no smile on his face. I called to him, but he did not move. He stood there, still and dark in his angered beauty, in a trance as though controlled by a force beyond himself.

When I looked down at myself, I gasped. My body was

no more than a transparent fog. I was a ghost, soulless and invisible, and as the wind picked up, I was completely blown away.

VISITORS

I woke abruptly in the darkness of my room. Lying completely still, I listened for some sign of what had woken me, but there was nothing. My eyes scanned the shadows, trying to breathe as quietly as possible. I had no idea what time it might be, but it was still dark.

There was sweat beading on my brow from my vivid nightmare. Feeling silly, I felt for my body, relieved that it was still here. As I released the breath I had been holding, there was a strange shuffling noise on the porch and my eyes shot to the window. Feeling suddenly alert, I listened intently, hoping the noise was only a small animal passing by. Beginning to relax back into sleep, I then heard the distinct flutter of wings outside the door. My eyes flew open once more, unable to ignore this new sound. My heart began to race as I stared through the darkness toward the source of the sound, waiting for further movement. Dim moonlight streamed through the small cracks in the shut blinds, notifying me of any shadows that may have been lurking.

"Is someone there?" I whispered, my heart pounding hard against my ribcage, my voice cracking with fear.

I did not blink as my eyes began to water, watching the handle of the door intently. The shiny brass was still, the sounds outside silenced. I finally blinked, but as I opened my eyes, I saw the brass handle glimmer as it twisted. My heart stopped and my hands gripped the blankets on my bed. A dark shadow moved behind the blinds now, and I sat up. Readying myself, I was quick to react as I reached to flip on the lamp beside me. My hands fumbled with the switch, unable to coax it to work. I heard the door begin to open now, the blinds clanking against the glass of the window. I was breathing hard, my eyes wide and frantic.

"Estella, it's me."

I heard the voice, and I stopped. It was Edgar's voice, a sound that was both relieving and frightening at the same time. What was he doing here?

"It's alright," he whispered in a soothing tone. "I didn't mean to wake you."

I said nothing, my breathing shallow as I tried to pretend I wasn't there.

"Apparently I'm not as stealthy as I'd hoped," he continued.

I gave up being still and let go of the lamp cord. I turned to face his silhouette, my body remaining rigid.

"Don't you know to knock?" My words were shaken.

His shadowed figure walked toward me, perching himself at the edge of my bed. He was careful to keep his distance, and I noticed that his eyes were glowing in the darkness. His inviting scent wafted across the bed and I breathed deep before reacting.

"You scared me," I hissed.

"Sorry," he apologized again, a mocking tone to his voice. "I just needed to come see you."

Shocked by the forward comment, I furrowed my brow, feeling violated. "And you think you can just invite yourself in to tell me this?" I asked in a sharp tone.

He laughed softly. "Well, no." He shifted on the bed and my heart rate quickened at his nearness. "I thought I'd leave a note." I caught a glimpse of his teeth in the dark as he grinned.

I was still trying to understand why he was here. "Okay," I paused, "That's still rather odd. If I woke and there was a note on the fridge, I'm pretty sure it would still mean you'd broken in."

He shrugged, still smiling.

He was acting as though this was a joke. I got that we had made some sort of connection earlier today, but it didn't warrant his intrusion. "So why did you need to see me?" I wrapped my blankets around me. I was self-conscious, sitting there with my hair disheveled and wearing my ratty pajamas. If Edgar was going to start making nocturnal visits, I needed some better sleepwear.

He sighed. "I have to leave for a few days, just until Sunday."

I intently listened, wondering what this had to do with me.

"I just needed to check on you before I left, make sure you were okay." His voice was full of sincerity.

"I'm fine," I spat. I didn't need him to protect me. Despite my attraction toward him, something about me still didn't trust him, especially now that he'd broken into my room. Then I remembered the lack of lock on the door, and realized he hadn't exactly committed a crime. I made a mental note to wedge a chair under the door in the future, to deter other unwanted visitors.

He laughed again, sarcasm edging his voice. "Yeah, seems like it."

I crossed my arms defensively, my eyes now adjusting enough to make out his pearly outline in the darkness. A part of me was strangely disappointed that he would be gone, but I wasn't about to admit that to him.

"Just..." a grave sigh seeped from his mouth. "Just don't leave the school grounds until I get back." His eyes flashed away from me and I could see him looking to the windows. "There are things in the world you shouldn't trust. There are things you need to know, but I don't have the time to explain." He leaned his elbow onto the foot of the bed. "I have to leave now. I know this seems abrupt, but trust me."

I nodded in acknowledgement of his request, remaining silent.

He stood and walked toward the door. "Just promise me, okay? Stay here, around people. When I get back, I can explain more."

I took a deep breath before answering, my head full of questions I'd thought up that day.

"I promise."

He exhaled, an expression of relief crossing his eyes and face. "Do you need anything? You know, before I go?" He was as still as a statue with his hand on the handle of the door.

His request was odd, and it occurred to me that this was my chance to ask a few quick questions. I knew he didn't have time, but they could no longer wait.

"What is it?" He had a perceptive grin on his face now.

I sat up as excitement pulsed through my veins. "I just wanted to ask something."

He waited patiently as I formulated the right words.

"I just need to know. What exactly do you know about me?" I blurted, blushing at the somewhat awkward question.

His hand fell from the handle of the door to his side and he walked back toward me. "What do I know?" He chuckled again, and his gaze fell to the nightstand. He stepped away from the door where he reached for the framed letter from my mother and brought it closer to his face.

I watched intently as he touched a finger to the glass. I was trying to read the strange expression that came to his face, but it was difficult in the dim light.

"Estella," his eyes were fixed on the words in the note. "You are amazingly unique. I don't even think you can grasp just how much." He placed the frame back on the table, bringing his gaze back to me. "Until you realize…"

I leaned forward, hanging on his every word.

He'd stopped himself before he revealed anymore. "You will see, Elle, I promise. When I have more time, I will explain all this." He stared at me with a look akin to adoration. "There just isn't the time right now." The way he said my name was as though he'd said it a million times.

Frustration gripped me. I wanted to urge him to tell me more but I could sense he wasn't ready, so I tried a different tack. "Well then, tell me something else," I uttered with urgency, trying to keep him here a bit longer. I began to think about the feather and how strong it had been, cutting into my finger like a razor. The right words were hard to find, so I gave up, quickly thinking of something else in my attempt to hear him talk a bit longer.

I heard his steady strong breathing as he waited with waning patience. I could tell he needed to leave.

"What more do you wish to know?" he asked, raising his eyebrows.

I looked into my lap, picking at my fingernails. "Well, this one's sort of childish, but…" I paused, looking back up at him as he loomed over me, "No one seems to know how old you are. I just want to know because you seem so young." I held my breath knowing it was a dumb question, but still one that had perplexed me all day.

His laughter filled the cabin. "Of all the things you could have asked me, you chose to ask me that?" He chuckled a bit more. "You know you could have asked me anything. I was in the mood to be truthful."

I cursed to myself for not asking the first question as he looked deeply into my eyes. He noticed my bruised expression so he leaned his head down toward me, his face just inches from mine. His eyes were glimmering. "To them, I look deceptively young, but am actually very old." He saw the shock cross my face. "I am like you, Estella. We are the same age."

I gave him a confused look as he straightened, my mind trying to wrap itself around his obscure answer. He reached into his coat pocket and retrieved a glowing feather. I further cursed as he handed it to me. Now had been the perfect time to ask. I looked at him with a reproachful glare as I gingerly plucked it from his gloved hand, examining it while avoiding its sharp razor edge. He had just affirmed his involvement with the pearl raven, but I was still unsure exactly what that connection was.

In one brisk movement, he turned and walked toward the door. "Just be safe, Estella, and do try to go back to sleep." With that, he closed the door and was gone.

I stared at the door for a moment, trying to process his abrupt visit. I looked to where my mother's framed note sat in the dark.

It was just the same as it always had been: the rumpled edges still ragged as though it were a hundred years old. I sat there in silence, reading the familiar words over and over. I tried to discern what had made him look at the words the way he had, perhaps some message I'd missed hidden inside them, but there was nothing.

In just a few short days, my life had changed drastically, becoming something far more than I'd expected. I figured being out here would be enough of a challenge for me, never mind finding a whole other world of mystery and a strange man that was half human and half something else entirely. I set the frame back on the table, flicked off the light, and pulled the covers up to my chin.

The quiet was growing on me, just as long as it wasn't too quiet. There were a few distant sounds of crickets, and they comforted me. I had learned that as long as they were singing, nothing bad would happen.

Sleep crept back in on me, and I could no longer force my eyes to stay open. I fell into my dreams where I once again returned to the field, but this time, to my relief, it was in full bloom. The weather was warmer than the current fall weather, more like mid-summer temperatures. As my eyes glanced around the misty dream, everything felt safe and my head was calm.

As I peeked down at myself, I was relieved that my body was still there. As my gaze filtered back up, Edgar entered into the opening. I instantly took notice, not just with my eyes, but in my heart. A true smile crossed my face as a feeling I'd never known came alive in my soul. I struggled to recognize the sensation. He was walking toward me now, and I brought one hand to my face, feeling a tear roll over my soft skin. I was happy. He was almost to me now, and the beating in my chest was stronger than anything I'd ever felt.

I reached out to touch him, but my dream dissipated as the morning light filtered into the cabin. The space rapidly grew brighter, beckoning me to wake. I opened my eyes and sadness rolled over me like a heavy wave. To my regret, the happiness I had felt had all been a dream. I sat up, more tired then I'd been since I'd arrived at the college, and I rubbed my eyes wearily.

The light of day had finally come, and I exhaled sharply, disappointed that the dream was gone, but relieved to find it was Saturday. I was looking forward to the fact that today I could at last take my time getting ready. I slowly stood, shuffling to the kitchenette where some sample packs of coffee sat next to the small coffee maker. I turned on the water, listening as it laboriously pumped out of the faucet and into the cup holder.

As I switched the machine on, the glorious smell filled the small space as I shuffled to the bathroom. I turned on the water to take the first shower I'd had in days, though I really didn't need it. I was always clean, always perfect, and it irked me. I stepped into the warm stream, allowing the water to flow soothingly over me for a few moments as I took an emotional inventory.

To my chagrin, my soul was just as empty as it had been. I tried to revisit the feeling of happiness that I'd imagined in my dream, but I felt nothing, quickly becoming frustrated and angry. I stomped my foot in annoyance, infuriated at my life. My chest rose and fell as I breathed hard, forcing my senseless anger to subside. I began to lather myself, attempting to wash away my discontent.

When the burning fury left me, melancholy took its place as I realized Edgar was gone. The familiar tingle I had felt when he was around was also gone. Clearly, wherever he was, it was too far away for me to sense him. I shut off the water and wrapped a towel around myself before tiptoeing

110

back into the room, trying not to drip water on the floor. There was nothing worse than putting on fresh socks and then stepping in a shower puddle. I rummaged through my bag for some clean jeans and a shirt, finally finding my last pair. Definitely time to do some laundry. Today was a better day than any other.

I quickly dressed and walked back to the kitchen. Grabbing the only cup from the empty cabinet, I jumped at the sudden sound of feverish knocking at my door. I put a hand to my heart and closed my eyes, hoping it wasn't Scott but knowing I wouldn't be so lucky. I shuffled to the door, swinging it open with a look of displeasure on my face.

"Hey!" he sang.

I sighed and stepped back so he could come in. All I had wanted was some peace.

"Hey, Scott." My voice was filled with obvious disappointment.

"You want to work a little on that paper today for Professor Edgar?" My hopes that he would go away, at least until noon, were fading as he bounded into my cabin, invading my space.

"Uh…" I watched as he began poking around the room. "Sure."

"Wow, this place is totally cool! You're lucky."

His energy was making me antsy. I watched him as he walked toward my bedside table, reaching for my framed letter.

"Hey!" I yelped, lunging toward him and grabbing his shoulders, distracting him by twisting his body around and plopping him on the bed. "Just sit, okay?"

He looked at me with a happy smile as I walked back to the kitchen and grabbed my coffee to take the first glorious sip.

"So, what do you think about the raven?" he asked, bouncing like a child on my bed as he sat there. "What's your theory?"

I thought for a moment about what could possibly sound logical. "He probably just got here by boat, some cruise line or something," I blurted carelessly. Or by magic, which was what I was beginning to believe.

Scott nodded, contemplating my theory. "Yeah, that's good." He looked to the ceiling. "My theory is he was brought here by smugglers. What do you think? Sound relevant enough to convince him?"

I gave him a confident look. "Oh yeah. I think so."

Scott's eyes dropped to his lap. "So," he paused, "I was sort of wondering..."

I leaned against the counter, wincing because I could predict what was coming next. I knew it was only a matter of time, especially after seeing how the nurse had looked at us.

"So I was just wondering if you wanted to maybe, you know, go for a hike? Or have dinner with me tonight? Or both?" The way he said it let me know it wasn't a friendly invite, and I squeezed my eyes shut in dismay. As I feared, he was looking for something more than friendship from me. I looked at him with sorrowful eyes as he fidgeted with his hands, looking down into his lap, avoiding my gaze.

I felt so bad, I didn't know what to say to soften the

blow. "Oh, uh…"

He looked up at me, and for the first time, I think he finally got it. "Oh yeah. I see. Just thought, you know, maybe I'd try." He smiled bleakly.

"I'm sorry, Scott." I paused, unable to formulate exactly what to tell him. He was my friend, and I liked it that way. "It's just that, I was an orphan and I've never had friends before…" I trailed off, really at a loss for words.

"Is it Professor Edgar?" he asked suddenly, taking me by surprise.

I looked at him with alarm, my face saying it all.

"Wow," he said, pausing as he re-grouped. "Then I guess that's cool." He stood and walked toward me. "Friends are a good thing." He gave me an encouraging smile, easing my discomfort.

I took another sip of my coffee, thankful he'd accepted my offer of friendship so easily. "I just would hate for things to get weird, you know?" I was pleading with him.

He nodded as he gave me a silly, overcompensating smile that said he was okay.

"Well, what about breakfast though? No harm there," he said lightly, his mood shifting.

I gave him a small smile, putting my coffee down and grabbing his hand. "Perfect, let's do that."

I playfully yanked him out the door, still trying to make myself feel less like the bad guy for not liking him like that. As we walked to breakfast, I thought about Edgar, and I wondered where he was. The feeling of separation was strange, as though now that we were close, we were never supposed to be apart. It just all felt so sudden, so out of the blue, like love at first sight or something goofy like that. I had a crush on my professor, how cliché.

Scott bounded along as though nothing had happened. I was hoping this time he'd finally understand and quit hitting on me. We opened the door to the cafeteria, and I glanced around at the occupants. Maybe if I helped find him a date, then he'd really give me my space, and also forgive me for being such a cold-hearted jerk.

I wasn't much of a matchmaker. Well, not at all actually, but it was worth a try. I felt so sisterly toward him, and not to mention responsible. We grabbed our food and took the same table as always. I scanned the room, my eyes searching one face after another. The pickings were slim, but I finally found a likely candidate.

"So, Scott," I ventured, noticing the lonely girl to my right, just a few tables over. I wasn't really sure where I was going with this, but it felt like the right solution. "How about that girl over there, sitting all alone? She's sure cute, huh?"

He blushed, and I knew I had caught him off guard.

"Yeah," he shoveled food into his mouth in avoidance.

"Oh, come on. I know you were just asking me because you're lonely." I stared at him while he chewed in defiance.

He looked hurt, but also seemed to be considering what I'd said as he glanced toward the girl. She was relatively cute with auburn hair and glasses that nicely framed her face.

"Go right now. It will be easy. Invite her to eat with us," I urged him.

He eyed her hesitantly as she ate her food. "I guess I

could." I knew his reluctance was a direct result of how I'd shut him down, but this would heal him. I could tell the girl was just waiting for anyone to talk to her, and Scott was bound to be that person. A look of confidence flashed across his face. He finished chewing and wiped his mouth, looking to me for approval.

I gave him a stern glare and a slight nudge. "Go," I whispered eagerly.

He stood up and smoothed his shirt over his cargo pants and straightened his glasses. He walked over in his typical awkward fashion and stood before her. I watched in amazement as they began to talk. I couldn't hear what he said, but she suddenly smiled and looked at me with friendly eyes. I watched her stand and they walked back to our table together. I was speechless as I shamelessly gawked, amazed that I'd accomplished such a social feat. They approached me with happy grins and pink cheeks, and a part of me wished I could be happy about this moment, too.

"This is Sarah." Scott was beaming. "She's very grateful for the invite."

I gave her my kindest fake smile. "Hi, Sarah. So glad you could join us."

She exuded the same hyper energy as Scott, and I was proud to have put this together. First Mother Earth and now expert matchmaker.

"Oh, thanks," she beamed. "I was starting to think everyone here was unfriendly." Her happiness was palpable, and I couldn't stop myself from envying her.

Scott moved his tray over to make room for Sarah at

the table. When they finally sat, they both kept eyeing each other like school kids on Valentine's Day.

"So, what is your name?" she asked with eyes full of youthful innocence.

I stared in disbelief, finding myself suddenly blessed with not just one, but two accidental friends. "Estella," I said shyly, taking the initiative to stick my hand out to shake hers.

She grabbed it and wobbled it with surprising vigor. "That's a beautiful name. Estella." She said it as though trying it on for size. "My mom was really uncreative," she said, making a discontented face.

I winced. Just what I needed - another mom comment sending me into internal turmoil. "Thanks."

Scott was beaming at her, almost on the brink of gawking. I gave him a stern look and he snapped out of his awkward trance.

"Well, I sure think Sarah is a pretty name," he gushed. And just like that, I was forgotten.

His cheesy line didn't impress me, but it sure sent Sarah into gales of giggles and blushing.

I watched them as they began to talk, and suddenly, I felt like a third wheel, and I liked it. I stayed long enough to be polite before strategically excusing myself. The love that was blooming was about all I could handle, and I quickly snuck out of the room.

My pace was brisk as I walked back to my cabin, excited for the solitude. I planned out a day of reading, laundry, and thinking. I was determined to accumulate as much info as I could before Edgar returned. Someone here had to know more about him. I wanted to find them and learn, so that I was certain I wasn't getting in over my head, or getting myself in serious danger.

Later that afternoon, after all of my laundry was done and I had read several chapters in my book, I found myself in serious internal debate. I'd promised Edgar I'd stay out of the woods, but today had dragged on longer than I'd liked and I was bored. What did it matter, anyway? He was gone. And like he said, the dead raven was just a weird sort of coincidence. I'd lived eighteen years without any problems, and in much more dangerous places than here, surely.

I was biting my nails, looking out the window of my cabin toward the woods and fighting my rebellious side. Finally, I couldn't take it anymore. This was my Saturday, my day to finally explore this place on my own. A voice inside was telling me not to, to obey Edgar, but I ignored it.

"Screw it," I said out loud, grabbing my coat and opening my door. I was going out, and that was that.

The air today was less obtrusive. At breakfast I had noticed a distinct change in the weather, and I was happy for it. I was used to the constant rain of Seattle, and at times I even liked it, so today, the somewhat cooler weather was nice. I sat on the top step to put on my boots, noticing there was also a strong, steady breeze. I stood determinedly, exhaling hard as I took off up the path and into the woods.

I passed the bench again, this time turning to the right. I decided the trail from before seemed far too familiar, not to mention still a little scary. I looked behind me with wary eyes. As before, it still felt as though someone was there, but as the wind came cold and fast up my back, I realized it was just its presence within the forest. There were large droves of sage dotting the floor and their scent was heavenly. The ferns rustled in the wind, their curling tips bowing to the floor in soft arches.

I walked on the path for what felt like a few miles. So far, nothing had jumped out at me. I fell into a comfortable rhythm. The path looked well traveled and cared for, which was a lot better than the somewhat rustic path to the meadow. The fact that this was the trail more heavily visited gave me a sense of security. Bad things were less likely to happen here.

My hands were pushed into my pockets, the wind chilling them despite their cover. I was humming to myself, something Heidi had hummed to me every night since the day she had taken me in. The plants absorbed my voice as they leaned toward me, the grass curling out as though kissed by the sunless sky. My body shook as the wind whipped through the evergreens again.

Suddenly, something very large and gray, almost the size of a small plane, flew like a silent cloud through the trees in my blind spot. I halted, my feet slipping on the gravel and my hum dying in my throat. I looked around but saw nothing. The swirling gusts through the pines disabled my hearing and left me senseless and blind as I strained to listen. I stood there for a few minutes, but nothing happened and so I carefully pressed on, continuing to twist my head from side to side, my senses on full alert.

I began humming again, though now, there was a noticeable shake to my voice. The path began to twist and a peak of rocks jutted skyward just a few feet ahead. Looking around, I was able to peek through an opening in the trees, catching the glimmer of the lake below. I tried to position myself in accordance with the dam at the head of the lake, but I found it more difficult than I'd thought as I looked around, lost.

Giving up, I began forward again, the soft rushing of water now audible in the distance. I wound myself around a large tree, stepping in a deep mud puddle that was hiding under a grove of ferns. I cursed to myself as I stamped off the dirt, looking at my boots in anger. As I inspected the messy damage, a large shadow dove overhead, completely shading the ground around me. I whipped my head up, seeing a group of branches shaking above the spot where I stood.

My breathing quickened, dragging hard in my throat.

"Hello?" I called, but as expected, nothing answered.

Irritated with myself for being so jumpy, I quickly decided that it was nothing more than the wind in the trees. For good measure, however, I still sprinted a ways down the path, looking toward the canopy as the branches churned in anger above me. I knew I was probably just being paranoid, and I also knew that turning around wasn't necessarily a bad idea, but my curiosity as to where the rushing sound of water was coming from was much more dominant.

I slowed my pace, the rushing sound even louder now, like a turbine engine on a plane as it flew overhead. I briefly thought of Edgar. If he found out where I was, he would be infuriated for sure. The way he had warned me to stay out of the woods was undeniably stern, but what did I really have to lose? As I rolled the idea around in my mind, I hardly noticed that the trail ended. I found myself on the edge of a very large cliff, a panoramic view of both the lake and the glacier in front of me.

I gasped. The view of the mountains was even more amazing here than it was from below. I looked to my left in utter astonishment. There, roughly twenty feet away, a river threw itself with ferocity off the cliff above me and plummeted to the lake below. I marveled at its sheer size, a feeling of vertigo washing over me. The roaring sound of water filled my ears, nearly deafening as it drowned out all other noise.

There was another sudden gust of wind and a cloud of mist blew across my face. I winced from the glacial chill of it against my skin, turning away from the falls and shielding my face.

As I opened my eyes, I was surprised to see that there was something there. It was large and grey, glowing as though lit by the sun. It was about the height of a human, except with large shoulders which were somewhat distorted. I tried to wipe the mist away from my eyes, but when I was finally able to see again, whatever it was had gone. Another strong gust fell across my face and I stepped backward, almost so far that I would have fallen over the cliff. I steadied myself and felt my nerves pounding in my chest, reminding me that I shouldn't be here. I ran my hand through my hair in agitation as I began to regret leaving the college. I should have listened to Edgar. Adrenaline took over, pulsing through my body and controlling my limbs. Lunging forward, I took off back toward campus, running as though being chased.

My feet were pounding the forest floor and mud splashed up all over my jeans. I heard something rustling through the branches behind and above me. I glanced up to see another shadow being cast around me, but as my eyes finally met the location of whatever or whoever it was, it had shot further skyward and only a large flutter of grey was visible between the open patches of sky. I pumped my legs harder, my thighs burning.

I heard voices ahead of me and was relieved to see two people on the path before me. As I flew toward them, they turned. I slowed to a walk as my feet sank into the mud, out of breath and surprised to see Scott and Sarah. Relief overcame me as I panted hard. Their eyes were wide with astonishment.

"Estella!" Sarah gasped, "What's going on?"

I struggled to catch my breath as Scott put his hand on my back. My side was cramping now, and I kept looking back into the woods, but there was still nothing.

"There..." I was heaving hard. "There was... something... chasing..." I let my voice trail off. Scott and Sarah were looking at me in utter disbelief.

Scott's face was almost comical. If I was in a different mood, I might even laugh. "Was it a bear?"

Of course it wasn't a bear. How can a bear fly through the trees? Still trying to catch my breath and eyeing the forest behind me with suspicion, I answered him.

"Uh, yeah." I breathed. It was a lie, but as far as level of danger went, it was probably the same. I needed to get them out of there, and fast.

Their eyes both got very wide and each hooked an arm through mine, now bracing me as my legs fell weak. "Maybe we should go," Sarah suggested, her voice shaking.

They led me forward, and soon, we were briskly making our way back to campus. I winced through the pain in my side, struggling to remember what I'd witnessed, but I couldn't connect the pieces. It was unlike anything I'd seen before: large, quiet, and fast.

We finally exited at the trailhead, and I watched as Sarah's face relaxed into a look of relief.

"Thank goodness," she gasped, her lips curling into a thankful smile.

I couldn't help but also feel immensely relieved.

Scott looked at me laughing. "Remind me not to be your friend anymore, okay? You're a magnet for trouble, Elle. No offense, but I have never felt more afraid for my life since I met you."

"You have no idea," I whispered under my breath. I had never been in fear like this either. I looked at Sarah's face, feeling horrible that on her first day meeting me, I'd already managed to put her in danger. I wondered exactly what she thought of me.

Sarah and Scott were laughing now, and I rolled my eyes. They were clueless, thinking they'd just narrowly escaped a bear when really, it was something else, maybe even something far worse.

Scott looked at me, smiling. "Well, what should we do now?"

"Monopoly?" Sarah suggested.

My heart was still racing. The fear in my bones wasn't yet gone, and I didn't feel the threat was over. How could they be thinking of stupid board games when there are weird things happening in the woods around us? I desperately wished for Edgar to be here right now. I needed his reassurance and his answers.

"Estella? Are you up for a game?" Scott looked to me with a questioning expression.

My eyes darted between the two hopeful faces. My body was still shaking. "No thanks. I think I may lie down."

Scott laughed. "Yeah, that's probably a good idea. You look a little faint, again."

Sarah giggled and I nodded. "Yeah, I think you're right. Thanks, though."

"Maybe next time?" Scott and Sarah looked at each other with a glimmer of relief. I knew they didn't want me tagging along anyway.

"Yeah, sounds great," I replied, faking a shaky smile.

They waved as they turned and began walking down the hill. I let out one last terrified breath before running into my cabin.

I slammed the door behind me, cursing at it for not having a lock. For good measure, I rushed to the chair that sat next to the window, dragging it toward the door and wedging it under the handle. For a moment I felt mildly safe, though, when it came to strange ghosts or other such phenomenon, I was sure my efforts would prove futile.

Since there was nothing more I could do, I sat on my bed, feeling helpless. Whatever it was that was out there had seemed harmless enough, and besides: it hadn't attacked even though it had ample chances to do so. I shuddered. What had I really expected by going out there today? Edgar had warned me, and I knew it was dangerous, so why? Was I that hungry for danger, or was I trying to prove Edgar wrong?

All my life I'd thought I was the only monster out there, but now, it seemed I was just one of many. Sighing, my heart rate finally returned to normal. I grabbed my book from the floor, hoping to lose myself in the story, but as I began to read, my mind only filtered back to the woods.

TRUTH

When I woke in the morning, I was surprised that I felt rested and calm, finding I had slept rather well despite the events of yesterday. I looked at the chair that was still propped under the handle of the door, untouched. After I'd left Sarah and Scott, things had become considerably less dramatic. I had at last managed to focus on my reading and even relax. Back home, I was so used to the screaming of my foster brothers and sisters and the general noise of a busy city always pulling my attention away during a climactic scene. Here, strange things in the woods were hardly a comparable distraction.

Falling asleep had been easier than expected, too, and my dreams had been blank, nothing like the night before. There were no strange visits from Edgar, or anything else for that matter, which was a welcomed relief. The incident by the waterfall began to feel like a hallucination, my mind's way of coping with all the change.

I sat up with a burst of excitement, remembering that today Edgar was due back at the college. I was eager to find him and continue the questioning.

I had decided as I fell asleep last night that I'd keep the incident in the woods a secret. It was stupid to compromise our somewhat interesting and budding relationship by showing Edgar he couldn't trust me. I was sure that in time, the answers I wanted would also find their way to the surface.

To my regret, I hadn't been able to dig up any dirt on him yesterday, as I'd planned. The grey figure in the woods had stolen my attention away from Edgar, bringing me a whole new set of things to ponder over. Today, however, I had a plan.

It had occurred to me that the nurse was British, and while being British did not make her an expert, I thought she might have some insight about the raven from the field and how he might have gotten here. She had also seemed like a veteran to the area, and her comment about having other students visit her infirmary after bad encounters with Edgar, had me curious.

It was a perfect coincidence that it was time my stitches were removed from my arm. I had peeked under the bandages the day after the incident, only to find that it was already nearly healed, another strange thing about my existence. Ever since I can remember, I've healed very fast. I had broken my arm in the first grade when a kid named

Andrew had teased and pushed me because the sandbox I was playing in had sprouted flowers all around me. A week later, my arm was already healed. Naturally, the doctors made me keep the cast on for another three weeks despite my whining. They were simply dumbfounded by the phenomenon, and to my dismay, they wrote me into some stupid medical mystery journal.

I jumped from bed and went to the bathroom to wash my face. As I looked out the small window, I noticed it was a rather dreary day. The windows had fogged and I could feel a noticeable chill seeping through them as small drops of rain ran like tears down the glass. The wind from yesterday seemed to have brought the bad weather with it.

I got dressed quickly in anticipation of Scott's arrival, but as the morning passed, I was surprised that he never came. I sighed, relieved but also saddened by the fact that he and Sarah had probably hit it off playing Monopoly, and I'd likely lost him as a constant friend and sidekick. Still, I was happy for him, and I now had a lot of free time to figure out my complex life.

After wasting half the morning thinking things over, I finally emerged from the cabin, driven by hunger and an eagerness to seek answers. I strode down the path toward the cafeteria. Most of the students had already come and gone, so I walked straight to the counter and grabbed two apples, figuring I'd save one for later.

As I chomped through the fresh crisp skin, I walked back outside, chewing my apple in sync with my footsteps on the crunching gravel. It was somewhat upsetting that I was familiar with the location of the infirmary, especially since I'd never arrived there fully conscious. Oh well.

As I walked through the door, Nurse Dee looked up with the same happy smile as always. "Well hello there, Miss."

"Hello, Miss Dee." I was trying to be as pleasant as possible so that she would allow me to pick her brain.

"All healed already?" She gave me a perplexed and doubtful look.

I tried to adopt Scott's same cheery demeanor. "I think I am," I chirped. All she had to do was look me up on the Internet. The extensive medical paperwork on me would explain it all.

"My, my," she clucked as she wheeled her chair toward me, grabbing my arm with a delicate touch and taking a peak below the white bandage. "You are!" She sounded flabbergasted, and I wasn't exactly shocked to hear it.

I laughed nervously.

She slowly began to unroll the bandages as she hummed under her breath. I worked to gain my confidence, thinking of what I could use to break the ice.

"Miss Dee," I began. "You remember when I came in here the first time, don't you?"

She chuckled merrily. "Oh dear, I don't think I could forget!"

I thought about her response. "Was I the first to be in such bad shape?"

She chuckled again. "You weren't the first, but definitely the worst off."

Okay, so I had my first bit of information: there was something different about how I'd reacted that day. The shortness of breath and the choking feeling in my chest was not an anxiety attack - I knew that - but then if I were the first to be that bad, it was likely the other students had just hyperventilated.

I nodded thoughtfully, hoping to find something as I continued to dig deeper. "So how long has the professor been here?"

She kept her gaze locked on my arm as she worked to remove the opaque tape that was covering the black stitches. "Oh, since the college opened, about four years ago."

I was a little shocked. "Wow, so then, was he just a student? He must have been rather young."

She tilted her head in thought.

"No." She slowly pulled back the tape, but the scar no longer hurt. "He was a professor then, too." She laughed a little to herself. "I always tell him he'll never look forty. He loves it when I say that, always gives him a laugh." She smiled with a hint of adoration.

"Hmmm..." I considered the fact. It was as though she was telling me he'd never aged, but that was impossible. "So do you know him well?" I pushed for more information.

"Oh yeah. The whole staff knows everyone pretty well. We're all rather discreet and independent, though. He usually likes to be alone in the lab a lot, and he lives in the adjoining apartment he had built." She began to snip at each stitch with a skilled hand. "Wow miss, you really did heal fast. I just can't get over it."

I respectfully ignored her comment. "So is he always so…" I paused, "Mysterious?"

She stared me in the eyes, a knowing look crossing her face. "Oh," she was struggling to comprehend. "He's different, yes. But I figure, everyone has their private things. I try to avoid asking and he never seems to volunteer. So, even if I did ask, I doubt he'd really give me an answer."

Her response was vague but did not suggest that she was hiding anything; more like bothered that she didn't know. She did strike me as the type to gossip, always eager to know everything. I moved on from Edgar, now further curious as to why he was there in the woods the day the raven had come.

I wanted to figure out more about the area, things not necessarily typed into a scientific journal or ranger map. "Things are so beautiful here, aren't they?"

"Mmmm," she cooed. "Isn't it magnificent?"

"It sure is." She was making this too easy. "Almost magical. I wonder why there are no legends written about these mountains." I paused, watching her face as I waited for her to take my bait.

She looked up at me, a surprised and excited expression on her face.

"Oh, miss," she cried. "But there are tons!" She smiled and looked back to my arm.

"Really?" I asked, excited to have finally struck gold. "Like what? I'd love to hear one."

She smiled gleefully. "Well," she said as she snipped another stitch. "My favorite is the story about the lakes."

I tilted my head and nodded encouragingly, so that she

130

could see I was interested in what she had to say.

"As the legend goes, the lakes here were created by magic," she whispered dramatically, "That is why the lake is named Diablo Lake, or Devil Lake."

My brow furrowed in intense concentration and interest.

"It is said that hundreds of years ago there was a fight here, a fight between two powerful beings. They say that these two being were devils, though some refer to them as angels." She yanked out the last stitch, reaching in her drawer and pulling out a scar cream. My skin would be flawless in just days.

I continued to stare at her and she smiled, pleased that I was so interested in what she had to say. If she only knew.

"Some say they were fighting over gold, some say power, and other skeptics claim they fought over souls."

Her words rang in my head. I touched my chest, finding it an eerie coincidence that I'd always felt soulless, her story taking my imagination to a place where a battle over souls may have been fought.

"They fought so hard that each place one threw the other down, it indented the ground, creating the tall peaks and deep lakes you see now. And, of course, the color." The way she said it told me that that was the most important part. "They say the color was that of their most prized possession."

I narrowed my eyes in anticipation, but her story had stopped. I sat back, allowing that last sentence to roll in my mind. "Then what was their most prized possession?" I asked perplexed.

She shrugged, her chuckle rattling the collection of bottles on her desk. "That's the mystery. What is a good legend without unanswered questions?"

I stayed silent, unsure of what to say.

Miss Dee looked at me in a motherly way. "Oh, but don't you fret or lose sleep over it, dear. No one has ever figured it out, not in hundreds of years." She patted me on the leg before she rolled her chair back toward her desk.

I pulled my sleeve over the faint scar and stood. "Well, thanks Miss Dee, for the wonderful story."

"Oh, my pleasure, miss," her chubby cheeks lifting in a smile. "Come back soon!"

I smiled one last time before closing the door behind me. I hadn't expected to gain so much information so soon, and I decided to file it away for further reflection.

I found myself compelled to go back to the lab. Something was there, something tugging at my mind but eluding me just the same. I walked down the corridor and into the courtyard where I stared at it for a long while from across the path, contemplating what to do. At last, I stepped forward and tugged at the door handle but it was locked.

Shifting my weight in thought, and only mildly discouraged, I rounded the building, determined to find an entrance. The lab was rectangular, but there was an area at the back that suggested an addition. I assumed that his office resided behind those particular walls.

I rushed toward the first window, disappointed by the blinds that blocked my view. I tested the latch and found it locked tight, refusing to budge even the slightest. No surprise there. Becoming frantic, I moved around the corner, looking for the next window. To my immense disappointment, each window I tried proved to be locked.

I leaned against the wall, sinking to the ground in surrender. My breathing was shallow, adrenaline pulsing through my veins like a drug. I urged myself to calm down and regain my composure. What was I doing?

As I sat there, a sudden deep and throaty laugh erupted from the woods. I felt a lump rise in my stomach as I looked toward the direction of the sound. A tall figure walked from the dark trees and I hurried to stand, now feeling my cheeks blush a vibrant red.

"Do you think I'd make it that easy?" Edgar's laugh echoed across the lake as the sun fell upon his face.

"Don't be ashamed, Elle." Edgar walked toward me, his stride confident. "I can understand your hunger, your desperation to know who I am. I'm afraid I haven't let you know too much about me yet, but I promise that when we get the time, I will."

I gaped at him in surprise. I had been terrified that he'd be angry with me for trying to break in, but instead he understood my desperate position.

"You think I should be angry with you, don't you? But I'm not." It was like he knew how I felt. "Like I said," his eyes were glowing, "I understand."

He approached me, bringing his face close to mine, sending tingles down my spine as I felt his heart enter mine.

"Aren't you going to say hello?" A smile spread across his face.

Mortified at my easy response to his nearness, I stiffened and turned away.

"No," I spat, walking toward the courtyard at a brisk and determined pace.

I heard his heavy steps behind me, gaining ground until he overtook my stride and stepped in front of me, halting me in my path.

"Look," he said, his voice soft, wreaking havoc on my will. "I'm not here to hurt you. I told you that." He gave me a small, tight smile. "I really do miss your fiery attitude, though."

"What do you know about my fiery attitude?" I scowled at him before I elbowed my way past him, again frustrated and confused by his obtuse remark.

He laughed. "I know you'll never do what I ask, that's for sure." His voice was trailing behind me. "How was your weekend?" he teased.

My heart sank and my pace slowed. He must have known I'd gone into the forest.

He caught up to me again and halted me. "Okay, so I messed up," he admitted, his hands shoved in his pockets, his shoulders raised. "I keep forgetting that you don't know me at all..." his voice trailed off.

My eyes blazed at him, and I noticed something give behind his marbled stare. A breeze blew off the lake and I shivered, a bit of rain riding on its tail.

"Listen," he pleaded. "Let me start over. Let's just get to know each other. Okay?"

We stood there, our eyes locked in some sort of staring

match, but I continued my stubborn silence. His face was solemn, sincere, and I felt my resolve began to crumble.

"Please?" His expression was so unsure, and I marveled at how I could make such a powerful man so insecure.

I sighed, giving in. "Fine." My tone was curt, but despite my abruptness, I was secretly pleased. The position of authority was a welcomed relief. I finally had the upper hand.

A smile spread across his face again, making my heart skip a beat.

Something inside me fought to remain rational, to stay away from Edgar and leave. I had never been full of this type of emotion, and I didn't understand what to do. It was almost as though he had a way to invoke things I never thought possible, as though he saw right through me like an old lover. I shook my head, trying to clear my wayward thoughts.

"Then what is all this about?" I spat, clinging to my stubbornness.

He shrugged, falling back to my side as I slowly began to walk forward again.

I rolled my eyes and tried again. "What is your deal?" My voice was shrill with impatience.

He looked at me, raising one eyebrow at my attitude. "Well, I'm not that easy," he chuckled. "Why don't we just start with names. I'm Edgar, Edgar Poe."

A sharp laugh escaped my lips. "Yeah, very funny. You think I'm really going to believe that? What, you're related to the famous nineteenth century poet?"

His eyebrows shot up in defiance. "No really! That's my name," he shrugged. "Then, what's yours?"

I rolled my eyes, shrugging him off. "Whatever."

One side of his mouth curled, as though he knew that my last name was unknown to me. I was an orphan, after all. I knew my first name had been Estella because of the letter my mother left when she had abandoned me, but leaving me without a last name had felt cruel, as though I wasn't worth having a full identity.

I pressed my brows together in irritation. "Well, at any rate, as you know, I'm Estella," I paused. "Estella Smith." I cringed at my lack of originality.

He laughed. "Well then, Estella *Smith*, nice to meet you."

The way he said Smith suggested he knew I was making it up. I took note of the fact that he made no effort to shake hands. I figured this had something to do with the fact he couldn't get too close, though I still didn't understand how or why that made sense.

We were now halfway up the hill toward my cabin, and I became aware of the fact that our chat was almost over, but I was still eager to learn more.

"So," he paused, and I could see the mischief returning to his eyes. "Are you happy to meet me?"

I gave him a wary glare. "What kind of question is that?" I saw his face sink, and I suddenly felt bad. I took a deep breath and regrouped, now attempting to be civil. "I guess it depends on what you classify as happy. That's not really a feeling I have a whole lot of experience with."

He snorted, removing his hands from his pockets. "I suppose you're right. So then are you…" I watched him as he tried to find the right words. "…at least relieved I'm here?"

He had hit the nail on the head, and I gave him a small nod in response.

A content smile filled his face. "Well then, at least that's good, right?" He winked at me as I eyed the woods behind him, still wondering if he knew I had gone there. He was acting formal and poised, his hands now clasped elegantly behind his back and his choice of words proper but vague.

We had arrived at the cabin, and as expected, he slowed to a halt.

Edgar turned to face me. "So, now I have a question for you. I don't want to be too presumptuous, but…" The expression on his face was indecipherable.

I stared at him unblinkingly, waiting for him to continue. I had a feeling that whatever he had to say was going to be pivotal to our fledgling relationship, if you could call it that. He cleared his throat somewhat nervously, and I could feel my palms growing moist.

"What should we call this thing between us?" he began.

I swallowed, now feeling the sweat in my palms. My heart rate surged, as did his.

"I think we both know that this is growing beyond a friendship." He glanced away and smiled. "I know that I am your professor, but that does not make me any older than you. I do still feel the attraction, regardless of the formalities."

He had commanded the conversation, so I said nothing.

"Now I can see that your friend Scott is sweet on you,

and I am going to be honest and say that I am not willing to share you, Elle." His words made my heart begin to hammer even harder. At this rate, I'd surely die of heart failure before twenty. I tried to keep my voice steady as I responded.

"Does it need definition just yet?" I squeaked, a mortified blush spreading over my face and down my neck. This was insane. I wanted to tell him that Scott was just my friend, but at this point, he should have been able to see that.

"I think it does need some sort of definition. Perhaps to keep the confusion at a minimum." He paused for a moment, as though finding the right words. "I would like to date you. That should cover it for now, don't you think?" Edgar was eyeing me with a combination of authority and uncertainty. I wanted to laugh at the absurdity of our conversation but at the same time, I was flattered that he liked me enough to even broach this subject in such a formal manner.

"Dating works for me," I answered in what I hoped was a nonchalant voice. I was intimidated, often boys just skipped around the subject in a formless manner, but here he was getting right to the point. I waited with bated breath for his reply. His eyebrows, which had been knitted together a moment ago, relaxed and he smiled.

"Great," he breathed, sounding relieved to have that behind us.

With that, Edgar turned on his heel, giving me a quick wave as he took off down the hill, leaving me hanging on his final words. I stood there stunned for a moment, my knees weak, trying to make sense of what had just happened. Did that mean that I was his girlfriend now? I was completely flustered as I finally turned and went into my cabin.

I threw my bag down on the bed, and the extra apple I'd gotten rolled onto the floor. I picked it up, feeling my stomach grumble. I was starving, wishing I could seek comfort with a large cheese pizza. Pizza always made my mind clear.

After a few moments of pacing, I finally gave in to my hunger, figuring the cafeteria would at least serve something that could distract me, even if it wasn't pizza. Anything that could take my mind off Edgar and the way I'd felt in his presence. I was muttering to myself as I walked back out the door and slammed it behind me.

As I pulled open the large doors to the cafeteria, I heard an excited yelp. When I looked to the sound, I was not surprised to see Sarah bouncing up and down in her chair, waving maniacally in my direction.

"Elle!" she yelled, causing everyone in the room to turn and look directly at me. Great.

My cheeks flushed in utter embarrassment. I rushed over to where Scott and Sarah sat, keeping my head ducked in hopes that people would quit staring.

"Elle!" Sarah sang again as I got close.

"Shh, Sarah. I'm right here. There's no need to shout!" I put my hands up to calm her.

She gave me a confused look as though she hadn't recognized she was being loud. She held a sloppy piece of something in her hand, and as I came closer, I realized she was eating a piece of pizza from a large round in the middle of the table.

"You want some?" she asked, apparently noticing my

covetous stare.

"Yes!" I breathed in delight. "You read my mind!" I gave her a thankful grin as she grinned in return.

"So, Elle," Scott chimed in. "How was the rest of your evening? Anymore life threatening occurrences?"

I wrinkled my nose at him. "No." My mouth was full of what I quickly realized was tofu cheese. Surprisingly it wasn't bad, actually tasting a lot like the real thing. It was food after all, and that was really all that mattered at this point.

"I was just kidding." He laughed and gave me a gentle nudge on the shoulder.

I swallowed. "Oh, I know," I added. "I was just giving you a hard time. So, what did you guys do?"

They eyed each other and smiled, and I deduced I probably didn't need all the details.

"Well," Scott began to blush. "She beat me at Monopoly, that's about all." The crack in his voice suggested otherwise, and I mentally cringed at the thought of them engaged in any sort of intimacy. TMI – too much information, even if he didn't actually say anything personal. His tone and look were enough.

"I could never stand Monopoly." I was trying to ease the mood, regretting the fact I'd even asked. "It's too long, and there are too many rules," I explained as I grabbed another slice.

"Yeah," I could tell Scott was working to change the subject. "So are you going to tell anyone about the bear you saw?"

I froze. The truth was there was no bear, but technically

you're supposed to report sightings so that other hikers are aware. "Uh huh," I grunted and shoved a huge bite in my mouth, chewing and nodding. I was lying, but he didn't need to know that.

He smiled. "Oh good, because if you weren't up to it, I would have done it for you."

"Yeah, or I could," Sarah chimed in.

They were like twins or something.

I waved them away. "Oh no, I got it handled." The last thing I needed was for them to tell on me and then for Edgar to find out I had been out there when I had promised I wouldn't. That's no way to impress the man I was now dating.

He laughed. "Yeah, I suppose Professor Edgar is the one who handles that anyway. You know, might give you a chance to ask him out." He winked at me in a way that looked more like a twitch; he wasn't all that smooth.

Regardless, I blushed, averting my eyes.

"I'm just kidding, Elle. Calm down. You look absolutely terrified." He nudged me and I almost choked.

Sarah gave us both a strange look. "Estella has a thing for Professor Edgar?" She crinkled her nose. "I mean, how old is he?"

"Oh, apparently he's only a little older than us," I blurted before I could stop myself.

They both stared at me with horrified faces.

"What? I asked him." I tried to defend myself.

Scott snapped out of his stare and whistled in disbelief. "You actually asked him that?" His face was turning red with laughter. "Elle, you really do have a death wish, don't you? I'm surprised he didn't decapitate you then and there."

This time it was me that shoved Scott.

"Hey, now," he chortled. "No need to resort to violence."

They were both giggling now, and I scowled at them playfully in return.

Sarah caught her breath, sobering a bit. "How does that work? He's been here for like, five years." She began counting on her fingers under her breath.

I shrugged. "Good genes, I guess. He must be the long lost discoverer of the fountain of youth." I was proud of the fact I'd actually made a joke, my first in history.

They both laughed as I said it, and somewhere deep inside my heart, I felt a flicker of happiness.

SOUL MATE

Later that evening, I found myself once again pacing in my silent room. The suspense was irritating and I wished that for a moment, I hadn't left Scott and Sarah so soon. I flipped through a few books but found that wasn't helping. As time crawled, my irritation only grew and my attention faltered. At dusk, I finally gave up and walked outside as the stars began to emerge.

The continuing cool weather signaled that fall had officially descended on the college, and I was amazed by how fast it had all changed over the course of one weekend. The mountains were dotted with orange where the occasional leafy tree emerged amongst the evergreens, but considering the cruel winters, there weren't many trees like that. I looked at the lake down the hill as the dawning moon lit a long stripe of blue-green across the surface. As I watched the rippling water, I thought about the story Nurse Dee had told me about the color and how it was created, wondering now, if something like that was even possible.

A part of me craved Edgar's companionship, yet another part of me couldn't help but feel cautious toward him. I needed to figure out how Edgar seemed to know me so well, how he already seemed to have an attachment to me after so short a time, and why I felt – despite my protests – so attracted to him in return. The idea that he was a sort of magic devil, as Nurse Dee had suggested, kept invading my thoughts. Surely he was no angel, he couldn't be. He was too dark for that.

A strong wind blew then, and I noticed a familiar scent that froze all my thoughts. I closed my eyes, trying to pinpoint its exact origin. It was something floral, yet warm, like spring would smell when the trees came back to life. I heard a few leaves blow past the cabin as I slowly opened my eyes. I jumped, grabbing my chest and gasping for air as Edgar now stood before me, appearing out of nowhere like a ghost.

"Hello," he said in a quiet voice.

I looked at him with alarmed surprise. I swallowed a few times, calming myself.

He laughed again. "Sorry. I keep sneaking up on you."

I gave him a reproachful look. "Maybe you should try approaching like normal people do. Maybe even make some noise. Footsteps are a good start, or take up whistling."

He shook his head as he walked forward and sat down next to me on the porch. He was close enough to converse, but still an arms length away.

"But then I'd be like normal people," he said with a sly smirk, "and normal people are boring."

His air had a strange effect on me. The way he moved exuded grace with a possession of power that made me feel fragile in his presence. I crossed my arms and looked toward the darkened sky, thousands of stars now glowing above us through the crisp air.

Edgar sighed. "Beautiful, aren't they?" He drew in a heavy breath, closing his eyes and drinking in the scent of the night.

I nodded, studying his movements.

He opened his eyes and dropped his gaze to me. "So, since we are still getting to know one another," he began, a crooked smile crossed his face, clearly enjoying the little game he'd started. "What do you think of me?"

I gave him a level look. "Truthfully? I think you're dangerous." I could tell my blunt remark took him off guard. He laughed. "Maybe," he paused, "But not to you. Like I've told you already, I won't ever hurt you."

The way he said it sent chills down my spine. No matter how hard I tried to believe that he'd never hurt me, I just couldn't shake off my doubt. "What…" I paused to gather my swimming thoughts. "What was it the first time I saw you, then? Why did I feel so…" I struggled to find the right words.

"Weak?" Edgar supplied knowingly.

"Yeah," I began to fidget with my shirt hem. "I felt so completely drained, and the pain," I put my hand to my chest.

"I felt like I was choking."

He nodded gravely, no spark of humor to his face now. "It's something between us, something powerful that I had to be prepared to control, but couldn't."

My curious gaze practically bore a hole through his face as I stared, hungry to know more, urging him to look me in the eyes. "Do you know what it is, this powerful thing between us?"

He shot his eyes toward me, their magnificence pulsing in my bones. "Yes, I do." He was searching my face as though remembering something about it. "But, I'm not sure you're ready to hear it just yet."

Frustration blazed in my eyes. "You keep saying that, but why not?" My tone was curt. "I need to know what I am, what we are. I can't do this anymore." It was times like this I'd wish I could cry.

Edgar looked shocked at my sudden burst of emotion and moved closer. I saw him looking at me from the corner of my eye, and I noticed a deep sadness cross his face. For a moment he seemed to be weighing his options, hesitating to make his next move. I heard him swallow as he reached toward my arm. My heart rate spiked. He halted for a moment as though he had changed his mind, but as my mind screamed for him to do it, his hand continued toward mine. He brushed one finger down the length of my palm. Holding my breath, I wasn't sure exactly what to expect, but as a tear formed in my eye and rolled down my cheek, I felt an overwhelming surge of emotion fill my darkened soul.

I gasped, bringing one shaking hand to my face in

astonishment, wiping away the tear. "What…" My throat was choked as he drew back, and I shot my gaze to meet his. "How did you do that?" I was frantic, almost to the point of hysteria. I had never cried before.

He smiled. "That's what I want to tell you, but I don't know how."

I searched his face. "You know, don't you? You know how to make me feel."

He shook his head. "No, I don't. I was hoping maybe you did, but apparently not."

I furrowed my brow. "I don't understand." I reached a shaking hand toward him, but he backed away.

"Elle, you don't know what kind of power you possess over me. You will kill yourself if you aren't careful." His eyes were apologetic but full of adoration. How could that be?

My gaze fell from his, and I dropped my hand as the emotion in my soul faded. "But, you touched me," I added, sounding like a child.

"Yes," he looked to the stars. "But it was hard. It takes a lot of self control for me to do that."

I nodded solemnly, not quite understanding but willing to accept his answer.

"You and I are opposites, of sorts. Like a battery. There is a positive end and a negative, but that doesn't mean they go together without their flaws." I hungered for his words as he continued. "Our history goes far beyond all you know," he said, watching my face for a reaction. "When I said we were the same age, I meant…."

He stopped, careful with his words as though trying

not to shock me, but I didn't care anymore. Life was worthless without my sense of happiness.

"Please, Edgar. I want to hear anything you can tell me." His gaze fell to mine, and I could see he was struggling to resist my desperation.

"It's just that we've been here a long time, if not in body, then in soul. I deeply wish you could remember it all." I saw the emptiness in his eyes. "But this is one outcome we had expected and it was a risk we had to take."

I didn't know exactly what his vague explanation meant, or what "we" entailed, but I was certain for the first time I wasn't feeling out of place. Something about this moment felt like home. Something about his words seemed believable. I had never felt a connection to the world, as though set apart. The things I could do and the things I felt, that was not normal.

"Then what are we?" I asked, rather bluntly.

A smile returned to his face. "Well," I saw his eyes grow bright with thought. "Some used to call us the Wiccan," he paused, watching the reaction on my face, "but the term seems cheesy, so I try not to use it. And there are some that called us the devil, and still others, the angels. I prefer the word *unique*. It sounds human enough that it doesn't seem so strange."

My thoughts flashed to the legend. "*Diablo Lake*," I whispered, and he looked sharply in my direction.

"You remember that?" he asked with excitement.

I stared into his eyes as adrenaline poured into my veins. "What do you mean by remember that? The story is hundreds of years old. Of course I don't remember that."

The excitement faded from his face.

"I just heard the legend, about how it was made," I added softly, thinking of Nurse Dee.

He sighed. "Well, yeah," he said as disappointment washed over him. "Maybe it's a good thing you don't remember that day. That was the last time I saw you."

My mind was swimming wildly, the words he was saying like a dream. "What do you mean?"

"When I saw you in your..." he paused, a weird look crossing his face, "Past life." The way he said it seemed unclear.

I could tell there was a strange connection between what he was referring to as then and now. "What was I to you in this past life?" My eyes searched his, but he again looked away.

"Just," he shrugged, "a friend." I saw a shy smile spread across his face, and I suddenly realized why he was acting so forward toward me: perhaps he had loved me.

He smiled. "But that was ages ago." He was changing the subject. "Right now, you don't know me at all."

"How am I to believe that what you are saying is true?" I didn't want to lose the conversation.

He nodded, "I know you believe what I'm saying. You know you can trust me because you feel it too, don't you?"

I licked my lips, watching his eyes as though in a trance. I felt so warm, his heart like a drum calling me home. "I do," I replied simply.

His lips parted and he exhaled. "Let's go do something

less depressing." He stood with sudden determination, urging me to follow as he briskly changed the subject.

"Like what?" I breathed, staggering to a standing position as the adrenaline inhibited my movement. He was tall, something I hadn't really noticed due to my overall fascination with his model physique.

"I want to show you some things from your past," he said.

At his urging, we slowly strolled down the hill. I watched him as he walked, his carriage poised and dominating. Every thought in my head had been jumbled, and it was hard to organize all the things he'd told me. I began to fear that if he were indeed some sort of Wiccan, then perhaps I was under a spell. I felt in control, not as though he had done something, but then there was that touch. It had filled me with a sweet feeling I could not explain, something I could not remember feeling before. It was then that I began to wonder just what a Wiccan even was. It was a witch, I thought, but what kind of witch? Besides, I had never once done a single magical thing, well, unless you counted the plants. I rubbed the muscles of my neck with my hand and shook the image from my head. This was absurd.

We walked the rest of the way in silence, and I saw now that he was leading me to the lab. He began fishing in his pockets for the keys as we approached. He was swift to unlock the door, inviting me in as he held it open for me. I entered the room with caution, still remembering my dream and the raven. I stood staring into the darkness, waiting just inside the door while he came in behind me and turned on a light. I followed him past the aisles of empty workstations until we arrived at the door to his office and what I supposed was also his apartment. He pulled out a second set of keys from somewhere near his lapel, unlocking the door and ushering me in.

The office was dark, but I somehow sensed that there was someone or something there. As I glanced around the room, I was shocked by the flicker of a half-dozen tiny flashing lights facing me. He walked into the darkness to my right and I was unsure exactly where he was headed, but figured he'd obviously known better than I. With a sudden crack, I heard the scratch of a match and a soft light filled the room. Edgar lit some candles and the six intense flickering orbs revealed three pairs of bird eyes as the candlelight fell across their downy feathers.

The first was the hawk from class, perched on a shelf toward the top of the tall office, its body poised as it had been in class. Its wing looked healed and relaxed at his side. The next was an owl that stood on a perch by the far window. The third was a snow-white hawk of some kind, an animal I'd never seen in his classroom before now.

The white hawk seemed to become flustered at my presence, its weight shifting from one foot to the next on the top of a large cage in the corner. Edgar watched as the white hawk ogled me, a smile crossing his face as he approached it and gave it a gentle nudge on its head, ruffling its feathers.

Looking around the small room, I wondered where he slept. Though the nurse had said that this was where he lived, there was no sign of a bed or kitchen. There was a large wood desk centered in the space, its design European and clearly antique, the top showing years of use upon it's roughened surface. The outer perimeter of the room was lined with various perches and shelves, stuffed from floor to ceiling with dusty books and manuscripts. I narrowed my eyes at the spines of the books, finding them shockingly old, and most of them rare first editions.

Edgar moved toward the large brown hawk I'd seen in class. "This is Henry," he said, looking at me with pride. "You've met him before, and yes, he is thankful you are here and thankful you saved his wing." Edgar motioned toward the owl. "And of course, that is Alexander. You've seen him before, too." The owl tilted its head at me, his eyes flashing like silver coins.

I made no attempt to move, afraid I would startle them.

Edgar walked toward the third bird, the white hawk. "And this is Isabelle." He looked at her with a soft smile on his face, her stare never breaking away from me. "She is native to warmer climates than this, but then again, her owner was a warmer being, so they were good together."

He looked at me with a sly smile. "Would you like her back now?" His face was amused by the shock that filled my eyes.

I stared at Isabelle in astonishment. Would I like her back? "She's mine?" I stuttered, nervous to be so close.

"Yes, Elle." His voice was strong and convincing.

Her petite beak was a deep grey fading to a snow white head and body. She blinked at me as she tilted her head from

152

side to side, still rocking back and forth in excitement on her perch.

Edgar put his hand on her milky feathers. "Can't you see how happy she is to see you? She's been waiting for centuries."

I felt my heart quicken. "Centuries?" I gasped.

He gave Isabelle a nudge and she spread her wings, pushing off the cage and gliding down toward me. Without hesitation, as though I had done it in another life, I put my arm up to catch her.

"So have I," he whispered, and I couldn't tell if he'd meant me to hear it or not. "See," Edgar's face was animated with delight and his marbled eyes twinkled. "She loves you. It's not right for me to keep her from you anymore, so now she's yours again."

My face was awash in disbelief. I had never kept a pet because they had always drastically changed under my care. It was hard to explain why my new kitten had grown to a full-sized cat overnight.

"Really?" I looked at Edgar with wide eyes, noticing his face was now somewhat sad. "What is it, what's wrong?" I asked, my brow creased with concern.

He took a few careful steps toward me. "I just miss your smile." He glanced away toward the hawk, closing his eyes as though concentrating on something.

I watched him with curious intensity, perplexed by the pained look on his face. When he opened his eyes again, they were a deep serene grey. He took a few steps closer as Isabelle moved to my shoulder. Despite her massive wing span, she was the perfect size, no more than one pound at the most.

I watched as Edgar lifted a hand toward me, letting it hover just inches from my cheek. My breathing quickened as he looked at me, focusing his eyes on mine. My heart was racing in fear and excitement, afraid of what I did not know, afraid to hurt him or myself, but at the same time excited to have him so close.

In measured increments, he brought his hand closer to my face and I closed my eyes, afraid of what would happen. Finally, his hand touched my cheek and a cold tingling pierced through my skin. The sensation was unbelievable as I felt it spreading from the veins in my cheek through my whole face until it hit my spine. From there a tingling warmth filtered through my entire body and something began to flicker in my soul.

Like lighting a match, the flicker burst into a fireball and the breath was torn from my body. My eyes shot open and I stared into Edgar's. His eyes went from a cool grey to a bright blue, and the warm sensation filled my every vein.

I felt my lips begin to curl upward, the sensation of euphoria causing my head to swim. My back arched in bliss, and instantly, I remembered this feeling. For the first time in what seemed a lifetime, I was smiling.

As the feeling spiked, I realized what was happening. Fear quickly washed over my body and I jerked away. "Stop!" I yelled, falling back against his desk. "Stop this."

His eyes were radiant but alarmed. "Elle, you're alright." He stepped toward me with his hands in the air.

I braced myself against the desk, my fingers gripping

the wood as the warmth in my chest slowly faded. "You're drugging me," I spat.

He shook his head, taking one more careful step. "I assure you, the reaction is not my doing. It's ours."

My nostrils flailed as I breathed hard, my jaw clenched shut.

I let him take another step toward me. "I'm not tricking you. Can't you see? That feeling is real. This is who you are." He was close to me now, his hand moving once again toward my cheek.

I longed to feel it again, my mind struggling between the feelings of happiness and my feelings of fear. He touched me then, the feeling bringing calm to my body as I relaxed into his touch. He pulled his hand away a moment later, his eyes again more brilliant.

A satisfied grin crossed his face. "See, that's what I was missing," he breathed. He stepped away from me, showing me that he meant no harm. His eyes were a shocking deep blue, and I was curious what it was that had caused the more than subtle change. Edgar looked away, his breathing now labored.

"Does that hurt you?" I asked, feeling composed.

"It does. See, why would I do that if it hurt me? I only did it for you, so that you could understand."

My smile began to die as the light in my soul faded to smoldering nothingness, Edgar's pained smile also leaving as he now focused on controlling whatever demons he now faced.

"What is it, Edgar?" I asked. "What makes that happen

155

to me?"

He sighed. "It's difficult to explain." He walked to his desk where he grabbed an apple he'd left there. "Watch," he held the apple in his hand and I watched as his eyes changed into the pure black I had recognized on my first day.

The apple began to quickly deteriorate as though all the juices were evaporating out of it. I was horrified as I pictured the apple as me, and my adrenaline pumped as I realized the lethal nature of his touch. His brows pressed together in concentration and his eyes flashed as the darkness faded back to the deep royal blue they had been after touching me.

"Here," he pushed his hand toward me.

With hesitation, I grasped the shriveled apple and brought it to my face. Just as fast as it had deflated, it began to prosper and heal. The skin re-constituted itself as though the hands of time had twisted back, returning the apple to its ripest youth. My touch revitalized the fruit in its entirety with little effort, even going as far as to bring it a certain light, as though it were glowing. My talents had never been this strong before.

"You see, Elle." There was a look of despair to his face as he spoke. "You give things life, all things," he paused as he hung his head, miserable in his existence. "I just take it. You are the positive end of the battery, and I am the negative."

I stared at the apple in amazement, allowing the sinister reality of his being sink in. "But it happened so fast, just now."

Edgar gave me little time to talk, "Yes. What I just did gave you strength, as it did me. Though for me it came with its trials."

"But, that's why you're afraid to touch me. You're afraid you will kill me."

He sighed. "Yes, my trials." Looking back up at me, he gently touched my hair. "But I can control it, especially with animals and nature, and even humans. It's just hard with you because the soul I crave most is yours."

A perplexed look crossed my face. "But I don't have a soul."

He perked up. "But you do!" A sly smile crossed his face. "You see, long ago, in your past life, you hid it inside me and only you know how to get it back. Even I can't access it without you." He was excited now. "This feeling that you just experienced, I haven't felt it either, not for a long time. That's what makes it so tempting and so hard for me to resist. Our touch unlocks this energy for the both of us."

I looked at him, confused.

His face again became solemn. "But what I fear is you'll never remember what you did to put your soul inside my heart. The only way you're feeling it now is through my poisonous touch."

I looked at him with extreme anxiety. "But why did I hide it in you?" I tilted my head in misunderstanding.

"To save yourself." He was walking away from me now, heading toward the wall where he grabbed a photo of a bird off the shelf, looking at it with mild interest.

I wasn't sure why I'd give my soul to the very thing that could kill it. "To save me from you? But that doesn't make sense. Then why would I hide it in you?"

He turned to look at me, his eyes fading to a pale blue grey. "No, to save you from something else."

He was being vague, and I could hear the sadness in his voice as he said it. Obviously, something had happened. Something had caused me to separate my mind from my soul. "But then..." I stopped. I had no idea what to say. Nothing made sense anymore.

"Elle," he took a deep breath. "I'm not complete without you. It sounds crazy, and probably a little more than you were bargaining for when you first laid your beautiful eyes on me, but it's a vicious and painful existence we've lived."

I nodded absently, feeling as though this was now my responsibility to fix.

"We are bound together by fate, by life. When one of us dies," his eyes fluttered to mine, "it's like losing the only thing that matters."

I touched my chest as Isabelle still sat, quiet and content, on my shoulder, her feathers fluffed as though asleep.

"I'm not sure if you want to hear the story, Elle, but I think its time you know." He placed the photo back on the shelf, turning to me and taking three paces forward.

I shifted my weight in excitement. "I want to know." I took a step forward, no longer feeling strange about the intensity that was between us. I believed him. I could feel the truth of it.

He sighed, collecting his thoughts. "When you were born into this world, so was I." He put his hand to his heart. "In the beginning we were one being. We were perfect: happy, strong, fast, and smart. But soon, the Gods grew angry and jealous at our utter perfection. One day, their rage became so great that they tore us all apart, and all of our kind was eternally damned to live a life of separation and turmoil."

He was pacing now, his hands clasped together in thought.

"One half became strong, fast, and intense, the bringers of death and war. The other half became smart, sharp, and gifted with life, and ultimately became the mothers, or watchers of our souls."

"But my half, the death half, was also blessed with power, and for some that power became an obsession and we took our gift for granted. It was these dark halves that became jealous of their mate and the proprietor of their most prized possession: the soul, the blue light of love and life. It's why I'm drawn to you, Elle. I can't resist it, but I can stop myself from taking it. But in this fact, we are also soul mates." He smirked at the word. "Literally."

I breathed slowly, my body tingling with a sudden release, all my fear and anger, as well as my attraction from the past few days, was all justified. "So basically," my voice was low and intense. "We share the same soul, in love?" I was trying to clarify his story somehow.

He looked at me with a glitter in his eye. "Essentially, yes. But also in happiness." He walked to his desk and lowered himself into the blue velvet chair. I could sense his exhaustion now. "Centuries ago we had it figured out. We had learned how to live with each other, to be happy as many of our kind also did. I learned to resist my jealous urge to kill you and steal the soul for myself. You see…" he leaned back in his chair. "I need energy to live, natural energy. Right now, the best I can do is gather it from the stars and nature." His face looked hallowed as though remembering a better day. "But you, before…" he paused. "All I had to do was be around you to get it."

I listened with unrestrained curiosity, my body breaking out in a sweat as the adrenaline pulsed undiluted through my blood. This was everything I had always dreamed to know, and now, it all made sense. It was as though all the suffering was somehow explained, as though I could finally move on from my sorrow, and live a life I could be proud of; a life I could finally feel.

His body was tense. "You have no concept of who you are, or what you can be." There was a fire in his eyes as he talked. "With your soul intact, you will be happy again." He sat forward in his chair. "The being I see in front of me pains my heart. You're nothing but a severed shell of your beautiful self. Your skin, your hair used to be so brilliant and so alive."

Under this new light, everything about Edgar seemed different. Despite the fact I'd only been here a short time, seeing him now made my heart feel tight with anxiety, as though longing to be close to him, to never be apart.

I slowly stepped toward him. "Then how can you be happy? How are you okay?" There was a passion to my voice I'd never known. If he couldn't access my soul, either, than why was he so alive with life and emotion?

He sat forward again, mulling over my question. "I may be happy, but I'm weak. Like you lose your happiness, I lose my strength." He sighed. "I'm tired, Elle. Every day is a struggle. I need your love, your life to bring me energy, not just your soul." He sighed again. "Even though I may seem happy now, I wasn't when you were gone, even when I could be. It's all an act, to keep people away from me, to make sure they fear me, though the strength barely lasts."

"So then, your weakness is why you were unable to help yourself when you first saw me." Something inside of me was grafting myself closer to him, pulling me in.

"Yes." He was fidgeting with a compass on his desk. "That first day in my class, with Henry, I was overwhelmed with desperation. I was weak beyond apprehension and hunger was driving me to try to kill you, but then," he paused, his eyes sad. "The love I felt deep inside, it saved you, and saved me. If you die, I'd never be able to live with myself. I couldn't do it again."

I stood there for a moment, overwhelmed with thought. I noticed the way his cheeks now seemed flushed, as though the time we'd spent here was already revitalizing his heart.

He sat up, giving me a bleak smile. "I think it's time I take you and Isabelle back to your cabin. It's getting late." He smiled at us as we stood there in the flickering light of the candles.

"*My girls*," he whispered softly under his breath.

BREAK OUT

The next day I woke to Isabelle's subtle purring. During the night, she had moved from the bed frame where I had perched her to a nesting position inside my arm. It was a surprise to see a bird cuddling as she was, but I guess it didn't seem inconceivable that they could, just inconceivable that a creature such as her would love a person so much.

I lay motionless for a few moments as I let the reality of everything sink in. I thought about last night, how Edgar had divulged a whole other world to me, things that I'd never imagined could exist. I had always figured I was the only one of my kind - my kind meaning, absolutely weird.

It was still pretty early and a part of me wondered if Scott would be showing up soon, or if he'd officially forgotten me in his love daze with Sarah. With extreme care, I drew my arm out from around Isabelle, moving as quietly as I could. After freeing my arm, I moved out from under the covers and tiptoed to the bathroom, closing the door behind me with a silent click and turning on the shower.

I washed my hair under the soothing water, my energy ignited and my soul longing to smile, though that ability still evaded me. There was a feeling of anticipation in my blood today, the adrenaline from last night still lingering. I was eager to get the hatchery class over with, anxious to see Edgar again. Now that I understood our special chemistry, it felt painful being apart. The string that was pulling me toward him was now yanking at my chest harder than ever. Something about being with him felt like centuries of life, centuries of some sort of comfort and completion that I needed to survive.

I felt the empty space in my chest, felt how desperate I was to get close to him and be whole again. I exhaled with eagerness and expectation. I needed that feeling back, and for the first time I felt I could finally see the end to my suffering, a solution that was true rather than another medication. Edgar was now all the drug I needed, and the only cure to the pain.

Shutting off the water, I jumped out of the shower and wrapped a towel around me as I opened my door. A low scream escaped my lips as I jumped back. Blinking hard a few times, I recognized the white thing was just Isabelle, standing like a stunned puppy on the floor before me, watching me with shocked curiosity.

I let out a relieved breath. For a moment, my mind had backtracked to that day in the woods and the grayish-white creature that had been following me. I stood there clutching the towel to my chest, my heart pounding. Isabelle was clearly much smaller than the thing in the woods, but when caught off guard, it's rather hard to control your mind's reactions.

Isabelle tilted her head up and moved aside so I could pass, her eyes apologetic as though sorry she'd scared me.

"Isabelle," I gasped. "Don't do that again." Her head tilted to the other side as though comprehending what I'd said. She scooted back, her claws clicking and sliding against the lacquered wood floors.

As I rummaged for something to wear, she hopped up to my bag, poking her head in. Isabelle was unlike any animal, let alone hawk, I had ever seen. Her mannerisms were more like a cat or dog, rather than a bird of prey. She nipped at my hand as I reached for a green shirt.

"Ouch, okay," I looked at her with my brow furrowed. "I'll pick something else."

I moved my hand from the green shirt to a red hooded sweatshirt and she looked up at me, her eyes glinting.

"This one?" I asked, amazed at how she seemed to understand.

She clicked her tongue at me and jumped around onto the floor.

A sharp exhale escaped my lips, almost like a laugh, but without the joy. "Wow, girl. I guess that's a yes."

I pulled the sweatshirt over my head as she watched, the warm fleece making my hair stick to my face with static from the dry climate. I pulled the rubber band from my hand and knotted my hair in a bun. I was sick of it tangling in the wind.

Content, Isabelle suddenly spread her wings, gently fanning them until she took flight, landing like an expert on the windowsill toward the back of the cabin and tapping her beak against the glass.

I stood, adjusting the sweatshirt around my waist. Approaching her, I placed my hand on her back. "Do you want to go out, Isabelle?"

She tilted her head to one side, her small eyes flashing as she blinked. I grasped the handle and threw the window open, filling the room with the crisp morning air. She seemed to look at me with gratitude as she took off, floating up the hill and into the morning mist. I shrugged my shoulders, figuring she knew what she was doing.

No sooner than she had disappeared, there was a sudden familiar knocking at the door. I whipped around, shutting the back window with a soft click then shuffling to the door. When I whisked it open, my eyes fell on two cheery looking faces and my mind raced with excitement.

"Elle!" sang Scott as Sarah stood, beaming next to him.

I quickly processed the scene, noticing the fact that they were now officially holding hands. "Hi, guys!" I tried to exude the same excitement my mind felt, feeling like an idiot as it came out awkwardly.

"Hey!" Scott boomed again. "Ready for class?"

"Yep!" I ran back to my bed and grabbed my bag. "Ready to go," I sang, still practicing the excitement. Shutting the door behind me, I grabbed my boots as Scott and Sarah stepped down onto the path. It would be easy for Edgar to see that Scott no longer held a glimmer of attraction toward me as he stared longingly at Sarah.

I pulled each boot over my heel, fumbling with the laces when I caught the sudden glimpse of a bird flying into the tree behind them. Careful not to attract attention, I glanced up, recognizing the milky white feathers glowing under the morning haze. A dead mouse hung in Isabelle's mouth and a glint of utter happiness flashed in her eyes. She was gloating about her skillful morning catch and I rolled my eyes at her as she again took off down the hill.

My gaze fell back to Scott and Sarah whom were now staring at Isabelle as she glided over the lake, enjoying her breakfast.

"Wow," Sarah gasped. "What kind of bird was that you suppose?"

I saw her look to Scott for an answer as he seemed to struggle to figure it out. "Um well…" A confident look crossed his face. "I'm pretty certain that was a white snow owl."

I bit my tongue as I tried to resist correcting him, seeing how impressed Sarah had seemed, not wanting to ruin the moment. A smug grin crossed Scott's face.

"Okay guys. Let's go." I walked up to them and the three of us turned onto the path and briskly walked to class.

The hatchery was as boring as ever. The professor had ended up being the environmental type that just liked to hear herself talk. I never realized there were five ways to explain the very same fact, but it did make it seem like she really knew more than she likely did, and I'm guessing that was her goal. I stood in the back row, shaking my leg impatiently.

I looked around the room, noticing the usual faces

staring like zombies toward the front. It was clear no one but Scott took any interest in this lecture, and it never made sense to me. If it was so horrible, then don't come. I thought about that point for a minute, realizing I was being a hypocrite. I actually didn't like any of it either, just the class with Edgar. As I rolled my eyes and looked to my left, my gaze fell on a fresh face staring at me over his shoulder.

Caught off guard, I looked away, feeling somewhat offended. I pressed my brows together and quickly glanced back, finding that he was still staring. I exhaled and looked away as I crossed my arms. This guy didn't even know me and already he was staring. Looking back for a third time, I glared at him, narrowing my eyes in hopes of scaring him off. My stare succeeded because he looked shocked and whipped his head back to the front. Intrigued, I continued to study him.

His clothes were not the type the students here usually wore. I glanced to his shoes, raising one eyebrow as I noticed he wore a pair of stylish sneakers, hardly the shoes you'd even wear to a muddy park, let alone the wilderness. Everyone in the room wore heavy boots and hiking shoes, even me. Moving my gaze upward, I noticed his jeans looked expensive and designer, and his coat was black leather, probably the only bit of butchered animal skin within fifty miles. He was clearly out of place. His presence certainly made the class more exciting than before.

As I sat there staring curiously, he once again looked over his shoulder at me, as though he knew I was staring. His eyes were an intense bronze and I quickly looked away, staring at a shelf behind him in hopes that he hadn't noticed the way I had been gawking.

His face was cold and mean, much like everyone else, except, he was shockingly pale. Most students had tanned skin, a result of the hiking and extensive outdoor activity that was enjoyed at the college. I quickly ruled out the idea that he was another Edgar-type based on the somewhat scruffy yet rich biker thing he had going, but still, he wasn't like everyone else, either. He had tousled brown hair that only made his features seem sharper. I watched him from the corner of my eye and marveled at how smooth and young his face was, the powdery complexion a far cry from the radiant glow Edgar seemed to possess.

He once again turned to the front as another student took notice, glaring at us as though we'd somehow disrupted his listening experience. I pursed my lips and began tapping my foot again. Something about this guy seemed too strange to let slide, and I made a mental note to keep my eye on him. As I thought this, the new kid seemed to laugh to himself, his back shaking. The kid next to him stepped away, as though he were a crazed lunatic.

Finally, the professor excused us and I dropped the mysterious newcomer from my mind as I rushed to hook Sarah and Scott by the arm and lead them out, my attention now crowded with thoughts of Edgar.

Scott looked at me with a knowing grin on his face. "Wow, Estella. You really do have a crush on the teacher, don't you?"

I gave him a reproachful glare, looking to Sarah for some support. As we walked through the door, I discreetly looked over my shoulder, noticing that the new guy had hung back. As I watched him, a voice echoed in my head and it took me by surprise.

"What?" It whispered, as though the mysterious guy had said it out loud.

I squinted my eyes at him, pushing my brows together even further, but he looked away. My jaw dropped in shock but I dismissed the idea that he had spoken to me telepathically. I must have just heard someone nearby.

"Hey, Elle. Did you hear me?" Scott was shaking my arm.

I whipped my head back forward, my arms still laced with Sarah and Scott's. "What?"

Scott rolled his eyes. "I said, you really do have a crush on Professor Edgar, don't you?" he sighed. "But it was sort of funnier a minute ago. You ruined it while you were staring at the new guy. Perhaps you have a crush on Edgar now."

Sarah gave me a sweet grin before giving Scott a sassy frown. "Scott, leave her alone. Besides, Edgar *is* pretty cute." I saw her glance at the new guy as well. A sour look passed over Scott's face and Sarah quickly back-peddled. "But not as cute as you."

Scott's face turned a vibrant red and I rolled my eyes in disgust. They were whispering and giggling to each other now so I stepped away from them, definitely not wanting to hear their lovey-dovey conversation.

We pushed through the doors into class and went straight to our station. Scott ran to get a third stool for Sara. I sat at the far end of the table, staring at the door and feeling the pull toward it become greater with each passing minute. I hardly noticed as the classroom filled and the voices droned all around me.

Thinking I could finally relax after the disturbing morning, my body went tense as I saw the new guy enter the room, pausing at the door. The air around him felt cold and foreboding, and I couldn't help but shudder. He looked around with a blank face before striding toward the front, taking a seat somewhere in the middle between the first and third rows at the only station that was empty. I was staring a hole in the back of his head. Something about him was not human, but this time, he didn't look back at me.

Silence fell over the room as Edgar emerged through the door and my attention was pulled away from the new guy to him. His face was more beautiful than the last time I'd seen him.

"Hello, class," he boomed, and I felt smug, knowing that he really wasn't as scary as most believed and that it was all for show.

His gaze was locked on mine and I could see happiness living there behind his serious expression. He was wearing a long-sleeved black shirt with jeans and a pair of nice black boots. He folded his arms across his chest as he leaned against the desk, crossing his feet with arrogance. His black hair was perfectly tousled. The pale blue-grey of his eyes told me he was calm, but the cloudiness told me he was anxious as well.

"How did we do with the research into the foreign intruder?" he asked in a dark tone, striking fear into the

170

hearts of all those with unfinished papers.

I hadn't written a paper, figuring there was absolutely no point, and if anything, he'd probably just laugh at my attempt at lying.

Everyone had their papers laid out before them as he went row to row, collecting each. He nodded at the new guy, giving him a free pass. When he got to my row his mouth curled into a seductive smile and he winked at me, his eyes flashing behind his lenses.

In a sudden flourish, his face turned to anger but his eyes were telling me otherwise. "Estella Smith," his voice boomed so loudly that it echoed in my empty soul. "Where is your paper?"

For a moment I was confused, but as I watched him eye me with playfulness, I realized he was just playing a trick on the rest of the class, as well as doing me a favor. I quickly summoned some terrified breaths, impersonating a scared student easier than I had expected.

"I, uh…" I stammered as best I could as I tried to formulate my next line. "I didn't find it relevant?"

An amused smirk crossed his face. "Are you saying you think my teachings are irrelevant?"

The pitch of his voice was frightening, and I found I didn't have to fake an elevated heart rate. I crossed my arms and lifted my chin, shocking the class with my defiance. "Yes," I snapped tartly.

I saw his eyes flash at me with a proud glimmer. "Well, then," he turned and marched to the front of the room. "I guess I will have to see you after class. And don't worry,

I'll make sure all your other professors know about your little indiscretion and that they take note of my disciplinary actions."

I tried to look horrified, but in truth I was relieved. He had rescued me from an afternoon of boring lectures and inevitable embarrassment. All I wanted to do was hang out with him.

He turned his attention from me to the rest of the frozen class. Everyone was terrified and Edgar looked pleased with himself, glowing with both pride and authority.

Scott nudged me as Sarah eyed me from around his shoulder. "Geez, Elle. You know there are better ways to get a date."

Sarah elbowed him in the ribs, and I saw him wince.

If I could have laughed, I would. I gave Sarah a thankful wink as she eyed me with pride. I could see that we were going to be more than just friends; we were going to be best friends.

After class, I sat rigid on my stool as everyone left, continuing the act. My gaze followed the new guy, but he didn't even glance my way so I gave up, only to see him look from the corner of my eye just seconds before he stepped through the door. I frowned, still curious as to who he was. Scott gave me an apologetic glance as Sarah dragged him off to the greenhouses. She gave me a sweet wave as the door shut behind her and at last, Edgar and I were alone.

I let out the breath I'd been holding as Edgar sauntered toward me, removing his glasses and grinning with enthusiasm. "For someone that can't feel emotion," he said in a sly tone.

"You were certainly a convincing victim."

I watched cautiously as he hovered near me, forgetting everything about the day as my mind melted into nothingness. Edgar brushed his finger down the length of my hand and a warm sensation burst to life in my chest. I smiled.

"You have no idea how good that feels," I sighed.

He gave me a gentle smile, his eyes full of life. "I think I have a pretty good idea."

His eyes were now deep, blazing a midnight blue as I looked into them. When he moved away, they began to fade.

"I think I'm getting better with that," he said. "With touching you." His voice was thick with emotion.

"I hope so." I was desperate to feel that way longer, forever.

"So, now that I have you all to myself for the rest of today, what would you like to do?" His gorgeous body was like a statue before me and I longed to nestle into it and feel his arms around me.

I shrugged.

He looked out the window thoughtfully. "I think I know just the thing." His eyes narrowed and a smile crossed his face. Beckoning me out the front door, I followed obediently. Once outside, he turned and took off up the hill, and I scurried to follow. As we passed my cabin, I realized where we were headed, and for a moment I felt unsure. We entered the woods and my eyes had a hard time adjusting to the darkness.

Edgar turned to look at me, his eyes flashing in the bleak surroundings. "Grab onto my coat," he breathed.

I reached forward, grasping onto the thick wool,

softer than I'd imagined beneath my touch. I reveled in the warmth of his body, breathing deeply as we walked past the bench where I had rested at on my first trip to the field. We continued on the same path, and I found that I felt at home here. I'd missed it. As the trees divided, the large expanse of the field opened like a blooming flower before us.

Edgar walked purposefully to a certain point in the opening, looking as though there was something there. The cry of hawks overhead grabbed my attention, and I shot my eyes skyward, seeing Isabelle and Henry fighting their way through the sky.

"They aren't hurting each other, right?" I asked, worry lacing my voice.

Edgar grunted. "Hardly." He stomped through the tall grass and I followed as it leaned in toward me, again blooming in my wake. My cheeks blushed, afraid Edgar would find it strange, but then again, why would he? I looked warily into every dark nook of the tree line. There was yet to be a time when I entered these woods without something horrible happening. As I thought about it, I grasped harder onto Edgar's jacket, trying to stay as close to his back as he would allow.

As we reached the exact center of the meadow, Edgar halted, throwing me backward as I jumped to avoid touching him. He turned to look at me, his mouth curled into a gorgeous grin.

"Here," he said abruptly, looking at the ground. His eyes were intense with excitement. "You didn't come to this field that day on a fluke. There was more that drew you here."

174

He paused, approaching me and now standing just inches away, his breath falling across my face. "It was also home," he finished.

As he spoke the words, something inside me flickered and my heart stopped at his words.

"Home?" I breathed, my eyebrows pressed together. I had never called anywhere home. What was the point when you never knew how long it would remain yours?

"Yes," his voice snaked through the air. "Your home, where you lived for most of your past life, and where I hope you'll learn to live again."

I gawked at him, looking around the field with wonder, confused as to what exactly he was referring.

He chuckled, touching his finger to my chin and turning my face back to him. I relished the feeling of his contact, the overwhelming emotions making my head swim.

"But, where?" I was scanning his eyes as he released his careful touch on my chin, his face now radiant with life.

"You do trust me, right?" His half smile was irresistible, and I found myself staring at his lips, falling in love at an alarming rate.

I nodded, my chin still tingling from his touch.

"Close your eyes, Elle." He closed his, and I quickly followed suit.

I was surprised when I felt him reach out and grab my hands, his skin smooth and warm, and his grasp firm. I smiled then, my body bursting to life.

I felt a gust of wind engulf us like a tornado, and I heard the cracking of a hundred trees snapping like twigs around us in the swirling vortex. I grasped his hands tighter, keeping my eyes clenched, afraid to see what was happening, afraid to die. As abruptly as it had begun, the wind settled and the only sound was the heavy, measured ticking of a clock somewhere to my left, a sound I didn't expect. I exhaled, and it was over.

"Ok," Edgar's face was right next to my ear, his wonderful breath falling across my cheek. "You can open your eyes now. You're safe."

I drew in a deep breath and cracked my eyes open. The gentle warmth of a million flickering candles were now dancing in my view. I looked to Edgar as he stepped away from me, his eyes turning from my face. I noticed him struggle for control, his pupils dilated and his eyes completely black. I stood there for a moment, allowing him to recover as I glanced around the room. After a moment, Edgar looked back, his body calm and relaxed.

"How did we...?" I gasped, still unable to understand what had just happened.

Edgar's mouth curled into a shaky smile, his body trembling.

I found myself standing in the front hall of a house, and when I looked out the windows of the front door, the field we had just been standing in was visible. Everything my gaze landed on looked ancient, every bit of furniture an antique. There were golden silk chairs and etched mirrors. A million candle votives hung on tenterhooks from the walls. The floor was dark granite, clearly its sheen coming from years and years of use. The ticking I had heard emanated from a large grandfather clock on the left end of the room, casting an

176

ominous mood upon the space.

"How is this…" stammering, I forced myself to find the words. "How is this here?" I couldn't understand what was happening.

Edgar finally spoke. "No one can see this. Only you and I know it's here." His chest rose with excitement, still watching me with a nervous eye.

"But I didn't know it was here," I retorted as I looked up toward the giant crystal chandelier that hung over my head and the spiraling stairs on either side of me.

"Something inside you did," he said frankly. "That's why you came here that day. Come in, let us sit for a while, get better acquainted and I'll show you around your house." His familiar personality returned, and his smile was brilliant and alive, as though finding the one thing his heart always desired. Together we turned, moving deeper into the house.

HOME

"Here you are." Edgar thrust a cool glass of water toward me.

"There's even plumbing?" I asked in a mocking tone.

He tilted his head, giving me a disdainful look.

"Very funny, Elle." He gulped down his water in three swallows. "So, nothing about this seems familiar?" he ventured with curiosity, setting his glass down on a nearby table. "Does it?"

I shook my head, guilt filling my body. I could see how much he needed me, how much he had missed whomever I was.

"Oh." His eyes fell. He sat next to me on an ancient

looking chaise lounge in what appeared to be the sitting room. He leaned his body across the back, his muscles flexing through his tight fitting shirt.

The walls were covered with elegant deep red wallpaper, and there were many different objects d'art scattered throughout the room. The large collection of clocks around the house was mind-boggling. Clocks of every shape and size, from every era of life. There were paintings, pictures, and rows upon rows of dusty bookshelves filled with centuries of literature.

I stood and he propped his head up with his hand, watching my every move. I walked to a shelf across the room. There was a small window in the wall and I noticed it looked through to a library. I turned my gaze back to the shelf in front of me, sidestepping as I ran my hand along the velvety wood.

There were objects from all over the world, from old Chinese fans, to small tribal looking masks. There was a framed bit of ancient looking newspaper, and as I squinted, I was barely able to make out 'Salem Witch Trials' typed in faded ink across the top. I looked at Edgar and he smirked.

"Yeah, I just thought it was funny. Humans are so paranoid." He looked amused, as though he'd looked at it every day for years, each time finding it funnier than before. I finally rounded the room in its entirety, feeling more like I'd visited a museum than the living room of a house I'd lived in my past life. At last satisfied that I'd seen enough, I sat back on the lounge, making sure to keep my distance.

The subtle ticking from the clocks was making me

anxious. "Edgar?" Saying his name broke the silence of the room and he turned to me, his perfect face serene. "If you don't age, and I do, what will happen?"

He laughed abruptly. "You don't age, either," he said directly. "At least, not once you get your soul back, you won't." He looked relaxed and content. "You will change, Elle. If you think you're pretty now," he paused, looking me up and down, "which I happen to think you're gorgeous, just wait until you see yourself later. You'll be simply breathtaking. Your body will return to its original form, the form in which you were designed."

I looked down at my body. The red sweatshirt Isabelle had picked for me was hardly the most attractive or revealing outfit I could wear. I looked at Edgar's effortless style and the way it made him look only further appealing. He had one leg hitched halfway onto the chair and one arm thrown over the back of the chaise, his other hand resting on his leg with his strong fingers spread. I squinted at a strange indentation on his left hand ring finger, but quickly glanced away.

I rolled the thought of eternal beauty in my head, shamelessly wishing I could have the same effortless appeal. I already didn't put very much, if any, effort into my looks, but what would it be like to look flawless and breathtaking, like Edgar always had?

I nodded, a dumbfounded look on my face. If I was never supposed to age, then how did I die in the first place? I looked at Edgar, puzzled. "But then how was I even born a second time? I mean, that probably means I died then, right? And if I was designed as an adult, then why was I ever a baby?"

My heart suddenly raced as he lifted the hand he'd had spread across the back of the lounge, reaching toward me and touching a wisp of hair that had escaped from my knot, twirling it in his fingers. His scent wafted to my nostrils and I breathed deeply. "You weren't really born, at least not the way you'd think."

He leaned in closer, my body now stiff. He tilted his head into the contours of my neck, just under my chin. His warm breath fell across my collar bone and my limbs froze. His lips were just a breath away from touching my skin and I shivered. I could feel his body heat as his head hovered close to mine. Slowly, without grazing my skin, he reached his opposite arm around my neck, grabbing my hair and tenderly pulling it out of its messy knot, allowing it to tumble down my back. He laced his hands into it, pulling it back, and flipping it over my other shoulder to further expose the skin on my neck.

Then he whispered, his breath tickling my skin. "When you died, eventually you were re-born." He dropped my hair and pulled away, somehow content with the new level to which he had brought. His eyes were a dangerous shade of navy.

I was hanging on his every word, my cheeks blushing from his welcomed closeness, my rebellious side pressing his self-control. I watched him as he sat there.

"How did I die, though?" My thoughts were racing. The way he smelled, his beautiful face - it was all so amazing.

His eyes turned to mine. "You killed yourself to save me, to save us." His voice was velvety smooth as he took a few deep breaths, still struggling to maintain his composure after getting so close.

I carefully ran my hand through my hair, trying not to make any sudden movements. He inhaled deeply. Then, eyeing me, he spoke.

"I can't resist being around you. You're intoxicating," he whispered, still leaning away from me, trying to recover.

I worked to distract him, quickly thinking of something else to say. "But I had a mother. She left me that letter…" I trailed off, now realizing that all I'd ever believed in was false.

"Estella," he said gently. "You wrote that note, to trick yourself, to give yourself false hope. We wrote it together." His eyes locked onto mine before glancing away. "Three hundred years ago, you wrote that, insisting that we were better off if we never knew each other, if we lived our own separate lives. I didn't want any part of it, but I couldn't resist the passion in your eyes." He was still hanging away from me, avoiding my gaze and watching my body language carefully.

Chills ran down my spine at those words. It was all so strange, so fantastic that this man before me, this devilish sorcerer had been my soul-mate. It was so dream-like that we had shared so much of a life together, and surreal that I was the only one that couldn't recall it. I felt cheated and lied to. But what was worse was that I only had myself to blame for my suffering.

"But why did I have to die?" My brow was furrowed in sudden anger. I had been cheated from a wonderful life, a life of magic and happiness.

He finally relaxed, his body leaning back toward me with a renewed comfort. "Because we are not the only ones of our kind. There was one other," he was leaning in even farther now, his desire to be close a bitter-sweet battle.

My heart rate quickened as I watched him, feeling my life hanging by a thread. He glanced at my lips, his head close to my cheek. "There was another one of our kind left, and he was coming for you." His voice was full of trepidation.

I sat very still as he whispered in my ear, his breath warm against my skin. "Didn't he have his own soul-mate, though?" I asked carefully.

He lifted his hand from his lap to my hair, his fingers combing through the silky strands. "He killed her."

The words caused me to shudder and I turned abruptly to face him, our noses perilously close. He looked at me with surprise and slight discomfort. His mouth curled into a half smile and his teeth glinted in the candlelight. I looked into his eyes with fear, now realizing his lethal power.

His breathing was steady and controlled. "He was evil, far more evil than any of the others. And greedy." Our breaths fluttered across each others lips, his ash-colored eyes searching mine. "He killed her first, and then in his thirst, came after all of us, killing us one at a time."

He leaned in further, his gaze never blinking from mine. I stopped breathing as his nose brushed against my cheek, the strongly anticipated feeling more powerful than anything I'd ever felt. I took a slow deep breath, delighting in the feeling before he pulled back for a second time, his eyes again a brilliant blue.

My chest was heaving as he watched me, pleased with his influence over my soul. "We were the last of our kind." His gaze flashed as he blinked. "You were terrified beyond repair, so I brought you here."

I watched him as my body still tingled, my cheeks burning.

He glanced around the room before settling his eyes back on mine. "He still found us, though, and for that reason, you made the decision to lock your soul inside me, against my strong objection."

He paused, his eyes dropping but not before I saw them well with pain. He rested both his hands on his lap and clasped them tightly as he forced back the sudden emotion.

"You were laying there lifeless before me. Your beautiful hair had lost its luster and life." he said, his gaze skimming over my hair. "And like I was saying, even now, it's not the same."

His eyes welled up, and I resisted the urge to wipe the tear that trailed down his cheek.

He looked deep into my eyes. "But I knew you would return. There was still life in those blue eyes of yours." He stopped himself, pausing to take a steadying breath. "Even then, you were always so stubborn and strong. You had the undying desire to come back. Besides, the Earth needs you."

He put his face in his hands and I sat there hopeless, the void in my chest unbearable.

"Then when he saw you," Edgar bit out, a disturbing look on his beautiful face, his eyes burning dark with hatred. "He just laughed at me, told me that now I was no better than him. I was suddenly overwhelmed with a hatred I'd never known, and I felt my body surge with pain as your energy began to leave me." He shook his head in regret. "I attacked him with so much force that it was quick to knock the life from me. The fight was brutal, far beyond anything you could imagine. It was my luck that he eventually ran like a coward; otherwise, I would have died as well. He was badly injured and bleeding, and that was the last I saw of him. The only thing that managed to save me that day was the thought of you, the hope that you'd return."

His eyes calmed and I leaned back, never breaking my sorrowful gaze from his.

"I flew back to you, as fast as my wings could manage, but your body was gone." The look on his face raised a painful lump in my throat. "All that was left of you was one feather."

He stood and walked to a bell jar that sat on the shelf, the dust on it thick, making it hard to view the contents. He lifted the lid, plucking something from it with care. He walked back to me and my mouth fell open at the object in his grasp.

"This feather." He handed it to me.

I took the white feather between my fingers. I held the feather as though it were the most precious thing in the world. Its color changed with a sudden glimmer, becoming a vivid white. The abrupt hue was much like Edgar's pearled black feather had been, with the same razor sharp edge. It was then that I instantly understood, my gaze jumping toward him.

His stare never faltered. "You were the last white raven," he exhaled. "And you were beautiful." The look on his face was one of deep despair. "It was hard to know exactly what happened to you. I had no idea if you'd ever return, but as the months rolled into years, then decades, and even worse, centuries, I began to lose hope. There was no real recorded history about our kind, so there was no way to know if you'd ever return. But then here you are, still alive."

I rolled the feather over and over in my hand, amazed that this beautiful object had been a product of me. "But then why am I not able to be a raven now? Is it because of my soul?"

He looked at me with hope, his brows lifting in thought. "Yes, I suppose that's why."

There was silence for a moment as the collection of wall clocks quietly ticked. I handed the feather back to Edgar, but he only shook his head.

"No, it's yours now. Keep it. Maybe it will help." He walked back toward me and knelt to the ground, his gaze meeting mine. His eyes were a gentle blue, like the lake on a rainy day. "I need you back, Elle." He reached toward me, slipping his arms around my waist, gently holding them away from my body as though in a hug.

I tilted my head down, his hair brushing my lips. "What happened to the other sorcerer, after he ran?" I breathed into his hair and this time it was he whom shuddered.

Edgar pulled his hands away from me, moving with fluid elegance to sit beside me, looking at me with dark apprehension. "Matthew is still alive. He lives in London."

His name sent terror through my heart, as though I had heard it before. "Won't he come back?" I asked, terrified.

Edgar sighed. "There is the potential that he could, if

186

he finds out about you. That's why I left last weekend."

I looked at him with alarm. "That raven, in the meadow." I gasped. "The English raven."

Edgar reached toward my hand, gently tracing it as I shut my eyes, feeling the rush of warmth rack my bones. "The raven was his spy," his voice was full of concern, "Matthew knows something about you. I'm sure he can sense you, but from London, it can't be very clear. He's been sending spies for the last hundred years in hopes that you'd return. My belief is that he has some sort of bargain with the Gods, a bargain against our kind in an effort to eradicate us. What I don't understand is that our kind can actually help, but the Gods' jealousy is so thick, they can't see beyond that."

I watched as he slid his hand across the cushion toward me, lacing his cool fingers with mine. I struggled to compose myself. Happiness hummed through my veins.

"I haven't seen anymore ravens, although he must have noticed that his spy was killed. When I went to scout out the situation last weekend, Matthew wasn't acting at all strange, just very sick and drained of life." His voice was soft, and he was concentrating on the touch of our hands. "The years had not been kind to him and in fact he has aged. His once youthful skin in now like leather and his eyes are no more than black marbles. At first, I didn't even recognize him. It was as though he had been replaced by something far more evil."

My breathing was labored as I opened my eyes, and Edgar smiled.

"There you are," he breathed, looking at my face with

187

strange recognition.

I felt a surge of memory flash through my mind, but none of it was at all comprehensible. His eyes were a deep blue and there was a warmth searing from him that I hadn't noticed before. Edgar was struggling to hold on, struggling to fight back his urge to take my soul away from me for good. Despite my fears, I desperately wanted to be closer. I needed this feeling.

His eyes darkened and he furrowed his brow, gently releasing his grasp with a trembling hand.

"I love you," he whispered, as though saying it not to me, but the fire that burned inside and the glimmer of a person that had flashed through my eyes.

My soul slowly flickered back to black and my chest ached with the pain of loss. I didn't know what to say so I found myself changing the subject in an attempt to retain my sanity.

"Will he come back?" I regained my composure, looking at him with controlled intensity.

"I hope not, but if he does, I will protect you. I feel I am stronger than him still, but if he's desperate enough, that may be worse." His voice sounded grave.

"Then you have to teach me to be me again." My voice was frantic. "I need to be able to protect you, too."

A smile curled across his beautiful face. "Or just try to remember how to get your soul back. That's probably easier," he laughed. "You're far too stubborn. I wouldn't want to have to teach you again."

I tried to smile, but nothing came. He brushed a hand

against my cheek, seeing my frustration and allowing me the chance to give him the reply I wanted. I closed my eyes and leaned into his touch, my heart finally filling with color and my soul shining a bright light through my heart.

"I'm just glad you're back, Elle. I should have never let you go. I just wish you had waited. We could have killed him together." He looked exhausted. "But you were always tricking me like that, always thinking of me before yourself. Your sacrifice was selfless and fueled by love, not reason." His face was now tormented and lost.

"But don't think about that," I sighed. "Just think about now. The past is over. Gone." I thought about the fact that to me, the past hadn't really even existed.

He forced a smile. "Yeah, easy for you to say."

I looked to the clock and then to the darkened field through the windows. I wasn't really willing to find my way back in the shadowy woods at midnight. I stood up. "It's getting late," I replied darkly. "I should probably get back."

Edgar raised his gaze to mine and I could see he felt awful. "I'll walk you home," he breathed, standing with pain, as though he'd just run a marathon.

I walked awkwardly to the hall and he took a deep breath. "Going out is a lot easier than coming in." He reached a hand out to me, and I grasped it as he walked for the door.

I closed my eyes as he opened it and led me down the front steps, still too afraid to watch what really happened when I returned to the field. My feet felt the familiar soft bed of grass and I opened them again. Looking around me, the house was completely gone as though it had been a dream.

I heard him laugh next to me in the darkness as he released my hand.

Looking to the sky, the full moon was halfway hidden behind a thick cloud, its light glowing around the edges like ripped tissue paper. As my eyes adjusted, I was able to make out Edgar's face, glimmering blue-grey in the moonlight. Edgar stared at the moon while I stared solely at him, finding his exquisite features far more captivating.

His breath formed small clouds in the cool night air and his eyes were luminous. I turned my gaze to the sky, feeling his eyes fall to me. I watched him staring at me from the corner of my eye, his eyes burning.

"Edgar?" I twisted my head, meeting his glowing countenance. "I don't want to be alone tonight."

A half smile grew on his lips. "Now you're the one being presumptuous."

I snorted with a playful chuckle. "Not like that!" I squealed, my voice echoing in the stillness of the night.

Edgar gave me a hang-dog face. "Well, that's too bad," he winked. "Because if you're feeling suicidal tonight, I'd be more than willing to oblige. Death would probably be the outcome."

I glared at him, shaking my head vehemently. "Yeah, I'll pass on that."

He walked toward me, half his face still illuminated in the lunar light. He brushed the hair from my brow, gracefully trailing his hand down my face and across my cheekbone, making me giggle nervously. The emotion he evoked in me was amazing. I had never felt anything like it before. It was like a tickle throughout my entire body, and I was addicted, heart and soul.

"I just couldn't keep that from you. It seemed like the right moment for a laugh. And yes, I'll stay. I'm always happy with sleeping on the floor. Besides, I don't think Isabelle would be too pleased if I stole her spot so soon." His smile cut across his face.

A soft breeze blew across the grass, and I shuddered, suddenly scared by the fact that we were in the woods in the dark.

Edgar looked to the trees. "Well? Shall we?"

"Yes, please." I paused, looking into the dark woods. "After you." My eyes were wide.

He laughed, taking one step forward. "Then grab my coat. I will lead the way."

Halfway across the field, he abruptly stopped. "Okay, this is going to take forever if you can't see like I can."

I yelped as he twisted around, scooping me into his arms as if I weighed nothing more than a sack of feathers.

"What's it like to be able to see in the dark?" I asked, adjusting his grip around my waist.

He laughed. "Like cheating. I can see everything, even if it can't see me. It's a great defense tool."

I nodded, longing to be able to see that well.

His grip tightened. "I carried you once. I can handle carrying you again. We'll just move fast." He was looking down at me, reveling in the fact that he held my whole life in his hands, his dimples now showing. "You trust me, right?"

I nodded against his strong chest, feeling so small. "I

191

trust you."

His walk was soft a lulling, his stride strong and heavy.

A few minutes later his feet hit gravel and he stopped, gently putting me down as he took a moment to regroup.

"Okay, that was hard, but definitely worth it," he gasped. He was winded as though he'd ran, but it was my proximity that had been the hardest part.

"Not for me. It was like flying first class," I teased. "Or what I would imagine flying first class is like." I felt happy.

He laughed between heavy breaths, his puffs of breath cutting through the cool night air.

"I am a little curious how you were able to handle being so close to me before. How did you not kill me that day when you carried me from the field?" I walked up onto my porch and he followed, noticeably distant as he still struggled to clear his mind. I opened the door to my cabin, searching through the dark for the switch to the lamp.

"Because I was more driven by the fear of losing you again rather than my hunger." I felt Edgar reach around me, immediately finding the switch.

"Okay, now you're just showing off," I complained.

He laughed. "Well, I mean come on. I can see the switch right there, clear as day. Why let you struggle?"

I grabbed a pillow from my bed and threw it at him.

"Here. Floor." I pointed to the middle of the room. There was at least a wool rug so I didn't feel completely horrid for making him sleep there, though I knew it wasn't ideal.

He eased himself onto the floor and I rummaged through my now-overflowing bag and piles of both clean and dirty clothes to find something to sleep in. My head shot up when there was a sudden subtle tapping at the door. Edgar sat up.

"I got it," he grunted as he rose to his feet.

He opened the door and Isabelle hopped in, followed by Henry.

I looked at them both incredulously. "It's like a zoo in here now." Henry looked at me with reproachful, beady eyes.

Edgar laughed. "I think if I were you, I wouldn't say that. I don't think he likes being referred to as a zoo animal."

I looked at Henry. "Sorry." My voice was sincere, and he tapped his feet over to Edgar as he eased himself back down on the floor.

I closed myself in my bathroom where I quickly changed and brushed my teeth. Glancing at myself in the mirror, I noticed that my face already looked brighter and my hair healthier. It seemed that whatever power Edgar possessed was already changing me in a small way.

I scurried back into the main room and slipped under my covers. Edgar twisted up off the floor and assisted with the lamp one more time, and then the room was dark. I listened to the soft breathing of our four alternating breaths, feeling for the first time that I wasn't alone and that I now had a life to live for.

Isabelle crawled up the sheets toward me from her position on the bed frame. I hunted in the dark for her head as my eyes adjusted. Turning on my side, I looked at Edgar's pearly outline as he laid on his back, one leg propped up and one arm behind his head on the pillow. His eyes were open and staring straight at the ceiling.

"What are you thinking about?" My voice cut through the mesmerizing silence.

Edgar turned his head to look at me. "Just you. Wondering where it was you went for so long, and why you came back now and not before."

I nodded. "Maybe I came back because I finally got lonely enough."

He snorted, his eyes blinking, "I don't think that's the case. You were always pretty independent. You couldn't stand the way I always hovered over you. My guess is that wherever you were, you were probably dying to get back. I just don't understand what kept you there for so long."

I leaned back onto my pillow. "Hmm," I tried to think, tried to remember, but there was nothing.

"Well, goodnight, Elle," Edgar's voice sounded tired.

"Goodnight, Professor," I teased.

Edgar groaned. "Now I really do feel old."

SAM

I shot up like an arrow causing Isabelle to click angrily at me. The knocking at the door had been abrupt, jarring me straight out of a sound sleep.

"Shoot!" I whispered harshly under my breath.

Edgar looked at me from the chair in the corner. "Don't worry. It's just that funny little friend of yours, Scott. He's so terrified of me, it cracks me up." His face was contorted with amusement and Henry was poised on his lap, enjoying being petted.

"Hold on!" I yelled, looking at the clock. "Why didn't you wake me?" I hissed.

Edgar shrugged. "I was enjoying the view."

I glared at him, flinging myself out of bed and mindlessly grabbing a pair of jeans and a black cotton long-sleeve shirt off the floor. I rushed into the bathroom and changed as fast as humanly possible, though the term "human" was a grey area at the moment. I stamped my feet petulantly as I crossed the room. Edgar watched with an irritating grin, lounging unconcerned in the chair.

"Shouldn't you be hiding?" I hissed.

He laughed. "Why? You don't want your friends to know you're dating the professor?" The look on his face suggested he was enjoying himself immensely.

I snorted. "I'm going to go to class, so don't let anyone see you leave. I don't need any more problems."

He gave me a sarcastic salute and I grumbled at him as I grabbed my bag. I refused to look at him as I marched to the door and grabbed the handle.

"See you soon," he sang. "You know, it's much easier to be a professor than a student. You should really try it. There is a lot less effort involved in looking normal that way."

I rolled my eyes. "I'd hardly classify you as normal." And with that, I bolted out the door.

The cool air felt amazing against my angered face. I looked at Sarah and Scott, tilting my head in shame, "Sorry guys."

They both looked exceedingly annoyed. Scott reproachfully thrust a doughnut toward me.

"Are you serious? They have doughnuts?" My face lit up.

Scott looked smug. "No. We stole them from the nurse's office this morning."

I gaped at him, giving him an admiring look. "Well

done!"

We walked down the hill toward the lake and I shivered as a strong wind whipped across my body. "Wow, it's really getting cold," I gasped.

Scott nodded. "Yeah, soon the snow will come. The change of weather happens so fast here. This is really a two season place: short spring and long winter."

I nodded in agreement.

Sarah looked at Scott with amazement. "What happens when the snow pack gets too high? Do they still hold class?"

Scott shrugged. "This is sort of a strange college as it is. Think of it like a renaissance classroom. People come and go as they feel or need. It's just a place to formulate information or spark ideas." Sarah's attention was locked on him. "But during the heavy snow, most of us go back to the lower grounds and then return in the spring. So more or less, the school closes."

I nodded. I hadn't known that, but the thought of going back to Seattle suddenly made my stomach lurch. My love for my foster mother was bitter-sweet. Though I knew I'd miss her, I never really planned on ever going back.

We arrived at the hatchery just in time for class to start. Most of the students were already there so we quickly pushed our way to the back before the professor arrived. I hadn't really been paying attention as I walked through the crowd. It was obvious everyone disliked me, even before they knew me; I didn't need another glaring reminder. I kept my eyes down until they landed on the familiar designer sneakers I'd noticed yesterday.

197

I froze, lifting my gaze cautiously to look at him. The new kid's eyes were still filled with curiosity as he looked me in the eye. He seemed as though he was uncomfortable being here, as though the students were invading his personal space. I scooted away from him a little, crossing my arms and moving closer to Sarah. I helplessly shrugged as she eyed me questioningly. This new kid had invaded my sacred space in the back of the room and I didn't like it. I thought I saw him smirk as he turned his gaze back to the front of the class.

The professor walked in then, her entrance just as dramatic as always and I sighed with discontent over the coming lesson. I felt the new kid look at me again, his face now calmer as I watched him from the corner of my eye. As the teacher began to drone, I kept glancing sideways, finally easing away from Sarah as boredom set in. After thirty minutes of biting my nails, I was taken by surprise when he leaned in toward me. I gave him a sharp, angry glare.

"Hi," he whispered. His voice was scratchy and gruff.

He laughed as I looked away from him, my lips pursed in irritation.

"I'm Sam," he continued with relentless dedication.

I refused to recognize his advances. He was making me uncomfortable, and I began to fidget with the buttons on the sleeve of my shirt. He seemed much older, probably closer to twenty-two or twenty-three.

He snorted.

I gave him another rude glare. "What's your problem?" I finally hissed, giving in and acknowledging his presence.

He smiled. "Nothing, just trying to make friendly

banter."

His amber eyes were happy but strange, piercing in a way I had never seen, even from Edgar. As I scanned his face, I noticed how shamelessly scruffy he was, and his hair was just as messed up as yesterday. I looked at his clothes, noticing that he wore the same leather coat and jeans as well.

Sarah looked at me sideways and I rolled my eyes at her. She giggled as she nudged Scott, but he only glared at her interruption.

When I turned my gaze forward, Sam was suddenly right next to me. "That wasn't very nice," he teased. "I saw you making fun of me." His mouth twisted into a smile.

I looked at him with antipathy, hoping to make him go away. I hadn't thought he'd notice my eye roll.

"This teacher is a nut job," he announced, rocking onto his heels with delight.

I squeezed my brows together, feeling embarrassed as a few students around us glared at his remark.

"So are you going to tell me your name?" he asked in a strong voice.

I let out a snort and he looked at me knowingly.

"Estella, right?" He had his hands casually behind his back.

I frowned at him. "How do you know my name?" I hissed.

He eyed the teacher to make sure she wasn't noticing the disturbance we were causing. "I just heard it around, that's all. It's an interesting name. Very old fashioned." He winked at me.

I recoiled at his remark, giving him a sour face. "Well, Sam. Then you don't have to say it, and actually, I'd prefer if you didn't."

He chuckled, pleased with himself. "Samuel is my full name. If you want to be fair, it's old-fashioned too." He was still smiling mockingly.

He was acting like an overconfident jerk, like he was better than all of this. He laughed like a mad man, as though he'd known what I thought of him. I rolled my eyes back to the front of the class and watched the teacher with faked interest. I could feel both Scott and Sarah watching me, but I didn't feel like hearing their thoughts on the awkward situation.

For the rest of the session, I was acutely aware of his presence. I refused to look at him, and thankfully, he never said another word. Despite the fact that I was pointedly ignoring him, I still felt him staring at me, his sharp eyes burning holes through the side of my face. I flushed a bright red. It was strange how he watched me. It felt almost protective and overbearing. When the teacher excused us, I quickly grabbed Sarah and Scott and used them as a shield against his advance.

Scott looked at me, his eyebrows shoved together. "What was that about?" he whispered, looking behind him. "Do you know him from somewhere? Because it sure seemed like he knew you."

I shrugged. "I can't figure it out. He doesn't seem like the type, you know, to be here."

He was striding a few paces behind us like a stalker, or perhaps body guard. We arrived at the bird lab and I watched as he brushed passed me and strode to the front silently. I sat and turned to Sarah, trying to ignore him.

"So, Sarah," I began. "Where will you go for the winter?"

She looked somewhat distracted. "Uh…" her face became terrified as she looked over my shoulder.

I whipped around, only to see Sam now standing behind me with a stool in his hand.

"Do you mind?" His voice was sharp and deep, his face permanently stuck in a stupid smirk.

"Yeah, I do mind," I spat.

He leaned in toward me. "I realize you hate me, but that's not really my problem."

I grumbled at him, crossing my arms and refusing to make room at the table for him.

He sighed. "Okay fine, but only because you forced me to." He placed two firm hands on either side of my seat and pushed me closer to Sarah. The stool scratched across the floor, making room for his chair. He took an annoyed breath and plopped on his stool next to me. The students that had taken notice of us in the hatchery class continued to stare.

Edgar entered the room then, his stride quick until his gaze fell on my grumpy face, and he paused. I watched angrily as his eyes shot to Sam's, but to my surprise, a crooked smile crossed his face.

I exhaled sharply in disbelief. What was this? I looked at Sam disdainfully, but he just sat there with a stupid content look on his face. I twisted my head to look at Sarah and Scott for some sort of consolation.

"Sorry, guys," I whispered. "I have no idea what this guy's problem is."

They both gave me looks of complete surprise as they shrugged, unable to help me discern exactly what was going on.

"Alright, class," Edgar's voice cut through the air like a knife. "Your papers were good and well thought out, at least most of them." His dark eyes fell on a somewhat grubby looking student whom began to shake with guilt and fear. "Though a handful of you insist on fairy tales, we all know that science is the only explanation here. I will not tolerate answers like that again. This is not a creative writing class."

Sam's body began to shake with laughter and Edgar glared at him over the top of his glasses. After a moment, however, he too began to smirk as though some sort of invisible exchange had occurred between them.

Throughout the rest of class they continued to have silent exchanges, and I only grew further irritated. It was like they were secretly talking about me through their body language, like old friends, and it was pissing me off. I tried to glare at both of them, but they ignored me and I was left staring at their two eerily perfect faces in complete confusion.

When class was over, Sam turned to me with a happy look on his face while mine was still distorted in bewilderment.

"Well, Estella. It was a pleasure to meet you. See you soon?" But before I could utter a word, he was gone.

Sarah and Scott looked at me with baffled expressions. I watched as Scott stood, but instead, I remained seated, sulking like a child.

"Are you staying behind for a bit?" he asked, a sly grin crossing his face.

Sarah glared at his smart aleck remark. "Scott please, what did I tell you?" she whispered, her voice harsh and grumbled.

He smirked again. "Yeah, I know, I know. I guess we will see you later, Elle." And with that, they left, their arms wrapped around each other.

Edgar sauntered over, smiling. "Are you giving up on college already?" he breathed, taking a seat on the stool that Sam had just vacated.

"What was that?" I finally spat.

He let out a deep laugh. "That's Sam. Didn't he tell you?" His eyes were bright with amusement.

I snorted, crossing my arms and pouting. "Yeah, but I think he's a jerk, and I also think he was hitting on me."

Edgar laughed at me even harder. "No, I doubt that."

I was steaming now, my face beet-red. "How do you know him?" I bellowed.

His laughter faded at my show of anger. "He's been a student of mine for a while."

"Well, Scott has never seen him before," I retorted. Edgar's mouth curled into the same grin as Sam.

"No, when I say a while, I mean a *while*." His head tilted down, his gaze holding mine as he waited for me to get what he was saying.

"Oh." I suddenly dropped the angry face as I realized that knowing him 'a while' meant that he was also like us: somehow immortal. "Well," I paused, unfolding my arms and placing my hands on the table. "Who is he and why is he here?"

Edgar leaned his face in toward me with his knees on either side of mine as he scooted the stool closer. He grabbed my hair from around and behind my head and draped it over my right shoulder as he leaned into the contours of my neck.

"He's doing me a favor, but he's not one of us. Sam is something else," he whispered, his hot breath so close to my skin that my body began to anticipate the explosion of life. Just then, I felt his nose graze a spot just under the curve of my jaw. He slowly trailed it down my neck where he pressed his lips against the ridge of my collarbone.

My mind went blank and Sam's face melted away. All I could feel was the way his lips felt on my skin, his breathing steady and calm. He rested his hands down on my legs as he brought his body closer. He stayed there for a moment before he finally sat back and I relished the beautiful color of his eyes.

"Thanks for that," he breathed, his chest rising and falling with control and ease.

I smiled for a brief moment before the fire died.

Edgar smiled back. "So, if you're skipping classes now, do you want to go back to the house with me?"

I felt a surge of excitement. "Yes!"

There was so much there to explore and learn. It was just the thing I was hoping he'd ask. He lifted me from the stool and placed me on my feet with ease, his muscles flexing. The existence of Sam was still bothering me, and I didn't understand who or what he was. I couldn't get over the way he had acted toward me, as though his sole duty was to drive me crazy. And besides, what kind of favor was he doing for Edgar?

I pondered over this the whole walk through the woods, but came to no exact conclusion other than if Edgar was trying to remain inconspicuous about who he was, I didn't think that inviting his tall, strong, handsome, and clearly out of place friend to the college was going to help his situation. When we reached the field where the house lay invisible, he turned to face me and I felt my body tremble in anticipation of his touch.

He grabbed both of my hands with a smile and I kept my eyes wide open, waiting for the wind and swirling so that I could see exactly how it all worked. A small gust tickled at my hair, quickly followed by a heartier blow, and then, it was like being in the eye of a tornado. Everything was now crashing around us in a way that would normally suggest the field was destroyed. I tilted my head back and looked up through the eye, watching as it danced and swirled.

Suddenly, the noise ceased and I heard the familiar ticking of the clock in the hall. I smiled and instinctively leaned in to hug Edgar. He pulled back abruptly, grabbing my hands and pulling them from around his waist, placing them at my sides. He gave me a warning glare and I noticed his jaw was tense.

I smiled playfully as I stepped back, giving him space to re-group.

"Elle, you really shouldn't do that. I am a warrior, and when I get attacked like that, my first instinct is to snap your neck. Do you know how horrifying that sort of thought is to have about the person I love and need?" He walked toward the library and I dutifully followed as he lounged down on the couch with a sigh.

I frowned, feeling my spirit die. "Sorry." I mumbled. "Are you tired?" I asked, changing the subject.

He gave me a reproachful look, his hand on his forehead. "How would you be if you'd slept on the floor?"

My guilt intensified. "Oh."

He laughed at my sad response, his happiness returning. "Tonight I'll sleep better in my own bed." He emphasized 'own' in a way I couldn't quite describe.

I frowned. "So you're leaving me all alone in the cabin?"

Edgar chuckled in a playfully menacing manner. "You think I'm going to let you out of my sight?" he mused. "I'm kidnapping you. Besides, this house is much better than that rickety cabin, and I happen to have a lot more comfortable surfaces, if you haven't noticed."

I gave him a disparaging look, feeling his power over me. I looked around, finding it undeniable that he was right. Every couch was luxurious.

"Besides, Elle, aren't you forgetting? This is your home, too." He looked up at me, an expression crossing his face that I couldn't decipher. "Last night felt like I was staying in a hotel room, and I never do that unless I have to. But, you were worth it." He gave me a reassuring smile.

I was blinking at him as an awkward silence grew between us. He leaned forward and grabbed me around my waist, pulling me onto the couch next to him. His face was full of emotion as he inched closer to my face, his breathing fast and heavy. My heart beat swift and hard against my chest as he drew closer, all playfulness gone. He was more than a warrior, but a hunter, and I couldn't help but feel as though at this moment, I was the prey.

I felt his breath fall across my lips and my lungs ceased moving. His eyes scanned mine urgently as he weighed the situation and the level of his composure. He too stopped breathing as he pressed his soft lips against mine. I sat there in shock, frozen by the feeling I had longed to experience. He exhaled as he let himself go, bringing his hand to my face. He gingerly cupped my cheek, gently curling his lips around mine and molding his body into me.

My heart burst open in my chest, the fire inside me blazing harder than it ever had. The pull toward Edgar became unbearable and I leaned against him, throwing my arms around his shoulders in my foolishness. He jerked away in one sudden movement. Breathing hard, his face was a mask of pain.

"Elle!" he gasped. "What are you doing?" His eyes were pitch-black and I sat back, giving him some space.

"Sorry," I smiled as the lingering fire inside me dissipated.

"I said it was getting easier, Elle," he teased. "That didn't mean go for it." His breathing slowed and his eyes faded to a brilliant blue. "At least I know I'm storing a lot of energy, so I'm strong enough to control myself," he laughed.

I gave him a sly look.

After that, we kept our distance. I spent a good couple of hours simply scanning the shelves upon shelves of books in the library. There were some that looked older than time and some that were surprisingly new, including books about the stock market. He watched me pace around the room as he pretended to enjoy a book he had sitting in his lap, but he rarely turned the page, suggesting he was more fixated on the company than the entertainment.

After another hour he finally stood, seeing I had grown tired of looking through ancient copies of travel books and Greek lectures.

"Follow me." His voice was sweet and soft as it cut through the silence. "Let me show you to your room."

ME

I followed Edgar out of the sitting room and we traced our steps back to the entry. It was already dark and I was relieved that I wasn't going to have to traipse back through the murky woods alone, especially not with droves of things out there hunting me.

The candles still flickered on the wall and the wax had burnt no further than it had been when we came. The chandelier above us sparkled in its antique glory as it reflected every glint of light and tossed it back toward us. There was so much history here, so many strange things that Edgar, and I suppose I, had collected through the ages.

The granite floors of the entry had given way to marble stairs that were also worn from time. The same brilliant red wallpaper that was in the sitting room continued up the stairs, covered in a substantial layer of dust. I placed one foot on the worn stone, imagining myself doing it a million times before. We walked up the staircase on the left that curved up to a top plateau where it met with the other curved staircase on the right

There was a shelf at the top of the stairs and my eyes were fixed on it as I followed him into the left wing. A very old book sat alone on the shelf and it caught my eye, making me stop with a sudden skid. I narrowed my eyes at the cover of the book, carefully approaching it as I wondered what sort of book could earn such a place of honor. I grabbed the book as Edgar turned to see where I had gone. He shuffled back toward me with a crooked smile on his face and his hands casually stuffed into the pockets of his pants.

I ran my hand across the scratchy black cover.

"Are you serious?" I asked, looking at him with alarm as I began flipping through the pages, gawking at the handwritten poems that formed in tangled masses before me.

"Well," he gave me a sly look of pride. "We were friends," he said frankly, shrugging his shoulders like it was no big deal.

I glanced at the signature page, running my hand over the deep pen scratches. Edgar A. Poe was scrawled into the thick parchment, and under the signature it read: "To Edgar, may you always be so obliged to steal my name…"

I snorted. "So, that was why you introduced yourself as Edgar Poe."

Edgar was gloating now. "He wrote 'The Raven' for me." His eyes glinted and his pearl skin glowed with joy.

He carefully pulled his hands from his pockets, taking the notebook from my grasp and flipping to the poem.

I watched as his face became hard and solemn.

"It was a dark time then, in 1845, and his friendship kept me alive. We suffered together, we suffered over life." He looked at me with shame. "You had already gone and I was considering..." he paused, the words catching in his mouth. "I was considering suicide."

Sadness washed over me as the thought sunk in. I saw Edgar alone and helpless, his energy fading and his life over.

His face remained cold and serious. "I was the forlorn student of the poem, the distraught lover slowly descending into madness, and Lenore was you, my lost love." He chuckled lightly. "He was so inspired by our story, our life."

Seeing the words, the disturbed and lonely handwriting, made me sad. I was angry about what I'd done. It was selfish of me to leave him so alone, so dead inside. Edgar reached over my shoulder and put the book back on the shelf.

"It was forbidden for us to confide in a human like that, to tell them our story, because it leads them to extremes, such as the paranoia of the Salem witch hunts. We have a certain responsibility, Elle, to protect them, even from themselves. We are some of the only beings on earth that are close enough to touch the Gods. Humans are our children. They were sprung from the same blueprints as us, but without the intensity of power, eternal life, and magic."

"This is why, in their world, you still see the same struggles as we have. The jealous husbands killing their wives and the wars between men are similar to ours. They are so oblivious to their creation and their importance on this earth. As you'll see, in time, they will destroy this place, and all of us."

I felt his body behind me, shadowing mine, his warmth radiating onto me. I stared at the notebook for a moment, lingering. He tilted his head down into the contours of my neck, his breath falling across the curve of my shoulder. I shuddered as he gently pressed his lips against my milky skin and the hairs on my neck reacted to his intoxicating touch, joy surging through my veins.

He whispered across my skin, "Edgar Allan was a different kind of human. He was in tune with his creation and because of that, he wrote these beautiful poems. Poems that touched humanity in a way no one could describe because it was a life they had long forgotten. I wish he could see us now," he spoke into my ear. "He would finally believe in the love in which he wrote."

I slowly turned to face him, my eyes scanning his. His smile was deeply affectionate and overwhelming, and his breath sent shivers down my spine.

He ran his fingers through my hair. "Let's get you to bed," his voice was inviting and calm.

I nodded as sleep began to tug at my mind.

I followed him into the left wing, uncertain as to what I would find there. No memories surfaced. He looked at the handles on the doors before us with a flash of sadness in his eye. It was as though he was remembering a painful time, a time before this new life, a time when we had a memory to share. I stared up at the large doors. They were Victorian, painted a deep blue with gold leaf framing and hinges. I turned to look behind me toward the other wing. The doors there were cracked open, suggesting that that room was more frequently visited. As he drew open the double doors, a cloud of dust rose before us.

"I'm afraid I haven't changed it since you left," he sighed. "I just couldn't bring myself to come here. It was too painful."

The candles burst to life as we entered the room and a soft light filled the space. As I looked around, my mind tickled with warmth, like I had been here before in some distant dream. Everything my curious eyes fell upon felt like me. Every picture on the wall and every color was a portrait of the soul I'd felt through Edgar's touch.

The room was organized, not cluttered as they had been in the rest of the house. The layout of the room seemed practical and pleasing. The ceilings were tall, probably eighteen feet, and for a moment, I thought it roughly resembled the Palace of Versailles.

The floor was a dark lacquered cherry and the walls were papered in alternating wide stripes of deep blue and light blue with gold pinstripes painted between each. The ceiling was black as the night sky, making the room seem roofless and open.

I walked to a portrait that was straight ahead of me. Its magnificence stole the breath from my lungs. Something about the striking blues and smooth strokes caught my eye. As I glanced at the signature, my eyes bulged in disbelief.

I twisted toward Edgar with wide eyes. "This is a Vermeer!" I gasped, staring back at the portrait and noting the date: 1588. Within the glazed layers of paint, a girl sat at a large piano. She was alone except for whoever she was looking at. As I looked closer, I realized she resembled me, right down to my shockingly bright hair, thin features, blue eyes, and pale skin. Despite the physical likeness, something was different. Peering at it some more, I noticed the difference was that all my features were beautifully enhanced. I was a vision, more so than I'd ever seen, and I found myself gawking.

Edgar's honey voice rose behind me. "You just loved him, his style," he breathed. I turned to look at him and I could see the elation flickering in his eyes.

Everything was so breathtaking, so unreal. "I can't believe this, I must be dreaming." As I walked along the walls from painting to painting, each was adorned with yet another famous name: Rembrandt, Rubens, and Van Eyck.

"Your love for art was insatiable, Elle. You were obsessed with its allure, its mystique." He stood near the door, careful not to invade my space, though it hardly seemed mine.

I watched him for a moment as I tried to decipher his mood. His body was almost shaking, and his cheeks were flushed. I realized then just how painfully difficult this all was for him.

"You only deserved the best, Elle." He was acutely aware of the way I was watching him and he tried to look away.

I looked back to the wall as shock overwhelmed me. I had always loved art, of every kind, but this? This was something I could have never hoped to see in my lifetime, let alone own it and also become the subject matter. I urgently wished I could remember what that was like. I wanted to know how it felt to physically see the faces of legend. Each much crisper than a photograph and obviously much more real than the distorted and idealized self-portraits you see now. I pulled myself away from the walls, finally satisfied that I'd given each painting a respectful glance.

Toward the middle of the room there were yards of rich fabric that canopied a large king size bed: lavish silks and velvet. The downy comforters were rumpled and I realized what Edgar had meant by never coming here. It was like a scene that had just been left, a life suddenly interrupted. He had literally shut the door on my past, trying with hopeless effort to forget something as familiar to him as his own face. My eyes fell on the disturbed coverings and I could just make out where I last laid. The indentation of my body was still wrinkled into the sheets next to another larger indent that was cradled around mine.

My heart ached with further sadness as the feeling of loss overwhelmed me. I felt like I'd walked in on a scene of someone else's crushed life. I looked to Edgar but he looked away, pain stinging his eyes. My stomach fluttered and I felt my body shake, my limbs going weak.

I walked toward Edgar. He leaned his strong body against the wall, his arm shaking. My steps were careful and slow as I approached and reached a terrified arm out to him, gingerly cupping his face in my hands.

"Edgar," I whispered, the grief overwhelming me as my soul burst to life and hot tears began streaming down my face. I leaned in closer so he could feel my warmth. "You're safe now. I'm home."

He drew in a shaky breath, his face hollow and worn. His hands dropped from the wall and he wrapped them around my shoulders. I carefully placed my head inside the curve of his neck. His breathing hitched as he placed his hand on the back of my head, cradling it as he pulled away.

I could tell he was plagued by his desires and fighting back his demons.

"Well," he paused, struggling with his words. "Goodnight, Estella." He smiled weakly, though I knew his sadness was far from gone.

I looked at him with eager eyes as he stepped toward the door. "But where will you be?" I asked with a hint of fear in my voice. I thought of the open room across the hall.

"I have my own room. I don't want to invade your privacy or make presumptions." He sounded so alone and so sad. He wiped the sadness from his face, forcing his playfulness to return. "Besides," he gave me a tight smile. "We're practically strangers, at least in your world."

I watched him with care as he nervously fidgeted with his hands, and I could tell this made him feel awkward. "But will you stay until I fall asleep?" I asked.

Love glowed in his eyes and his smiled widened into a genuine one. I watched as he walked to a chair that was near the bed, and he lowered himself into it. He politely folded his hands across his chest. He smiled at me, and I was content.

I removed my jacket as I walked back toward the bed, hanging it on the enormous frame post and kicking off my boots. This moment felt a lot less awkward than I'd expected.

I could feel the room tickling at a memory deep inside, but I couldn't manage to bring it to the surface. I looked down at my clothes. Sleeping in jeans was never my favorite pastime, but considering he had suffered on the floor, I figured I could make do.

Edgar seemed to notice how I was weighing my options.

"I think you have something you can sleep in over there." He pointed toward a large four-door armoire in the corner that was shielded by a screen.

I looked at the screen in fascination. There was a golden scene of gently rolling hills embroidered into it. The details came to life before me as I admired every stitch. I ran my hand across the silk thread, so delicately placed. The thin fibers were rich and soft, and each weave was expertly sited. I trailed my fingers on the threads as I rounded to the back.

My hands moved to the magnificent armoire that was covered in gold leaf with a matching scene painted on the front. I placed my hand on the latch and it gave with a gentle crack as the doors opened. My eyes were met by a glamorous collection of clothing. My mouth fell open. I fished through each hanger with excitement as I noticed that the styles spanned decades of time, from renaissance to late Victorian and even Icelandic. After delighting my senses long enough, my eyes fell upon a simple looking nightgown and I pulled it from the closet, holding it before me.

I glanced at Edgar. He was nibbling on his fingers in a nervous fashion and watching me rediscover my past with curiosity and wonder, remembering what it was like to have me here. Turning back, I timidly snuck behind the screen to change. A part of me still saw Edgar as a complete stranger, and I felt awkward. I wriggled out of my jeans and ripped my shirt over my head. The soft cotton fabric of the nightgown made me swoon with delight as I pulled it down over my body.

I kicked my jeans to the side as I always did, glancing down and realizing there had also been other clothing kicked there, though it looked old and dusty. I shuddered, thinking it was probably the last time I'd changed, my last day in that life.

Feeling exposed, I popped my head around the screen. Edgar was still watching intently. As I emerged, a look of both happiness and despair crossed his face. I watched him as another tortured tear rolled down his cheek. He did nothing to brush it away.

I could only imagine how it felt for him. The stinging irrationality of the whole experience and the three hundred years he spent alone, only half of himself.

Walking to the bed, I looked again at the wrinkled impressions. A part of me was scared to disturb something so beautiful, scared to destroy something I didn't think was mine. I heard Edgar stand up from the chair behind me, standing close to my back. His breath blew across the back of my neck and he carefully wrapped his arms around my shoulders. His tender touch filled me with happiness. I could almost remember the love.

He pulled my hair away from my cheek and placed his cheek next to mine.

"Elle, don't be sad." He brushed his lips across my face to my ear as he whispered. "This is how you should feel. Happy."

The feeling of love pulsed in my veins as he slowly let go, forcing himself to back away. He sank back into the silk chair. I turned and glanced at him over my shoulder, looking for affirmation that all this was indeed mine. Raising my hand above the sheets, I noticed it was trembling. With a soft touch, I placed it on the sheets which were silkier than anything I'd felt before. I slid my other hand across the fabric as I smoothed away the beautiful indents and gingerly crawled in.

I reached for the covers and pulled them up to my face. As they fell around me, I could smell the lingering scent of Edgar wafting out from underneath and it affirmed his presence was once here. I rolled myself onto the pillow and the smell there was also eerily familiar and intensely comfortable. Edgar watched me with eyes blue as the sky, and slowly, although I tried to force sleep away, my lids became heavy and I fell asleep.

MEMORIES

When I woke in the morning, I didn't open my eyes right away. Fear gripped me as I wondered if it had all been a dream, a fabricated life that my desperately fogged and depressed mind had created. Everything was very silent except the quick breathing of something beside me. I reached out and my hand fell upon a warm, feathery lump that was curled into the curve of my hip.

With a surge of hope, I peeked open one eye and saw the curtained canopy that hung above me. Feeling braver, I opened the other eye, blinking a few times to focus. The feathery lump to my side was Isabelle. Looking down at her, I noticed how her beak was gently tucked under her chest and her feathers fluffed along the length of her back. Her eyes were closed in repose, and excitement pulsed through my body. I was thrilled that it was still real.

My eyes darted to the chair beside me, but it was

long vacant. My heart sunk as I found myself alone again. The morning light poured into the room, brighter than I'd ever seen. For a moment I thought about Edgar, and the life I had now found. Was this life really mine? It still felt too much like a fairy tale to believe, but it was still happening, and as long as it did, I would go along for the ride. The fear of sudden death was so prevalent in this new life, but to feel was more important. I now found that if being with Edgar was dangerous, it was worth it. I would honor my tortured life and fight to save it.

I slid from under the silky covers as Isabelle yawned, rolling her body onto her side.

Sliding my feet along the smooth wood floor, I moved toward a dusty shelf of books that sat directly across from my bed. I squinted at the bindings as I brushed away the cobwebs. The books were different shapes and sizes, but each was stamped with a date. I tilted my head to get a better look at them and my eyebrows pressed together in concentration.

Glancing over my shoulder to be sure no one was watching, I gingerly removed a random book labeled "1356". I carefully lowered it into my hand, brushing my fingers over the thick leather cover and feeling the indent of the large numbers that were burned into the hide.

I opened it to the middle, the ancient smell of paper wafting up at me. Dust motes danced in the air around me. I breathed deep, admiring the ancient smell of paper, a deep musty scent that seemed to take me to the time in which it was written. I stared at the familiar writing for a moment, then I began to read:

March 11th

Today Edgar and I came across another couple, just like us. They were the first we'd seen in a few years. We had begun to fear that our population was decreasing, but this was the first affirmation that perhaps they were all in hiding. There must be something after us, never the less. Either that, or they're losing their self control and killing each other off. Edgar seemed only mildly concerned, but I couldn't help but be fearful...

My heart stopped as I read the words, written in my careful and unique handwriting. I quickly flipped to another page:

July 9th

The heat today was unbearable. Though I begged Edgar to leave Paris, he refused. He said he had a surprise for me. I nearly died when he took me to the bird shop! She's gorgeous, just the perfect white I'd always dreamed of...

I felt warm, finding this passage much more positive. The happiness reflected in my words was almost palpable, and I touched my fingers to the indentations my pen had left, evidence of my excitement. My body was now filled with an intense feeling that washed over my thoughts as a million voices began to ramble through my mind. Voices I'd heard before and people I'd met.

I slammed the journal shut, my head now splitting in pain. The dust flew out of the pages and settled around me. I was squeezing my eyes shut so tightly that all the light was gone. Each voice that was rushing back to me was like a surge of electricity to my brain, shocking every receptor. Everything was so loud that I barely noticed the doors to my room open. Edgar entered and quietly moved behind me.

I felt a surging fire burst in my heart as he put his hand on my shoulder. I screamed, spinning around and jumping back, suddenly feeling dizzy and fogged.

"Elle!" Edgar grabbed me as I fell, but his toxic touch kept the emotion burning inside me and the voices clear.

I fell to the ground and he released me, stepping back with burning dark eyes. My hip hit the wood floor with a resounding thump. I winced and the journal flew out of my hand, sliding across the wood and under my bed. My breathing was heavy as Edgar stared with a horrified look on his face, his instincts ignited with a dangerous spark of fear.

I put my hand up to calm him as the voices and fire faded.

"It's okay Edgar." I took a deep breath, bringing my hand to my chest. "You just scared me. You really need to learn how to pre-warn or something. Like I said, take up whistling."

Isabelle was perched on the edge of the bed, gazing at me with blinking eyes, her head tilted curiously as I sat on the floor.

Edgar's terrified face began to relax and his lips curled into a smile. "I'm pretty sure you were the one that startled me," he retorted tartly.

I glared at him as I pushed myself off the floor and stood.

"Sorry, it's just that so many things suddenly collided in my mind all at once. I couldn't help but scream. The voices, the journal, and your lightning touch." I steadied myself on the bed frame.

"The voices?" Edgar approached me slowly, wrapping one hand around my neck and lacing it through my hair, avoiding contact with my skin.

"I was reading those journals, my journals." I pointed to the shelf. "It was like a rush of memories, of people I'd met, coming back to my mind."

He furrowed his brow. "Well that's good. You're beginning to remember."

I shrugged. "Yeah, but I still don't exactly get it. It's like spying on someone else's life. It feels so wrong, so voyeuristic." My voice was forlorn and dejected.

Edgar's eyes were glittering. "Don't feel that way, though. Just believe in it." He put his hand on my chest and I breathed in the feeling. "Believe in yourself. This is your life all around you." He put his head into the nook of my chin, tracing his lips upward until they met mine.

I shuddered, the feeling infinitely better than I could ever describe in words. He released his hold on me and stepped back. My eyes fluttered open again, tears staining my face.

Edgar fished the journal out from under the bed and flipped it over. He glanced at the page and smirked, looking at Isabelle before walking to the shelf and sliding it back in its place respectfully.

I ran my eye over the multitude of journals before me, my mind swimming at the thought of all of the information contained in the pages.

"How old are we?" I asked, thinking about the dates I had seen in the entries I read.

Edgar's laughter boomed across the room, causing Isabelle to fluff her feathers in alarm.

"You are so amusing, Elle. Especially now."

I gave him a blank stare, finding no humor in my question.

He beckoned to me to come closer as he grabbed the first book from the shelf. Opening it to the very first page, he read:

Rome. Winter 1006

There is no way to describe this strange place I've suddenly found myself, or the strange partner beside me, but something about him scares me. Something in his

225

dark stare. I've been running from him all day, but he keeps coming closer, this black raven. Just staring...

Edgar ran his fingers lovingly across the page.

"You were always recording our history. It was your thing, your way of keeping your soul open to the world."

I stared at him in disbelief. "We were born in 1006?" I gasped.

He chuckled.

"No, technically in 986. You were born in Rome and I was born in what is now Verona, but you only began writing the first day we met. It was like you were afraid to forget. Like some outside force was compelling you to do so." He snorted. "I guess that all makes sense now."

"So we weren't born in the same place?" I was confused. None of this was fitting together. If we were in fact each a half of one, we should have been discarded on Earth in the same place.

He smiled. "Like I said, we weren't really 'born'. We just appeared one day, eternally the ideal age of eighteen and very lost. The Gods scattered us when they discarded our two halves from the Heavens in their jealous rage." A smirk crossed his face. "I always figured this was all a game for them and we were the pawns, just struggling to find each other."

I nodded in confusion. "What happened when we realized we were on Earth?"

Edgar shrugged. "We just began living. There was no memory of what happened, almost like having amnesia. I can

226

only imagine what it was like when the early couples found each other. They had no knowledge of their lethal attraction. The first to actually survive their initial meeting was a couple named Gloria and Alek." He smiled at some unspoken memory. "They became rather egotistical about it, too, but how can you blame them? To us, they were like celebrities. We owe them our life. Because of them, we all began to figure it out, and I'm sure it enraged the Gods when we began cohabitating."

"So then, you knew about the lethal attraction when you first saw me?" I thought about my journal entry, how I had ran from Edgar all day while he chased me in his raven form.

He rolled the journal around in his hands. "I had literally just heard about it, and I was skeptical that something like this even existed. But when I found you, I felt the murderous jealousy welling in my heart, right along with the undeniable feeling of love and power. It was strangely bitter-sweet." His face suggested he was thinking of the day and his eyes glimmered with remembrance.

I watched him as he placed the journal back on the shelf.

"So," he said with a renewed tone to his voice. "Not to change the subject, but I really came up here to ask you if you've looked outside."

I gave him a perplexed look.

"Why?" My voice sounded curt and a little irritated.

Edgar motioned me to the tall window draped in silk curtains. It was very bright outside, as I had noticed before, but I didn't think that amounted to anything important. The condensation on the window was thick and it beaded in cold bands down the glass. I lifted my hand to the pane to gently rub the moisture away. My eyes fell upon a meadow of white, completely untouched and pristine.

"Snow?" I gasped, my mouth gaping as I took in the scene before me.

Edgar stood at my side, defogging his own pane so he could take in the view with me.

"Yes. Beautiful, isn't it?" His breath fogged up the glass again as he spoke.

A light snort escaped my lips.

"So much for fall." My eyes were wide, drinking in the pureness of the snow, each drift like whipped cream.

Edgar let out a merry laugh.

"Fall is a dreary time of year, anyway. So over-rated. Everything is dying around you – it's depressing, actually. So really, what are you missing?"

Since I agreed with him, I merely nodded, turning my attention back to the scene outside. It was so utterly beautiful. I had never seen anything like this. It was just so clean and perfect.

"Shall we go outside, then?" he asked, a crooked smile on his face. "I doubt there's any rush to get you back for class. It's likely no one will go."

I nodded with eager anticipation and his eyes filled with elation.

"Well, then, get dressed." He pointed toward my closet as he briskly walked to the door. "I'll just be downstairs. I need to get a few things ready." With a wave, he left.

Isabelle playfully clicked her tongue at me as I walked away from the window. I scratched her on the head and she fanned her feathers. I'd had Isabelle for hundreds of years, and now, she felt much more significant to me than just a mere pet. She was kin.

Feeling a surge of energy, I was quick to dive behind the screen. When I opened my closet, I was still amazed by the vast collection before me. Sighing with delight, I rifled through what seemed like yards of silk and cotton. The task of finding something appropriate seemed daunting, and I actually broke a sweat as I searched. Finally, I was able to find some almost modern pants. In fact, they resembled riding pants you would wear to ride horses, but would have to do. Besides, I wasn't about to wear a dress. I made a mental note to go back to the cabin later and collect my jeans.

Pushing back a row of ball gowns, I found where I'd stashed my shoes. I riffled through cluttered piles of custom tailored dress heels and slippers before laying my eyes on a pair of shearling boots toward the back. They looked handmade and I couldn't help but wonder where I had acquired something so artistic and beautiful, but at the same time functional. I pulled the boots out. They would definitely do.

I stood back for a moment to regroup before delving back in. There was a large collection of shirts, each eerily perfect for me. I chose a cream wool blouse and a twill vest that showed off my figure. I walked to the mirror, admiring my choice of clothes. They were far richer than anything I'd ever worn.

Going to the vanity, I grabbed a brush from the top and patted it against my leg to remove the dust. I ran it through my hair a few times before placing it back in the exact spot I had taken it from. Reaching up, I twisted my hair up into a knot.

I took a deep breath and turned away from the mirror, walking swiftly out the door. Isabelle flew up behind me and landed on my shoulder just before I shut the doors. As I trotted down the stairs, I couldn't help but feel amazing. It was like the fire Edgar had lit in my soul earlier had left a smoldering ember that allowed me to feel a hint of excitement and joy.

Edgar was standing at the base of the stairs, leaning casually against the railing. His eyes blazed a beautiful blue against his dark wool coat. He watched me with admiration as I descended and finally stepped onto the granite of the entry with Isabelle poised on my shoulder. His eyes were now smoldering seductively and his body was shaking as though he'd seen a ghost.

"I just can't believe it. It's so surreal, seeing you like that." He looked at my outfit with approval. "Beautiful," he whispered as he moved in close, raising his hand to pat Isabelle on the head before turning his gaze to me.

He tilted his head toward my ear and leaned into my neck. I shuddered as he brushed his cheek along mine, his lips grazing my chin before resting gently on my nose. I giggled, the soft touch tickling my senses and igniting my soul.

His lips curled into a smile against my skin, his breath warm and inviting.

"Are you ready?" he whispered as he stepped away, a mischievous smile snaking across his face.

"What exactly should I be ready for?" I tilted my head inquisitively.

He chuckled secretively. A white coat materialized from behind his back. I gave him a skeptical glance as he draped the thick wool around me. The pure white fur on the hood brushed against my cheeks, and I found it was softer than anything I had ever felt. He pulled the hood over my bare head, making sure that I was properly bundled.

"You know, fur like this might make some of the students down there a little angry." I brushed my hand from one side of the hood to the other. It was so sumptuous.

He laughed.

"Well, this coat was made when it was a matter of survival, not just a luxury, so they can deal." He kissed me on the forehead before leading me through a door to the far left, just beside the grandfather clock.

"Where are we going?" I asked with immense curiosity.

He turned his head and looked over his shoulder, the glint of his eyes just visible. "To the garage."

I crumpled my brow. "There's a garage?" I asked in disbelief.

He chuckled.

"Of course there's a garage. What did you expect? A barn full of Clydesdales?" His voice was playfully sarcastic.

I looked at his back with a sour glare.

"Well, everything else you have is so old fashioned, how was I supposed to know?"

231

He glanced over his shoulder. "I will agree, there are some things that never should have been modernized, but there are other things, brilliant things, I couldn't imagine we ever lived without. It's all about finding a happy medium, Elle." He winked and then turned back forward as we continued down a long hall.

He had a good point. Candlelight was certainly more attractive than halogen.

"I built the garage in 1885 when Mr. Benz and I finally discovered how to apply a combustion system to a hunk of rolling metal." He was talking as he faced forward and his voice echoed through the dark space before us.

"Mr. Benz?" I gasped, my gate breaking to a slight run in order to keep up with him, "As in Mercedes-Benz?"

We had finally arrived at another door and he opened it with a gruff pull, "Yes, but Mercedes came much later, in 1901 when he merged ideas with Wilhelm Maybach."

Candles again flared to life on the walls and my gaze fell on a long narrow alleyway. My mouth hung open in disbelief. There before me was a very old car, something I didn't recognize, but knew was valuable.

"What…" I choked on disbelief in my throat. "You, or I mean, we have cars? But we live in the woods!"

A surprised laugh filled the room. "Doesn't matter. I take them out at night, anyway."

"But there are no roads!" I gasped, walking toward the first car in a line of about fifty that stretched as far as I could see.

He laughed at me again. "You really don't remember,

do you? You just have to visualize the roads, Elle. Where's your creativity? We're magical. We can do a lot of things you wouldn't think were possible." He had a teasing grin painted on his perfect face. "Just think about it, you'll see what I mean soon enough."

"Gas?" I ventured.

"Don't need it," he said simply.

I looked at him and rolled my eyes in disbelief. My fingers ran across the familiar three point star Mercedes-Benz logo I had learned to associate with the well-to-do upper class, but never me.

Each car in the line looked successively newer as we strolled down the length of the long garage. I noticed he seemed to have a thing for black, finding every car appeared sleek and sharp as a result. Each panel of highly waxed aluminum glowed like gems in the candlelight. I was amazed at how all this could possibly fit in the field unnoticed, but then again, if I used my imagination as I was told, I could manage to make it feasible.

Edgar watched me as we approached the end where I gasped, bringing my hand to my mouth. There, in all its rusty and worn down glory, sitting between a nineteen eighties El Camino and a first generation Hummer, was my green Datsun. It stood out like a sore thumb amongst the pristine beauty of all his black cars and I cringed, suddenly embarrassed by my once proud buy. My eyes whipped toward him, silent in my embarrassment.

He raised his eyebrows comically.

"I must say that your addition to our collection is

surely…" he paused as he struggled to find the right words, something that wouldn't hurt my feelings. I had worked so hard to earn it, and to think, all that torture for nothing. "It's definitely colorful," he mused.

I stared at my car for a moment before ripping myself away, watching Edgar as he approached the last thing in the garage, exponentially smaller than all the other vehicles and covered by a thick canvas tarp. The shape looked vaguely familiar, but not anything I had ever seen in person. Edgar looked at me excitedly, grabbing my hand before ripping off the cover. My eyes lit up and a brilliant smile crept across my face.

I yelped in delight and felt a charge of adrenaline pulse through my veins.

"It's a snowmobile!"

SNOW DAY

Edgar slowly released my hand and practically danced with eagerness. He folded the canvas tarp and tossed it aside. The black snowmobile looked brand new, and I assumed it was because he had upgraded to a model made for two passengers instead of one.

"I've been dying to take this out." The look on his face was purely male, an inherent craving for speed and danger.

"No horses, then?" I teased.

He laughed.

"Oh we can do that, too, but unfortunately, you'd have to go out and find some first, and these days, wild horses are hard to come by."

It felt good to be silly with Edgar.

He threw his leg over the saddle of the snowmobile and reached out for me with a gloved hand.

"Don't worry. It's safe. I promise." His eyes were a

stormy blue and he winked at me. His beautiful smile made me weak.

My fingers touched his gloved hand and I was surprised that only a faint fire emerged in my soul. I glanced down at our grasp, confused.

He chuckled again.

"It's the gloves, Elle. Skin on skin is the most powerful connection for us, but this way, I will be able to handle your terrified iron grip around me as we fly through the woods, much like when I carried you from the field." There was a dangerous yet playful glimmer in his eye, and I gave him a warning glare.

"You better not kill me, Edgar Poe." I gave him a mock angry look and he grinned in return."

I swung my leg over the seat and locked my arms around his chest, squeezing them together as hard as I could. His body felt amazingly strong under my touch. I could feel every muscle flex as he moved. This was more contact then we'd ever had, and I reveled in the moment, locking it away for future meditation. I shuddered, my soul pulling me against him, becoming one.

There was just enough fire in my heart to muster a smile as I closed my eyes. The garage door rumbled open automatically. My eyes opened, then, and the crisp air poured in over us.

"Can't someone see this? Or even hear this?" I asked, yelling over the roar of the engine.

He twisted his head to shout over his shoulder.

"Nope. Not until the snowmobile hits the snow. Right

now, we're still invisible to them, even the noise." His voice boomed over the engine, both reverberating through my bones.

I felt Edgar press down hard on the throttle and we jerked forward as we burst out onto the blanketed white meadow. The loud whining suddenly became muffled by the thick billowy snow that churned through the belts. A few flakes fell like cotton from the sky, hitting my face with a cold sting before they melted onto my skin. Edgar drove with control across the untouched fields and into the woods. The trees shook the snow from their branches onto us. He expertly dodged trees and fallen trunks, and I slowly felt my grip relax. I allowed myself to sit up and view my surroundings.

I became aware of what Edgar had meant as I noticed the trees and roots make way for us, as though creating a sort of path or road, the perfect size for us to pass. Because of this, the ride was very smooth, and I found it easy to enjoy myself and the magic of the day. My soul was flying and I took a few deep breaths as I absorbed the sensation, trying hard to remember every glimmer and pulse. To my right, I caught a glimpse of two elk that loped playfully alongside us, just a few feet away. They darted through the trees with an expertise I wish I could possess, the forest floor like a trampoline.

We drove for a ways up the gently sloping mountainside, passing scenic frozen rivers and icy cliffs covered with sheets of glassy waterfalls. Wherever we were going, Edgar seemed to know the way.

As we rounded onto a sort of plateau, he slowed to a halt and cut the engine in one seamless movement. He easily pried my iron grip from around him as he looked at me over his shoulder. My ears felt as though they had been stuffed with cotton, the sound of the snowmobile still reverberating in my head. His brilliant eyes glimmered against the white backdrop, his gaze searching mine in silence, roaring with intense desire and love, death and fury.

He stood from the snowmobile, grasping my hand and hoisting me off with ease as he lifted me into his arms. His breath flowed across my face, his eyes still watching mine. As he stared, the muted colors of the white forest allowed for the blue hues of our existence to brilliantly shine. I could feel his chest rising against mine as he tilted his head down and pressed his frosty lips against my warm skin, causing me to shiver.

He smiled against my lips as he released his strong grip.

"Amazing, isn't it?" He watched as my gaze fell from him to the trees.

We had stopped in a grove of maples that had been stripped of their summer leaves and were seemingly shivering under their cold dusting of snow.

"I've never seen anything like it in my life," I said as a sharp breath of amazement passed my lips.

I noticed Edgar smirk as he grabbed my hand and pulled me toward one of the trees.

"Sure you have." His eyes urged me to look at the trunk more closely.

I struggled to focus on the shapes that had been carved into its bark. I reached my hand up to the markings

238

and traced the outlines of two ravens, both looking skyward and to the right. He then pulled me to a trunk a few paces away. Two other ravens were etched there, facing toward the sky and to the left.

When I'd had a good look, he pulled me back to the center of the two trees, still grasping onto my hand with an urgent grip. I looked up and saw that the trees mirrored each other, like a couple, as though each other's perfect halves. Edgar gently released his grip on my hand, pulling his glove off and stuffing it in his pocket. His warm hand laced through my icy fingers. My soul burned brighter.

"What can you see here?" he asked, a smile still touching his lips and his eyes calm.

I gave him a confused look as the warmth inside me began to pulse through my veins.

"What do you mean?"

"Imagine anything you want. Imagine what you'd wish for these trees to be." His eyes burned like sapphires, testing me.

I thought hard for a moment, finding it easier than ever to clear my thoughts. I closed my eyes, imagining the trees twisting, shaping themselves into an embrace, and finding their happiness as one. I kept my eyes tightly sealed as I heard the sound of crackling branches, much like the sound of burning wood in a hearth.

When I opened them, Edgar stared proudly at the trees before us. A few tufts of snow fluttered to the ground from the branches above.

"Just as always," he whispered as he released his grip

on my hand and dropped it to his side, giving it a shake as though our touch had hurt him.

I looked at the trees in utter amazement and a weak smile tugged at my lips. The trees had intertwined their branches, braiding into a large arch. In the middle of the arch two branches cascaded down in the middle and leveled out into a swing.

He pulled the leather glove back over his strong hand and then grabbed my cold fingers again. Stepping forward, he pulled me toward the swing. I sat down with care as the trees swayed under my touch, bursting to life in an instant shroud of brilliant green leaves. I laughed as amazement and love filled my soul.

Edgar took his seat next to me.

"See, Elle? I could never harm you. All the magic and beauty in my world would be gone if I did. My love for you is too great and so much more brilliant than anything else." The look on his face was genuine and soft, and his hand was warm as he cradled mine inside it.

I still did not fully understand my own power, nor could I imagine what it was like to have it as my own. Edgar had kept things a secret, as though afraid to let me know the real truth, but at this point, I didn't really care. This was information enough.

I looked above me, admiring the branches as they continued to twine themselves together, full of life. I saw the power of our being, our existence, and how important it was for us to be together. We had a pre-determined love greater than anything in human existence, and I knew the strength of it would keep me alive forever.

We swung for a while in silence, and my mind began to clear. Suddenly, I thought about Scott and Sarah, and I turned to Edgar with apprehension swimming in my eyes.

"What about class?" I asked frantically.

He laughed. "Like I said, with the snow, I doubt anyone is there. Besides, I don't think you'd really be learning a whole lot more right now. Not more than this." He motioned with his hand to the trees. "There is no point for you to ever go back, if you don't want to. You already know it all, but your mind is trying to keep it from you. That's why learning comes so naturally."

"Yeah," I paused, accepting what he was saying as a truthful statement. It was true I never needed to go back, other than to see Scott and Sarah. It was so amazing to finally have friends, and I didn't want to have to give that up. It was hard to decide.

"But then what about your class?" I asked, remembering there was more to this than just me.

He snorted.

"That's not really my top priority." He looked at me, love boiling in his gaze, "You're all that matters now. You are my life." His face looked pained and urgent. "Besides, I have a very good substitute," he said playfully, a grin returning to his smooth lips. "And in about two weeks, most will be going home for the winter, anyway."

I looked at him, confused. "But won't they wonder where you went, where I went? Even just for the week?"

His lips coiled in amusement. "Oh, I'm still teaching.

I just made a sort of hallucination of myself, a holographic replacement, sort of like a ghost. And as for you? I told all your professors I was going to be teaching you personally because you needed the discipline, and you had a lot of potential."

I was satisfied with his response, so I did not carry that conversation much farther. I changed the subject to something new.

"Edgar?" I asked quietly. "Will we ever die?" I held my breath as I awaited his response.

His face grew solemn.

"No. We will live forever," he replied with a sudden smile. "Together."

Despite his mutual happiness and despair, his reply reassured me. The idea of eternal life seemed so sweet, yet seeing Edgar's suffering also offered me the bitter side, and the possibility of eternal pain. We rocked in silence as we both considered the matter. Edgar's grip tightened on my hand, almost crushing my fingers, but it felt safe, secure. I felt so natural with him, so at home, and I was going to try my hardest to protect him as well.

An hour passed of complete silence before Edgar finally stood. "Shall we get back?" his voice sounded distant.

I nodded, swallowing hard as I pushed myself off the swing. Immediately, the branches began to untangle and revert to their previous position. The leaves withered and fell to the ground, leaving a blanket of rusty foliage at their base, slowly being buried in the snow that was now falling in heavy drifts.

We crawled back onto the snowmobile and I wrapped

my arms around Edgar, lacing one hand into his coat and pressing it gently against his ribs. I felt his heart racing as we took off, and I tenderly rested my head against his back.

When the trees finally opened into the meadow, I sat up as I wondered how we'd get back inside. He was racing full speed toward the center of the opening as a watery wall suddenly appeared before us. We crashed through the screen as it rippled. Edgar twisted the handlebars and the snowmobile began to skid, almost crashing into the back wall of the garage.

I gasped, digging my fingers into his jacket. He cut the engine, wincing at my painful grip.

"Geez, Elle," he groaned, his face contorted into a pained mask. "With that claw-like grip I'd figured you found out how to become a raven again."

I laughed. "Yeah, sure. I wish." I rolled my eyes as he pried my hands apart.

He twisted in his seat, throwing his legs around until he faced me. He placed his hands on my knees. "You will remember," he breathed.

Without hesitation he grabbed my face between his still gloved hands, his eyes a steady blue. He leaned in and pressed his lips against mine. Our breathing became fast and urgent. His breath was intoxicating. Our lips molded together and his hand moved to my back, pressing our bodies together. I grabbed at his coat, my need driving all logical thought from my mind. I wanted to be as close to him as I could.

He stiffened under my attack, and I froze, dropping my hands to my sides as if I had been burned. I quickly stood and backed away, a tightness forming in my chest and throat. Edgar was gripping the seat of the snowmobile, his face twisted as he struggled for control. I pouted slightly before finally laughing when I noticed his navy eyes return. The feeling in my chest subsided.

"It seems I do have the ability to save myself." I put my hands on my hips with a smug smile.

His face was still strained, but he managed a smile.

"Good thing, too." He shook his head and stood.

He looked away, grabbing the tarp and throwing it over the snowmobile. Turning to me, he grabbed my hood and pushed it off my head.

"Thank you," he whispered, leaning in and softly kissing my forehead with renewed control before resting his head against mine. He lingered there for a moment before pulling back, his face cheerful once again.

I smiled. "You're welcome."

His eyes glittered slightly. "Are you hungry?"

MATTHEW

"So what would you like?" Edgar stood across the gleaming copper counter from me, his long sleeves pushed up to his elbows, revealing his strong forearms.

I had a thick silk and fleece robe wrapped around me and my hair was still damp from the searing shower I'd subjected my chilled body to. My cheeks were rosy from the wind and the heat of the water. It had felt so good to be warm again after the freezing temperature outside.

I shrugged, unable to summon an idea, my stomach too hungry to think.

He pursed his lips and narrowed his eyes.

"I know just the thing." He went to the antique icebox where he retrieved three small blue eggs from within. He balanced them on the counter before untangling a towel in a basket to the far right and retrieving two pieces of bread.

I looked around the kitchen as Edgar worked.

Everything was covered in copper sheeting, from the counters to the antique Victorian hood that hung over an open fire, molded with a beautiful scene of two ravens in a field of fruit. The kitchen was U-shaped and located just to the right as you walked from the left of the front hall to the back of the house. The island I sat at was located in the middle of the space accompanied by two bar stools.

Behind me was the sitting room he had brought me to the first night. It looked through to the library that was toward the front of the house. The whole layout didn't make much sense, but being that the house was invisible in space, almost like part of a whole other dimension, I guess it didn't have to.

The fire crackled, filling the room with warmth. I felt cozy and safe. Edgar cracked the three eggs into a pan and set them close to the heat to cook. He then hung the bread in a basket above the flames to toast.

He sighed, noticing me as I watched him.

"I could never get used to the modern stoves. You just don't get the same flavor." Laughing, he strolled back toward me where he reached across the cold counter and cradled my hands between his.

I smiled at him.

"Have you begun to remember anything, about your former life?" he urged as I felt his toxicity pour through me.

I searched my mind, finding it silent and clear. There were faint voices hanging in the distance, but I still could not match them with the faces that flashed like cards before my eyes. The house only seemed vaguely familiar, as though I

246

knew my place here, but still couldn't recall exact moments.

"Sort of," I crumpled my brow. "But none of it makes any sense."

His eyes reflected the burning candles. He let go of my hand and gave me a crooked smile, standing back a bit and positioning himself in a strange manner. I watched in amazement as he began to spin. There was a swift burst of energy as wind whipped around the room, papers and pans shaking in its wake.

I gasped, a nervous giggle bursting from my throat as the residual flame in me faded. Edgar stood on the counter before me, his eyes a beady blue and his pearly feathers glittering. I reached out and carefully rubbed the feathers on his head, knowing that they were sharp. They instantly fluffed and my soul surged as a laugh echoed through the house.

"You're so beautiful," I announced with amazement.

Edgar's talons scratched against the copper as he spun before me, modeling his new look. As I looked at his claws, I saw that counter was now deeply etched and I laughed.

"You're ruining your house!" I yelped and he lunged toward me with a sharp "caw!" "Okay, our house," I giggled.

He stepped back, blinking with his beak open.

The raven that stood before me was no longer threatening or sinister. As I looked at him, my heart smiled. His beautiful armor was more stunning than the singular feather. He was strong and proud. He spread his wings and began slowly flapping them as he lifted off the counter and twisted back into his human form.

Edgar ran his hands through his ruffled black hair,

smiling slyly.

"That's so amazing!" I looked at him, wide-eyed. "I wish I could do that."

He smiled. "Of course you can." He furrowed his brow. "But I don't think you could do it without your soul back. It's not like I could hold your hand through all the commotion. But I would love nothing more than to see you like that again, in your changeling."

I thought about it for a moment. "What is it exactly that you do?" I paused, clarifying my question. "To turn like that?"

Edgar turned to the fire and flipped the tiny eggs in the air. "You have to visualize it. See yourself as the raven and your body being weightless." He returned to the counter.

I glanced at him, finding it hard to envision his large body becoming weightless.

"It's a feeling that comes from inside, from your core." He looked so passionate when he talked, and I could see how it would be near impossible for me to accomplish the transformation, like he'd said. I didn't have that passion yet.

"It's like you're indestructible. All your feathers are like knives." I looked at my finger where I had previously cut myself.

He knelt again and adjusted the eggs. "It's pretty handy and certainly makes it easy to kill spies."

I shuddered, thinking of the sound that day in the meadow - the sounds of death and cracking bones.

Isabelle landed on the counter next to me, startling me as she began clicking her tongue.

Edgar snorted. "Greedy little thing, aren't you?" He

gave her a reproachful smile. She clicked her tongue again as Edgar picked one fried egg up with a fork and tossed it to her.

Her beak snapped as she dodged to catch the egg before it hit the counter. She tilted her head at me and her eyes were full of satisfaction. She seemed to wink. The egg hung from her mouth, flapping as she twisted her body around and took off, flying across the room and through the window between the sitting room and library before she zipped up through the loft ceiling to the railing above.

Edgar grabbed two crystal plates from the cabinet, putting one toasted piece of bread on each. He then stabbed the eggs and placed one on each of the two toasts. He placed one plate on the counter before me. The robin's egg was small and delicate. I watched as he walked to the cabinet where he grabbed a bottle containing an amber liquid from within. He shook it gently before uncorking the top and I pushed my brows together in frustration, huffing as he poured the thick syrup over my egg and toast.

"What are you doing?" I squealed.

He laughed. "Trust me, you love this. Just try it."

I winced as he pushed the plate that was swimming in maple syrup toward me. He handed me a fork with an amused grin on his face as he leaned down and put his elbows on the counter, cradling his head in his hands to watch.

I eyed the plate he had sheltered between his arms with a hungry desire, his egg and toast void of syrup. With disdain, I lifted the fork to the center of the yolk, pressing down so it popped open, spilling into the syrup and over the bread. I gagged slightly and Edgar choked back a laugh.

With extreme apprehension, I brought a small piece to my mouth, the smell surprisingly sweet and almost smoky. As I touched it to my tongue, I furrowed my brow as I concentrated on the taste alone, ignoring the texture completely. Chewing slowly, I found myself utterly surprised. The flavors were beyond amazing, and the sweet syrup mixed with the thick yolk and grainy bread burst across my mouth, hitting every taste bud.

My eyebrows shot up. "Wow."

Edgar's hearty laugh filled the room. "I told you," he snorted. "I guess I know you better than you know yourself." He gave me a playful wink.

Still skeptical, I took another bite, finding it as delicious as before. "Well, when you don't even know yourself, that's not very hard," I added with a full mouth.

Edgar nodded. "Very true." After that, time passed quickly.

* * *

Later that afternoon, I sat quietly in my room with a dozen journals lying open around me. There was no sound anywhere except that of my furtive swallows as I scanned my words, trying hard to remember my life. Every entry was loaded with emotion and happiness. The discovery of my gift, the way it grew over time, and then the day that I even created this forest with my talents of nature.

And then there was the end where my writing turned

sinister and scared. I flipped through the pages, my heart pounding hard in my chest, as though remembering the feeling and the uncertainty. It was suspenseful as the last few entries turned frantic and short:

October 10th, 1708

> *He's coming closer. I can feel his hunger in my soul. My mind is fogging. The evil that seeps from his blood is dark and sinister, a hundred souls dying because of his thirst. Edgar seems unfazed, but he's the rock, my protector. I just hope when the time comes, I'll know what to do...*

That was the last thing I wrote. I gave myself no clues, no way of knowing how to unlock my soul and get it back. I looked toward the paintings on the wall. How could I give up this life so easily? How could my stubborn heart surrender before the fight?

Closing my eyes, I slowly brought each remembered image back into my peripherals, noting the facial structures and mannerisms of each. One face kept flashing into my view. Someone deeply disturbed, with eyes so hollow he may as well be nothing more than a corpse. The memory caused fear to well in my chest, and it began tightening my lungs as I tried hard to remember his name.

As the image lingered, I remembered what Edgar had told me - the name of the sorcerer that had come for us and had murdered so many others. Deep in the back of my mind I uttered the words as the face nearly fell away: *Matthew*. My heart lurched as a fire seared through it, and I struggled to hide the pain. I closed my eyes and forced myself to concentrate on the face, making myself recall the horrible day I'd suppressed so painfully.

There was a soft knock on my door and I snapped back to the present, instinctually wrapping my robe around me even tighter. Edgar peeked in and then entered the room, afraid to startle me again. He was freshly shaved and now wore a finely tailored suit. My eyes fell upon him with hunger. I had never seen him look so handsome, so beautiful.

"Am I disturbing you?" He looked sheepish and lonely, tired of spending time by himself for so long. It was unfair of me to lock myself up here, away from him. I could see in his face he was desperate to see me, desperate to spend time with me and have me back.

I shook my head.

He leisurely approached my bed, sitting on the edge. "I was bored." A smile crept onto his face, his powerful back slouching over slightly.

The candles in the room came to life with the receding daylight. I looked around at the new light that was now cast upon the walls, and his face took on a warm, romantic hue.

"I had an idea." He looked at me with fire in his eyes. He stood eagerly and walked to the boudoir. I heard him rustle through bolts of fabric before finally halting as he pulled a massive sapphire-blue pile from within.

I gave him a questioning look. "Exactly what are you

proposing?"

He smirked. "I'm not proposing anything. We hardly know each other. Something like that would be highly inappropriate."

I nervously exhaled at his reference to marriage, and a notion crossed my mind that hadn't before. I had never thought to really bring it up, nor did I really want to, but a part of me still wondered if we'd ever been married. There was nothing that I had found in the journals, but there had also been missing pages.

As he held the gown in his grasp, I saw that he was hiding something, something I figured he'd know I'd refuse to do. "I was just wondering if you'd like to dance," he said lightly, a look I couldn't refuse crossing his face.

I snorted. "Yeah, right. I've never danced in my life."

He glared at me. I knew I'd loved to dance - my journals spoke of nothing else, but I still figured I'd try to deny it. There was no way my current self could recall dance moves. I faked a smile as he tilted his head and gave me a look of disbelief.

"Oh, come on!" His eyes flashed seductively. "It will be fun."

I sighed and gave in, figuring it was better to do physical activities to try and jog my memory rather than just sit here locked in my room, desperately searching books and trying to force it from my blocked mind.

Crawling from the bed, I grabbed the pile of silk and gave him a sulking look of surrender as I stormed behind the screen. He laughed at my less-than-thrilled attitude, diligently standing on the other side of the makeshift wall and waiting as I wrestled with the fabric.

I finally slid the bodice over my chest and reached to try and fasten the string. Edgar bravely walked around the screen behind me and I could feel his gaze as he watched me. I froze, and for a moment we just stood there in silence. Slowly, his fingers touched the small of my back, tracing up my spine before finally resting at my neck. I felt my skin tremble, giving in to his soft, warm touch.

A deep exhale escaped his lips as his hands worked at the strings, tightening them each with a soft and forceful tug, the whole time remaining silent. When he reached the top, I felt him tie a perfect bow. I was breathing in measured increments as he twisted his hands into my hair, grasping it and gently pushing it aside so that it cascaded down my chest. I tilted my head to the side as he leaned toward me. His lips parted and he kissed me at the base of my neck, his hands skimming down my arms.

With a shaky exhale, he stepped away and I opened my eyes to look at myself in the mirror. An image flashed across my mind, one of happiness. In the memory, I was wearing this dress but the look of my eyes and skin were different, unreal.

"You look beautiful, Elle." His silhouette was reflected next to mine in the mirror and I watched his eyes intently, wondering what came next.

The dress was exquisite, fitting me as though it had been tailored only for me. There were Tahitian blue pearls lining the hem and deep blue opals sewn down the bodice, and I instantly recognized why he'd picked this particular gown as the gems complimented his eyes, and mine. The overall weight of the fabric and gems was incredible, but I wasn't about to take it off.

I had never been the type to go to school dances, finding them childish and strange, let alone the fact that I'd never been invited. My mind had always rebelled against anything that was group-related, anything that reminded me of the fact I didn't belong. In my journals, however, it had seemed as though I was always the center of attention in my previous life. It was hard to fathom this other being: a strong and confident woman, not the scared child I saw today. I envied her.

Edgar reached into his pocket and slowly drew out a matching string of blue pearls from within. He laced his hands around my neck as he softly draped his fingers across my collarbones.

My heart melted and I turned to face him. He smiled once before taking my hand and pulling me toward him. The heavy silk grazed the floor and I stood on my toes, barefoot. He led me downstairs, one hand behind his back as his other cradled mine. As we descended the stairs, I felt like royalty. Time fell away. He rounded me into the front entry. The cold granite chilled my bare feet. He stepped toward me with a measured step, and like a forgotten instinct, my feet moved as though controlled by a puppeteer. His firm grip guided me, twirling my frame as my dress flew out around me.

I laughed as music began to play. "Where is that coming from?" I asked.

He laughed, lifting one eyebrow. "The CD player."

I giggled as he pulled me toward him and rested one

hand on the small of my back, the other still cupping my hand.

"So you don't believe in light bulbs or own a TV, but you do believe in cars, and you have a CD player?"

He nodded with an innocent look on his face. "CD's don't take up as much space as a piano." His expression was priceless.

I snickered before sobering.

"I want to stay here forever." I looked at him, and this time it was me who leaned toward him, standing on my toes to kiss him.

A deep exhale left his lips as I pulled back.

"I want you to stay, also." His eyes were sad. "I will never let us part again. Life without you is too painful. It's not worth living." He pressed his lips to my forehead as we slowly spun. "I realize now that I had no clue how I did it for so long."

He twirled me away, pulling me back and cradling my head with his hand as he dipped me down, slowly curling me back up.

We danced in silence and I remembered every step like it was something I'd done all my life. He held me close and his scent surrounded me, intoxicating my senses. Closing my eyes, I felt our bodies fusing into one and it was there that I found the comfort I'd longed for all my life. It wasn't just happiness I had been missing, but also love.

As the evening came to an end, the music ceased and he gave me an elegant bow. I giggled lightly, my head spinning and my limbs tired.

"Are you ready for bed?" His eyes were thoughtful.

I nodded as he led me to the stairs.

Entering my room, Edgar delicately helped untie my dress, giving me privacy as I struggled to take it off. I hung it in my closet, the weight of the fabric now taxing my tired arms. Feeling the cold breeze of the house, I quickly grabbed my nightgown from the pile of clothes on the floor and pulled it over my head as my teeth chattered.

When I emerged, Edgar was once again slouched in the chair by my bed. He had stacked the journals on the side table and pulled back the layers of velvet and down for me. Shaking, I ran to its welcoming warmth.

I crawled in and turned to look at him as he smiled. I flipped away to face the other direction as I thought about the day's events and the many things I had come to understand about my past. I froze as I heard Edgar slowly stand from the chair, worried he would leave until I heard the distinct rustling of wool as he removed his coat. I listened as he draped it over the chair and removed his shoes. Slowly, the comforter lifted and I felt him slide in. I shuffled over to give him space as he settled behind me.

He reached his arm around my torso, gently grazing it as he kept his body at a safe distance.

"I love you," he whispered into my ear.

I inhaled one delicate breath.

"I love you too." The words were thick on my tongue and my throat was choked with emotion.

He nestled his nose into my hair and my soul warmed to a smoldering burn. Though he wasn't touching me, having him close was comforting and intimate. As I began to fall asleep, I thought about Scott and Sarah. Their love was so simple and easy, but at the same moment I thought about Edgar's outlook on life. He resented normalcy and instead relished the simple elegance of challenge and the element of forbidden love. I knew that what we had, what we felt, was so much more than their love. It was enduring and intoxicating to know that one truly could not live without the other.

THE BEGINNING

In the morning I woke alone, the acute feeling of danger and fear on my mind. My head was clouded and my mouth felt numb. I sat up with sudden terror ripping through my heart as I looked around the room for Edgar, but the sheets where he had laid were already empty and cold.

Rushing from the bed, I donned my robe. I noticed Isabelle at the window, her feathers fluffed and her angry eyes darting across the field. My heart pounded in my chest as I turned and ran out the double doors, my feet sliding on the stairs in my hurry. As I stepped onto the foyer floor, I glanced out the front windows and halted abruptly. Frozen by what I'd seen, I lifted my hand to my mouth, stifling a scream.

My eyes were fixed on the meadow where a single matte black raven was standing like a statue, the wind whipping at its feathers but its body still as stone. There was a sudden movement in the front hall to my left and I jumped, my eyes darting toward the dark corner. My gaze met Edgar's black gaze and my heart leapt in fear. He walked toward me with a look I hadn't seen since that first day of class, his jaw angrily fixed and his fists clenched at his sides.

"Edgar, what is it?" My body was shaking with anxiety.

His face was solemn.

"It's another spy. Matthew knows you're back. He must. I've never seen more than one a year."

My breathing accelerated. "But how? How does he know we're here?"

Edgar arrived close at my side, but still distanced in his vulnerable state, his face cold and unchanged.

"He can feel us." He exhaled as a low growl escaped his throat. "I feared this, Elle, but there was no way to know until now." His voice sounded distant and sharp. "His senses are far stronger than I'd expected and I can feel him now, too. He's gaining strength as we are."

I took a calming breath.

"It's only a matter of time," he predicted grimly.

I slowly stepped toward him, looking at him with apprehension as I approached. He outstretched his arms and I took it as an invitation, running into his grasp and wrapping my arms hard around his chest. When I opened my eyes, I was horror-struck to see three more ravens land in the field, their black wings fanning the snow in waves of misty crystal plumes, a stark contrast to the brilliant white of the snow.

Edgar firmly grasped my arm and dragged me through the hall and into the sitting room. My arm ached where he grabbed me, but I didn't dare object.

"Sit here," he hissed, and I noticed his eyes were still

perilously black. "Don't look out the window, Elle, and plug your ears." His expression was murderous. "I'm sorry about this," he added in an attempt to revive some sort of human compassion before storming around the corner.

I pulled my knees to my chest as I heard the front door slam. There was a low rumbling as I heard Edgar change into a raven, and for a moment, there was a silence. My breath dragged in my throat and echoed in my head. Like a sudden crash of thunder, there was a shrill screaming of birds and I plugged my ears, terrified by what I knew was happening.

My body shook against the leather of the chair, sweat now beading on my forehead. I was beginning to feel faint. This was entirely my fault! Why had I been so dumb? Why had I thought that giving him my soul would make this stop? My head ripped open in pain, aching more than it ever had. The voices in my mind were screaming and I found no way to relieve the onslaught. I sat huddled in the chair, unable to breathe. I began singing in a loud voice, trying to muffle my thoughts and the sounds from outside.

After a while, I trailed off. All I could hear was my muffled breathing and I listened as a door slammed somewhere in the distance. A heavy exhale escaped my trembling lips as I chanted over and over in my head that Edgar was okay.

I heard his heavy footsteps as he rounded the corner into the room. I lifted my head to look at him, noticing the bloodied sweat glistening on his forehead. I quickly struggled to discern if the spatters were his blood or that of the other ravens. Then, as my eyes scanned his body, I noticed the deep scratches gouged into his neck. The fresh wounds oozed thick, red blood into his shirt, leaving dark stains that contrasted with his pearly skin. I gasped and ran toward him with fogged desperation. I was horrified when he held up one bloodied hand, halting me in my path. My shocked gaze fell to the lifeless lumps hanging from his other hand. Blood dripped on the black granite, glimmering under the candlelight like an ebony pool.

"Don't get their blood on you," he growled. "It will make it easier for them to find you, for him to find you." His face was cold and hard, as were his eyes.

Terrified, I stepped back. I saw his face suddenly change.

"I think I managed to kill them all, but I can't be certain. They could be hiding." His eyes were beginning to calm. "But it's only a matter of time before more come. We need to be careful."

I followed him as he walked to the fire that was blazing in the kitchen, tremors of shock still coursing through my body. He threw the four dead bodies into the hearth without a glimmer of remorse. The flames exploded into a deep purple. I watched as their feathers curled and melted. A smell like rotting wood and curdled milk soon permeated the room.

Washing his hands in the sink, I watched them tremble as he reached for a towel. He struggled to wet it as he cleaned his face and neck of blood. He turned off the water and leaned against the sink, water dripping from his open lips. After a moment, he walked toward me and wrapped his arms around my shoulders, placing his chin on my head.

I began to sob.

"Edgar," I struggled to form words through the well of tears. "I don't want this to happen. It's entirely my fault. I'm so sorry!"

His hands pulled me roughly away from him. He looked me in the eyes, his fury burning deep into my core. "Estella, this is not your fault. Don't think that." His brows were pushed together and deep creases cut into his smooth skin. "Don't start blaming yourself. You've had enough sorrow."

I gave him an unsatisfied glare. "And so have you, and it's all because of me!"

He grabbed my face, his hands like steel against by cheek bones. "Stop that," he snapped and I shook with despair, seeing the fine line on which I was dancing.

He pulled me into him again and I leaned against his stone chest, wiping the tears from my cheeks. This was my fault and I refused to be told otherwise. I should have never come here; I should have killed myself as I'd thought to do a thousand times. He had learned to live without me, and now, I was bringing trouble back to him, dragging him into my sadness in my selfish desire to feel something.

I pushed him away, shaking my forehead in denial and finding myself unable to look him in the eyes. I glanced back at the flames where only bones now sat atop the fire, the grotesque reality of it making me feel ill. Irrationality swept over me and I spun on my heel, filled with a sudden need to get away, taking off toward my room.

"Elle!" Edgar yelled behind me, his voice frantic and scared, as though he knew the thoughts that swam in my mind.

As I reached the stairs, the tears had already dried. My soul turned dark and cold, the need to punish myself somehow healing the guilt. I touched my chest in sorrow, grasping it hard and allowing the pain to seep into me. I ran into my room and slammed the doors behind me in a thunderous rage, my chest heaving.

I wanted to scream and yell. I wanted nothing more than to rip my body limb from limb. Why had this happened? I never should have come here. I should have let my life take its course, let myself suffer for how much pain I had caused and all the trouble I had brought upon this world, and these lives I've lived. I walked to the shelf containing my journals. With strength I did not know I possessed, I grabbed the back of the bookcase and threw it to the ground in my violent wrath. The tomes slid across the wood boards and sprawled open.

My breathing slowed as a sense of calm came over me. All this life, all something I couldn't remember. It was such a waste. I fell to my knees, the pain sharp as I hit the floor. The desire to punish myself was now greater than my desire to live, but all thought seemed to cease as my body took over, protecting itself from my mind. I knew what I had to do, but I still didn't see how. I was not going to allow us to live in fear. This time, I was going to fight.

There was a knock at the door and I ducked my head in shame. I said nothing in reply, my heart torn and my black soul charred too deeply. Edgar knocked again but still I said nothing, just stared at the floor in a complete loss. There was no third knock. Edgar opened the door despite my refusal to allow him entrance. He looked miserable, his shoulders hunched in despair.

He walked up to me on soundless feet, kneeling to the floor and wrapping his arms around me as he lifted me into his lap. His hand grazed across my cheek as he pushed my face toward his. His eyes scanned mine with calm before he kissed me, his grip like steel. I couldn't help but feel calm and safe. He lifted me off the floor and set me gently in the chair. He knelt before me and his eyes met mine.

"Elle," his voice sounded shaky, yet calm. "Please, don't do this."

I felt the anger in my heart reignite with a sudden crack. I didn't need his rationalizations, and the feeling welled in my throat.

"Why? You would have been fine without me. You would have learned to live on."

I watched him as my spiteful words stung his heart and he bowed his head into my lap. His face was still stained with faint spots of blood and his hair was messed. I felt no remorse for my words. It was all true, and our fate was already sealed.

"Elle, you don't understand how dark it is without you. I was hopeless and lost." He lifted his eyes to look at me, and I was shocked to see they looked empty and cold. "You are so important to me, so important to everything. You still don't understand."

"Then help me understand!" I breathed hard as my arms went limp at my sides.

He tried to comfort me further but I shied away. Irritated, Edgar grabbed me against my will and held me hard in his stern grasp in an attempt to make his point sink in. I struggled futilely for a few moments before resigning myself. My anger melted away to sadness and heartache. He clenched his jaw hard against my cheek, his strong arms unwilling to let me go.

"Just calm down," he breathed into my ear, his voice lulling me into tranquility. "We can beat this. We will."

I remained silent, staring stonily at him.

"Estella," his voice was firm. "We're going to be okay. Just be calm. We have time until he gains enough strength, until he formulates a plan. Be strong for me. This is only the beginning."

I looked up at him as he held me, my limbs heavy with emotion. I wrapped my arms around him, grasping him as though he were my life. It was then that I remembered that he was my life, and it was all worth living if living was what I was here to do. I could not waste what little time I had left.

WAITING

For the next few weeks, Edgar held my hand and remained by my side with relentless resolve. Still, I remained wary, treating every slight movement like a threat. I winced as he adjusted the coals in the fire, and I thought of the four lives he'd taken and the four carcasses that were long gone.

"I'm going to have to forbid you to leave the house," he finally spoke one afternoon. It was already clear that I wasn't leaving, but hearing him say it made it seem like a jail sentence. He was becoming impatient with the silent treatment I'd subjected him to, but what more did I really have to say? In my anger and hatred for myself, I had receded into silence. We sat quietly on the stools in the kitchen as the winter light streamed through the window and reflected onto his sad face.

I sighed. Over the past weeks, I had prepared for death, for the end.

"This is how it all happened last time, isn't it?" My voice

cracked with sudden emotion.

He squeezed my hand hard, his eyes meeting mine and blazing a deep sapphire blue that glowed brighter than they ever had. I knew there were likely two reasons he was refusing to let go of me. One was in hopes of making me remember my past, and the other was so that he could gain strength, as though preparing for a coming battle.

My appearance was already altered. My hair had taken on a new sheen. His constant grasp was mystifying and it had begun to change me back into my former angelic self. In his attempts, I was also ceasing to age, my skin becoming a radiant pale pearl and my eyes beginning to reflect the light like a creature of the night.

He touched my face, brushing his warm fingers across my chin.

"Yes, this is how it happened last time," he exhaled. "But he was more powerful and more dangerous then."

I nodded. "But now he's hungrier, and you can't underestimate that."

A sudden frustration flooded his face and I could tell that these were all grim facts he already knew were true, and that he found infuriating. Since the morning the spies came, Edgar had seemed drawn and distracted. His mind was now crowded with thought and his blue eyes were stormy. His cold demeanor frightened me, making me wary of the world around us as though it was all out to get me. Despite his motives, the constant touch was nice and I felt complete for long periods of time. I was afraid to tell him that it wasn't helping, at least not like he wanted. There were no new memories coming back to me, still just the few faces flashing across my mind.

I sighed as I dropped his hand. He gave me a look of surprise and I just shrugged.

"Sorry, Edgar. I just need a break for a second. It's all very hard to handle. I'm sure it is for you, too."

His face was gloomy. "Yes," he agreed. He tilted his head down, leaning against the copper counter in the kitchen. "I'm exhausted."

"I'll be fine," I reassured him. "I'll keep working on it. I just need some space." My eyes were locked on his, begging for him to understand.

A familiar gloominess slowly seeped over me and the house seemed to grow even colder. I walked away from him down the hall. I missed Scott. There was something about the simplicity of his life, and Sarah's. I missed their childish smiles and playful, cheery lives. They were so naïve. I envied the fact that they had nothing to fear.

Though I had been prepared to dig deep and find my life, I had at least figured it would be somewhat traditional: a mother, a father, maybe even some brothers and sisters. I was hoping that in finding that, I would also find what my soul had been missing. I never expected I was actually missing my soul and my other half. It pained me to think I'd never have a mother, never have siblings, or even friends. Scott and Sarah would eventually age, and in time, die. I would be forced to leave their companionship behind out of fear they would discover my true self.

When I thought about Edgar's life, I knew that he was

frustrated also. All the friends he had ever made - Mr. Benz, Edgar Allan, and numerous others - were all lost in history now, never to return to their former selves. There had surely been a time in Edgar's life where he thought this would be easier. There was probably a day, after my death, that had felt like he could heal and move on like humans often could.

I saw how inwardly upset he was when he found I remembered nothing about my former life. His eyes fade when he thinks of it, and to him, it's probably like holding onto a dying flame. I used to be something amazing, but now I just pale in comparison. He hides it though, out of his love for me, and when you share a soul that's certainly something you can feel: each other's deepest pains.

I can see how I've improved him, though, and I can see my purpose in his life. His energy was so low before I came, but even since I've been here, I've noticed a change in him - a strength returning. At night, he still lays away from me, safely distanced in his undying fear of killing me by taking his anger too far. I often stay awake for hours, just listening to him as he murmurs in his sleep. Sometimes he says my name, other times he speaks in Italian or French and I can't understand.

It's strange to imagine that all of the anger in our soul resides in him. I often wonder what he acts like when he's not around me, and I wonder if he's any different. It is clear that of the coupling, I was the most important, but alone I would be weak and vulnerable, unable to accept dangers in a way that could be fought. In this, I felt scared.

I traced my hands against the velvet stamped wallpaper in the hall as I walked its length. I stopped at the library where

270

I rested my hand on the doorframe, digging my nails into the wood. The lofted room was intimidating and filled with shelf upon shelf of books that spiraled up to the second level and the gold leaf ceiling. One wall gave way to large arched windows that reached two stories, pouring an ominous light onto the already faded books. Straight ahead, there was a ladder that took you to the separate upper level. I decided to climb it.

I shuffled in and put my cold pale hands on the mahogany wood of the treads. Hoisting myself up, I placed my feet on each ancient rung, careful not to get Edgar's attention from the other room. The previous time I had tried to climb up here, he had warned me that the ladder was old and somewhat unstable, and he ultimately forbade me to climb it. I remember thinking that maybe under his weight it was, but I was so light, I knew it was fine. Rung by rung, I silently ascended into the overhead space, my rebellion pulsing hot blood through my veins.

Once on the second level, I placed my hands on the iron railing and looked down on the worn leather couch and Thomas Edison lamp Edgar had received in 1879. It was the only light bulb in the entire house, and with just cause. Edgar had explained his reasons for resorting to candle light, beyond its simple beauty. He had argued that if all light bulbs were made like the original, then he would use them, because like Edison and Humphrey Davy, theirs would never burn out.

The second level platform was narrow and angled at a ninety-degree angle toward the right from where I stood, around the square room. I touched my fingers to the dusty volumes on my left. There were old dictionaries and encyclopedias, surely all much too outdated with today's technology. I tiptoed tentatively as I rounded the corner, and I noticed something I'd never seen before, perhaps because of its obscure angle to the room below.

There was a small archway tucked back in the corner, about the size of a regular doorway, but with no door. I balanced myself against the wall, peering around the corner with a curious eye. I twisted my head to peer down to the ground floor, making sure no one was there. Satisfied that I had gone undetected, I turned back and walked toward the archway without hesitation. My breathing was shallow as I slid into the small nook unnoticed, and the sound of my breath quietly echoed off the cold stucco walls.

As my feet crossed the threshold, candlelight fell upon the space, shining on a chair that was pushed into the back corner and reflecting off a large gold frame on the wall. The room was no bigger than a pantry, and I found myself mildly disappointed. A part of me had been hoping to find more than just a small sitting room. I threw myself down into the leather armchair and closed my eyes in defeat as dust flew up around me.

Despite the disappointing discovery, I felt I'd found a place to hide, a place Edgar wouldn't think to look. There was one lit candle and it flickered against the walls, making me feel like I was in a cave. I slouched down and folded my hands across my chest as I looked at the very large painting that stretched from knee to ceiling, clearly not designed to fit the space. The layers of paint beneath the thick dust tickled at my memories, catching my attention. I stood, brushing some cobwebs from the surface. I immediately recognized the signature: Vermeer 1667. I brushed away some dust so that I could get a better look at the scene. The overall theme was of everyday life, a group of people gathered in a sitting room for a party.

I brushed more of the thick dust away and looked closely at each face. My eyes scanned with delight until I was shocked to recognize the familiar features of Edgar, staring out from the scene with bored eyes. His jaw was clenched and his hair was tousled. I noticed that his eyes were a deep blue, like they were now, like the deepest ocean. I tried to smile slightly but couldn't quite manage it.

I followed his arm with my hand where I saw it was placed on the shoulder of a beautiful blonde woman in a familiar sapphire blue gown. My eloquent and balanced features gazed out at me with a knowing stare, as though telling my current self a secret that only I would understand. My skin was young and smooth, just as it was now, and my eyes were a light and striking crystal blue as they beamed from the canvas with life and happiness. My lips were rosy red, my features glimmering in the filtering light from a window. Vermeer's use of bright colors and light made the scene seem so life-like.

My focus fell to the other attendants of the party, each face flashing through my murky memory, each someone that I had been trying to recognize for weeks. I squinted as I brushed at the canvas with a brisker hand, now intrigued. The pearly skin and finery of each couple was eerily familiar, and

I deduced that they had also been like us: eternally locked in longing and alive for what they'd hope would be eternity.

All the men were dressed in black, their coats and vests dark as night with matching black silk ties. Their white shirts were the only difference, but the monochromatic ensemble accentuated the pearly reflection of their eyes, allowing the colors to show with greater brilliance.

One couple was adorned in velvety green, the gentleman's eyes glowing like a forest of evergreens, deep emerald and heavily faceted. The lady's hair was a deep, radiant burgundy, the color complimenting the luminous greens of her dress and eyes, making her pale skin and blushing cheeks blaze like the sun. She had a small black cat perched on her lap and her delicate hand was placed on its head. The cat's eyes were a matching green.

Another lady wore a brilliant bronze, and not surprisingly, her partner's eyes flashed like gold coins. Her hair cascaded in curling gold strands down her back and her cheeks also appeared to be lightly flushed. They both stood, the gentleman shadowing her to her left with two large English greyhounds at their sides.

The last couple leaned casually against the wall, the lady leaning against the lapel of her partner's coat and her hand resting on his chest. I noticed her fingers were crowded with diamonds. There were strands of pearls dangling from her neck and she was the only one smiling, other than me; the only other attendant enjoying the afternoon.

Her white gown was radiant, gleaming like a perfect silver pearl in the sunlight, and her hair was a billowy platinum blonde, as though she were my perfect twin. My attention flashed to her partner's face, deeply hollowed. His jaw was clenched and his silvery white eyes stood out like diamonds against his pitch-black hair. There was a white owl perched on the lady's shoulder, much like the owl Edgar had in his office, and for a moment, I wondered if that was exactly what it was.

In sudden revelation, my jaw fell open as I remembered the face of the man with the silvery stare. The face in the painting was much more youthful and alive, but the blistering eyes were unchanged, and just as lethal.

"Matthew," I whispered, my heart beginning to pound in my chest. I struggled to make sense of it all. According to this painting, he had been an acquaintance - our friend. My eyes darted again to his beautiful partner, angelic in her love toward him. I felt sorrow tug at my heart as my mind willed me to remember her. A warm sensation filled me and in that subtle response, I knew I had adored her like a sister. In a flood of anxiety, I dashed from the tiny room. The candle flickered out behind me with a tiny gust of wind. I carefully bustled down the ladder and ran into the hall, skidding on the floor in my hurry to flee.

I heard Edgar's voice somewhere in the distance as I raced up the stairs.

"Elle? Are you all right?" he yelled.

I froze midway up the steps.

"Yeah, I'm fine!" I yelled back as I stood there for a moment, but he didn't reply. In a few swift movements, I threw myself the rest up the way up the steps and through the colossal doors into my room. As fast and quiet as I could, I went immediately to my shelf of journals that Edgar had helped me categorize after my explosion a few weeks back. I tried to keep the floorboards from squeaking, knowing Edgar was directly below. I pulled out the journal marked 1667 from between '68 and '66.

With deep concentration, I flipped through each entry. My heart drummed against my ribs. At last, I caught a glimpse of my flagrant handwritten "V" on a page about halfway in. Eagerly, I held it open and read aloud:

September 1667

The lot of us gathered today for a portrait. I had convinced them of Johannes Vermeer's talents for texture, and they agreed it was a lovely idea. Hazel was more than excited. She even bought a beautiful new silk dress in a magnificent bronze...

I paused, noting the name of the lady with the gold hair: Hazel. It rang a strange bell inside my soul and I felt a fleeting sense of achievement. My eyes quickly darted back to the page:

... Gloria was snottier about the whole thing. She wanted to look the best, so she had a professional apply powder and blush to her face, making her burgundy hair stand out, and her *skin more radiant than it already was. I couldn't help but feel self-conscious near her, despite my naturally glowing features...*

There was another familiar click inside me: Gloria. I said her name over and over, locking it in my mind and my heart fluttered,

... Only Margriete was unworried about her appearance. She and I spent the afternoon snickering in the corner at the others' vanity. I should hope if I had a sister, she could be it. We are eternally joined at the hip and I shall miss her greatly when they go away to London for the summer, but come spring, we will be right again in Rome...

I put my hand to my chest, feeling the pain surging through my throat and stealing the breath from my lungs. A sudden illness overtook me and my mind began to fog as a memory flashed before my eyes: Margriete's laughing face that day. Though my soul could not feel the severed friendship, my body trembled from the loss, and the sorrow.

He had killed her, killed us. The way his face burned in the painting looked so evil, so angry. How had we not noticed his dark secret, his internal burning desire? I remembered the way my face had glared out of the canvas, as if I had known a secret. I gasped for air as I struggled to stay conscious, struggled to hold on to the feelings that now felt so real.

We were all so innocent and careless, so flagrantly in love with ourselves and our world; but the promise of endless life and the power we held over everyone was too intoxicating to see the evil among us. We had ignored every sign, ignored the possibilities of treachery and greed that went beyond our own vanity.

"Hazel," I whispered lightly. My chest ached as her glorious face flashed across my mind, her soft laughter lingering in the echoes of my empty soul. "Gloria," I whispered again as her tartness stung my mind and her vain existence tickled my nose with envy.

There was an abrupt knock at my door and I looked up from where I knelt on the ground, the journal clutched in my angry hand. My arms were trembling as Edgar entered, his eyes falling on mine, heavy with concern.

"Elle, are you okay?" He rushed toward me and put his warm hand on my back as I tried to catch my breath.

Tears poured from my eyes and my body began shuddering uncontrollably. I clenched my eyes tightly as tears stained the pages of my journal, leaving water marks and smearing the ink on the thick parchment.

Edgar pried the book from my desperate grasp. His eyes glided across the page and lit in understanding. He sighed.

"You found it, didn't you?"

My throat was swollen with sadness and a familiar dread overtook me. The world went dark and I fell to the floor.

As I came to, Edgar was carrying me to my bed. He laid me down on the soft sheets as he brushed the hair from my face, the strands matted against my cheeks from my tears. He was gently humming, trying to calm my hysterical state.

"Shhh, Elle," he cooed, his voice silvery and soft. "I'm so sorry, so sorry you had to feel this again." He gently rubbed my back as I faced the window, snow falling from the sky in thick flakes. "I never meant for you to see that."

My eyes began to dry as I felt my body give out, the fear numbing my muscles. The same despair and guilt rushed over me and I began blaming myself again. It seemed like the only logical notion. I had known what was happening back then, sensed the end nearing, but did nothing to stop it. Why? It was then I realized why I had the painting commissioned. Just as I had recorded our history in journals, I had also desired to record all of ours, to record that day so that I could look back, and recognize my own solemn stare.

Edgar sighed, his hand tracing mine.

"After that picture was painted, they began dying." His voice cracked and he paused for a moment. "You ordered me to immediately burn the painting, but I couldn't. You loved Vermeer, you loved them. I see now that it was a mistake to keep it."

Fresh tears formed in my eye and my notions were suddenly affirmed. There was a reason I had commissioned the painting, wanted that record of life. I was glad he hadn't burned it. I needed to see that moment, I needed to remember it.

"Margriete was like family to us, as was Matthew." There was a sudden resentment and a cold twinge to his voice, "But he used us, Elle, to lure them all in. I assure you I never knew, and neither did Margriete. She had no idea of the fate that was waiting for her." He touched my ear with the tips of his fingers.

He settled the covers over me and I felt him tuck the blankets under my sides before sliding next to me and placing his arms around my waist. He was distancing his touch, allowing my emotion to cool.

I struggled to speak. "Why…" but the words came out in a choked muffle and I cleared my throat and tried again. "Why do I remember these painful things? Why nothing wonderful or happy? How did I not do something to stop this?"

A light laugh filled the room and his breath fell across my ear.

"But that was a wonderful day, one of your happiest. The way you smiled, the way you looked," he stopped, his warmth relaxing me.

I thought hard to remember it, he was right. It wasn't the day that had been horrid. It was the days that followed, the darkness that would soon descend upon us in a shroud of death. The Gods were sadistic and cruel to do this. All we wanted was to be together, to live in love forever.

"I don't want you to think I'm protecting you from your past. I couldn't keep that from you. Your life is your own. It just pains me to see you this way, but perhaps if I told you some things, now while you're already upset, would that help?"

I felt him run his hand down the length of my arm. My body was still shaking, but I needed to know; I wanted to know. Nodding my head, I let it softly rest on the pillow, my hair tangling around my face.

He sighed, and I could sense he was going to hate this moment as much as me.

"Margriete, Gloria, and Hazel were your best friends, your sisters. You were each as different as the next, each unique and beautiful. When you were together, you seemed to make up every kind of personality, the perfect friendships." He exhaled. "Gloria was obviously very vain and conceited. Do you remember the story I told you about the first couple to succeed, to live after meeting for the first time?"

I nodded, now putting the pieces of my past back together.

"Gloria and Alek became our friends and her vanity came with a certain understanding. In her mind she was royalty and could not stand anyone being better than her. But to you, she was your…" he paused to think of the right term, "your Barbie doll, of sorts."

A soft laugh escaped through my tear-stained mouth and something inside me believed him, somehow knew how furious she was for not receiving the praise she'd believed she rightfully deserved.

Edgar leaned in close to my ear, brushing his lips against my cheek as they curled into a grin.

"And Hazel was envious, always jealous of everyone. She always thought her bronze hair and eyes were bland and boring. No matter how hard she tried, she could never fly like the rest of you. She had a short attention span, and as a result, she was clumsy." He laughed in my ear. "You treated her like your little sister. You were always protecting her, watching out for her when she wouldn't, or couldn't."

My heart was bursting with warmth, but also frustration. I could feel that her death had been the hardest on me and my body shuddered in pain.

"And then, of course, there was Margriete." I could hear the deepening despair in his voice. "She was your best friend, and the only one that was just like you. She was carefree and never worried about her beauty or her belongings, and because of that, you were both far more beautiful than the rest."

My body went cold as I waited to hear his next words.

Edgar squeezed me tighter.

"She was the last to disappear. You instantly suspected Matthew, but I didn't believe you. I realize my fault in that." He paused, his voice breaking. "You were the first to notice when Gloria and Hazel were killed that their partners were also brutally murdered alongside them. But Matthew hadn't died with Margriete, and you didn't believe his stories, his lies about how she'd run away in fear. Your eyes were far sharper than mine. I was furious with you, horrified that you could blame someone that was like a brother to me."

My eyebrows furrowed as the anxiety of that fact made my body feel rigid and angry toward Edgar. How could he manage to make friends with someone that held that sort of fury? But then again, perhaps they all had, and the notion of murder was just over the threshold of their understanding.

"You knew he had taken her and was just hiding the evidence of her body. I should have seen it in his eyes, but he was adept at hiding it all." He brushed his nose across my face. "It's my fault, Elle, you see. Not yours."

A wave of guilt washed over me, and I took a deep breath as I closed my eyes and allowed it to clear my head.

"No," my voice was surprisingly stubborn. "It was Matthew's fault, his alone." I wiggled out of Edgar's iron grasp. "I understand now. It wasn't me that caused all the pain and the suffering, not even us. It was you and I that saved our species, and we still can." I rolled over to face his stormy eyes. "Edgar, this time when he comes, I will have the guts and fury to help kill him. I can't run anymore, and I don't want this to happen again."

He traced his finger across my furrowed brow, and I could see my flashing eyes reflected in his. A grin crossed his face.

"There's the fire I knew you had." His breath fell across my lips, and I found it warm and intoxicating.

I smiled back as I wiped the last tear from my face. I was done being afraid, done running away from life as it tried to knock down the door on me. Edgar stared deep into my soul as he bent forward and pressed his lips against mine, sliding his hand alongside my back with a controlled but firm grasp. I gave in, realizing that I was being reckless, but as I pressed closer, his lips curled into mine and his teeth gently grazed my lip. The kiss felt desperate, as though our lives were suddenly fleeting. I thought about the day I had died, wondering if we'd even had the chance to say goodbye. The memory was still too painful for Edgar to share.

We molded together for a brief moment before he pulled away and untangled himself from my grasp, his eyes black, and his breathing shallow. "I really think you ought to reconsider your motives," he joked, leering at me.

I giggled, enjoying the fine line I was walking and the rush of adrenaline it pumped through my heart. I laughed, quickly pecking him one last time. A low growl escaped his lips.

He stood, grabbing my hand and pulling me from under the covers in one gruff move. I squealed with laughter as he twirled me out into the room, curling me back into a low bow, his strong arms cradling me with little effort.

He sunk his head against my chest. "But, I do love your sense of adventure," he whispered, his scent swirling around me. His touch was delicate as he pulled me into his arms and looked at me with adoration and a deep love.

As he set me down, I gave him a smart smirk. The fear that had crippled me all week was gone, and I realized that I was safer than before. We had the advantage. Besides, I was a delectable piece of bait, soullessly deceiving to my predator. A plan began to form in my head, a plan I could never tell Edgar. There was no way he would allow for it. He was too protective of me and too cautious to ever allow me the chance to get that close to Matthew, to touch his skin. A sudden power filled me and it was there that I vowed to avenge my friends, my family.

FREEDOM

It had been over a month now since the ravens had appeared. Christmas was only a week away. I sat looking out the tall, arched windows of the library as Edgar held my hand, flipping through a large book about Alaska that sat balanced on his lap. His CD player blared opera throughout the house and the clocks on the wall ticked. I stared at the snow-covered field, thick flakes falling on the already saturated ground. I rested my head on the back of the sofa with my legs curled under me, biting the nails on my free hand with anxiety.

I had spent endless hours thinking about my plan to kill Matthew. Ever since I found the painting, the idea had been formulating in my mind. I had ceased trying to figure out how to get my soul back. It was in Edgar for a reason, to keep it safe. I had already figured, three hundred years ago, that I had meant it to be that way. Our soul was where it was in order to make me free, to give me the ability to take the risks that are needed to end this once and for all.

The meadow was empty and cold, and the wind whipped the snow in wavy drifts, gathering it into invisible dunes around the eaves of the house. Things were beginning to feel ominous as we waited. It was just a matter of time before things would come to a head, and as we sat there helpless, the stillness weighed heavy on my mind.

I was growing increasingly anxious. Would Matthew come here? Or was it better to hunt him down first? If I made myself the bait, I would have to be prepared for the outcome, and whatever pain may come with it.

I sighed heavily, but Edgar didn't seem to notice. As I glanced back outside, my eyes caught the glimpse of something moving in the snow. I sat up straight as an arrow and squinted through the misty window, my lips parting and my breath coming fast.

My first thought, as I darted my eyes across the field through the panes, was that it was only the swirling snow playing tricks on my mind. I caught the sharp flash of my eyes reflecting in the glass, the crystal blue piercing back at me. I shook my head in annoyance, figuring it was just the glare of the light off the snow and I relaxed my chin back down on the sofa.

Edgar hadn't moved, still locked in his stony silence toward me. My wary eyes scanned the treetops and again something flashed across my blind spot. I furrowed my brow as I tried to make out what I'd seen. My heart rate quickened, pulsing into my hand as Edgar grasped it. I sat up again, this time eagerly watching, refusing to look away. I thought about that day in the woods, when something had followed me to the waterfall, but whatever this was, was too small.

Another minute passed and I felt Edgar watching from the corner of his eye, beginning to sense my unease. He tightened his grip on my hand. Concentrating my gaze back on the field, something again moved, and that's when I finally saw it. A white cat darted across the meadow between two drifts of light snow. I jumped and Edgar looked at me in annoyance.

"Estella, what is your problem?" he boomed.

I looked at him wide eyed. "Did you see that?" I gasped.

He turned and looked out the window behind him. "See what, Elle? I don't have eyes in the back of my head, you know." He gave me a sly smile.

I snorted. "I'm not joking, Edgar. There was something out there."

He squinted through the bright glare on the glass. "I don't see anything, Elle. Was it black?"

I looked at him with aggravation in my eyes. "No," I said tartly.

He touched a finger to my nose and I swatted it away. "Seriously. It was a white cat or something."

A mocking laugh grumbled in his throat. "You really think a cat could live up here in the frigid wilderness?"

I didn't like his condescending tone and my eyes blazed at him.

He lifted his eyebrows as he leaned back in surprise. "Wow, okay then," he breathed. "I guess if I were to tell you that you were probably seeing things, you'd rip my head off, right?"

I glowered at him. "You're such a bully," I hissed.

Looking back outside I saw the distinct pop of a tail as the cat jumped through the trees and into the woods. My jaw fell open in disbelief. I wasn't crazy, this I knew for sure. What I saw was really there, but as Edgar said, that was absurd. I stood and tried to peer further into the woods, standing on my toes and leaning against the couch for support.

"Elle, really! Please sit down." He was treating me like a child and I disliked it. "We are in the woods, you know. There are wild animals."

I snorted. "I didn't realize cats were wild," I said under my breath. Edgar looked at me with one eyebrow raised, his face threatening but his eyes a soft blue-grey.

Plopping down on the couch, I crossed my arms across my chest in annoyance. I glanced up toward where the small arched room was, filled with a desire to view the painting again, to see my friends and stare deep into the eyes of my enemy.

I shot out of the chair in one fluid movement, dropping Edgar's hand with a forceful thump and darting to the ladder.

"Elle, I've told you that's not safe. I wasn't just saying that so you wouldn't go up there." His voice was nagging and it only fueled me more.

Gingerly, I navigated my way up the creaky ladder.

"Then maybe you should get me a new one," I shot toward him in a bratty tone.

He snorted and dropped his gaze back to the book.

I popped up to the top rim, my soul fading as the playfulness began to leave me. I eyed the field again, now getting a better view, but to my dismay nothing was there. Each time I touched Edgar, the feeling of happiness seemed to linger longer than before. I was like a rechargeable battery of sorts, only, you wouldn't want to leave me unplugged for too long, because then I just became self-destructive and bratty.

I curled my fingers around the rail, walking like a toy soldier in a bored attempt to make Edgar laugh. I rolled my eyes as I finally gave up, feeling the depression begin to grip my chest. Rounding the corner of the narrow walkway, I delved into the small sitting area and plopped down in the chair, now drained and tired.

Isabelle flew up to the top railing where she tilted her head and looked at me with bored curiosity from outside the space. I patted my thigh and she floated down onto the chair, nesting herself in my lap with delight. I scratched her head and she furled her feathers, her eyes slowly closing in bliss.

"You saw the cat, right?" I scratched her in vigorous strokes as she kept her eyes shut, uninterested in my trivial question.

The candle streamed a gentle light on the photo and I looked at Margriete, her hand eternally resting on the chest of her two-faced partner, her murderer. The tiny white owl that rested on her far shoulder still perplexed me, its sharp yellow eyes gazing out from the canvas like a statue.

In the painting, I recognized Isabelle perched at my feet as I sat in the blue silk chair from my bedroom. I glared with anger at my face in the painting, still annoyed with myself for being so vague. Edgar's arm on my shoulder looked proud, his love for me stronger than his thirst for our soul.

I took a deep breath and exhaled with dark rage. I missed having friends, even if I couldn't remember them. I thought about how easily Scott and I seemed to get along, and my heart tugged as I began to feel sad about leaving him and Sarah behind. But come spring, they would be back, and hopefully so would I. Despite my initial social clumsiness, I had fallen into their friendships with comfort and ease.

I sat up then, Isabelle looking at me with annoyance as I gently pushed her off my lap and onto the chair. I shuffled to the railing just outside the archway where and looked down on Edgar.

"Do we have a phone?" I said bluntly, remembering that Scott and Sarah had given me their cell phone numbers. Not that they worked out here, but it was worth a try, just to check in.

He dropped the book in his hand and looked at me with parted lips.

"Uh…" he was struggling which only meant one thing: we did have a phone. "No?" His voice cracked.

"You are such a bad liar," I narrowed my eyes at him.

He pretended to be hurt, but I wasn't so naïve.

"Oh come on, please? I miss my friends, I won't tell them where I am, I promise." I stuck my bottom lip out in a pout.

He laughed, shaking his head at me. "Well, you're supposed to be back in Seattle."

I looked at him curiously. "What?"

He tilted his head back and he looked sheepish.

"Since I forbid you to leave the house, I just told everyone you refused to take my nasty personality, and you left the college forever. That's why I had to take in your colorful car."

My jaw fell open. "You had no right!" I squeaked, "You can't just bottle me up and wait. I didn't even say goodbye!"

He scowled at my words.

"Well, what should I have said? I kidnapped you? I had to make them believe that you hated them so much that you would never contact them again."

I was glowering at him. "How do you do that, anyway? Make a hallucination or holograph…" I struggled to find the right word. "Or whatever you call it."

I walked around the second level toward the ladder. Edgar stood from the couch with a lazy yawn and walked toward me as I began to descend. His large hands grabbed my waist and lifted me down before I even got half way.

"And how come you get to be so strong?" I spat, lashing out in my anger. He rolled me around in his arms and cradled me in such a way that I couldn't fight back.

He grinned widely. "Because, Elle, we're opposites. Whereas I am strong, you are sharp."

"Yeah, well, whereas I am smart, you are boring!" I spat, giving him a playful glare.

He tilted his head down, giving my forehead a gentle kiss before dropping me on the couch. "Well, you're impossible." He shook his head, walking out of the room in his hope to avoid the conversation.

"Don't think you're getting off so easy, mister!" I yelled over my shoulder. "I will find that phone!"

I heard him chuckle from the kitchen over the banging of pans.

"And don't think you can shut me up with your cooking, either!" I yelled again. Blood was pumping through my veins and I was enjoying this little spat far too much.

In truth, I loved Edgar's cooking. Over a thousand years of life had taught him well. As I sunk into the soft leather, I finally began to calm down. My thoughts shifted to the white cat. Maybe it really had been my imagination. After all, I was bored to tears trapped inside this house and yet, it was also nice being so close to Edgar. If I was going to face imminent death, at least I would have known what it was like to cry, love, and laugh.

I thought about what Edgar meant by opposites. It was like, besides sharing a soul, we also shared a body. He was strong, I was sharp; he was able to create illusions, and I could manipulate the earth. That's when I realized, it wasn't being cooped up that was driving me mad, it was the fact that I was so far from nature, like the fish in the tanks of the hatchery, right next to the lake they so longed to swim in.

I sat up as the delightful smells from the kitchen filled my nose. I shuffled into the room already glowering.

"Edgar, I need to get out," I sighed.

He gave me a cautioning look. "Elle, please don't start being difficult again. I'm afraid if you go out, they'll see you. Or worse yet, he will see you. For all I know they're already out there, waiting for you to be dumb enough to go outside and expose yourself."

An angry growl rumbled in my chest as I sat on the stool and looked at my reflection in the copper counter. My eyes were like tiny pearls and I found myself staring. Edgar wiped his hand on a towel as he threw some pasta into a giant pot over the fire. He walked around the island and stood behind me, tracing his strong hands down my arms and placing his chin on my shoulder.

"What would happen if I just didn't eat? If we live forever, why do we?" I asked with sudden interest.

He laughed. "That's a good question. Remember how I told you Matthew was drawn, tired and old? That's what happens. We may live forever, but everyone needs nourishment."

"Oh, that's too bad. I was hoping if I didn't eat maybe you'd give me some freedom." I sighed.

"Come on, Elle. Soon you can do whatever you want, we just need to wait." He traced his finger down my spine and it quickly clouded my mind. I sulked into the counter and he only made it harder for me as he wrapped his arms around my stomach, grazing my ear with his lips.

"Edgar…" I paused, my mind becoming cloudy and distracted and my anger leaving me.

"I love you, Estella," his voice was like a drug seeping into my blood mind, numbing every receptor and making me forget.

I melted into his arms. "Do you really, though? You always get close, but then quickly back away." My words were sassy, yet soft. "I want more."

I felt his mouth curl into a smile as he laughed. "I do think about other things, Elle. I am a man after all. But I also have the desire not to kill you, and I think that's what's most important." He spun me on the stool, grabbing my knees and wrapping them around his torso.

I blushed, realizing where this conversation was going. Edgar had succeeded in stupefying me, making me forget what I'd marched in here to say. His warmth was wrapping me in cotton, stuffing my thoughts and confusing my anger. He ran his fingers through my hair from front to back.

"Yeah, but I mean, even when we sleep, though you're right there, you're still so far away."

He exhaled with an amused chuckle. "Exactly. I'm trying not to kill you."

I heard his point, but it wasn't enough. "But you used to," I pried. I remembered the shape of the sheets that first day in my room.

He sighed. "Elle, you sound like an addict, and that's what concerns me." He pulled my legs from around him, though I protested against it. He stepped back and rounded the counter to look at me with deep blue eyes. "I understand your point, but we need to be careful. If we are the last of our kind, that's really important," His voice sounded taxed, but there was something else there; something he needed to tell me.

I kept watching with a skeptical eye, waiting in silence.

He walked back toward the fire, averting his eyes from mine.

294

"I need to go down to the college for a bit this afternoon. It seems the teachers that are still here are getting suspicious." He was frowning. "I guess one of them was actually dumb enough to try and touch me, but instead their hand passed right through me, the hologram, you know?"

I felt a sudden burst of rebellious thought run into my head, and I saw him take notice. He glared at me, his eyes a much darkened shade of blue grey. "And don't start thinking that means you're going to find the phone," he said bluntly.

I gave him a mischievous grin. "What makes you think I'd do that?" My voice was pitchy and fake.

He snorted. "I'm serious, Elle. This is for your own good. Don't do anything stupid."

I breathed hard through my nose and slouched into the stool. "Fine."

He looked at me then, his eyes still serious and dark. "Promise me, Elle?"

I exhaled, refusing to agree. "Yeah, yeah, okay. I'll be safe." I was swatting him away with my hand, but my mind was racing.

He served me a bowl of juniper berry pasta, and I winced at the smell.

"This smells like a pine tree!" I protested.

He looked at me sideways. "Seriously, you're really testing my patience today, Elle. Just eat." He pointed at my bowl with a spatula in his hand and a stern face.

I took one bite and my taste buds were again bursting with flavor. Rolling my eyes with joy, Edgar looked at me with relieved approval, gently kissing me on the cheek as he went to grab his coat. I looked around the room when he left for a hidden closet, trying hard to search out where he could possibly stuff a phone. If he could so easily hide a giant painting, it was hard to say what else was hidden as well.

When he walked back into the room, he had his black boots and wool coat on. My chewing slowed as I watched him. His handsome and unearthly beauty was breathtaking. Every day was like living with an angel, but as I looked in the mirror, I too was amazed at what I'd become from the almost constant touch of his pearly skin.

My eyes darted to his hand and I let out an annoyed sigh. In his grasp he held an old looking dial phone, the cord still attached to the back, as though ripped from the wall.

"Just in case," he smiled, dangling it before me with sick satisfaction.

I gave him a sour frown.

"Whatever," I spat, but he just laughed at me. He was obviously pleased with the torture he was putting me through.

Edgar walked up to me and kissed my temple before turning and leaving the room. I heard the door slam as he left the house through the garage. I dropped my fork in the bowl with a loud clatter and ran to the window. I saw him walk out the side door, his black figure loping across the field with the grace of a mountain lion.

He looked back briefly before disappearing into the trees, obviously content that there was nothing behind him and the house invisible in its massive glory. I moped back to the kitchen, throwing myself down onto my stool. I stabbed my fork irritably through another bunch of noodles and shoved it in my mouth.

The ticking clocks all over the house were beginning to make me crazy. Every day without fail: 'tick 'tick 'tick. It was enough to drive the sanest man into insanity. Maybe Edgar Allan wasn't writing about Edgar's decent into madness over lost love, but his stupid love affair with clocks.

I kicked the wall below the island, furious beyond reason. I threw my fork in the sink and stormed upstairs. I was tired of being trapped. This was stupid and childish. For goodness sake, I was eternally eighteen and by human standards, a legal adult a few times over. I rifled through my closet, firm in my determination to do as I pleased. I searched until I found my shearling boots and a sweater.

I stormed downstairs to the hall closet and grabbed my coat, wrapping it around me and pulling the hood over my head. I fished in my pocket for my gloves, pulling them gruffly over my hands without a second thought about what I was doing. Tromping to the door, I grasped the brass handle with determination, letting out an annoyed grumble as I twisted it and quickly walked onto the porch, letting the door slam behind me in my stubbornness. I had no idea where I was going, but I figured anywhere was better than here.

My body was still invisible as I stood on the stoop, looking around the field with caution, but also a soaring heart. Everything was silent, but not too silent, and that was good. I raised one rebellious foot and planted it in the deep snow. A sense of utter satisfaction flooded over me. The soft crunching sound my foot made was inviting. I repeated the action with my other foot, stomping it down with the same force right next to the other.

Exhaling, I twisted my head around and looked at the now-empty field behind me. As I turned back, I looked up at the expanse of blue sky. I let the sunny sky soak into my skin and warm my face. I shifted my gaze to the ground as I began walking forward, my eyes watching how the pristine snow collapsed under my weight. Keeping my eyes on my toes, I noticed that the footsteps behind me magically re-inflated, leaving no trace of my presence. My face was bright with amazement, and as I put my hand to my chest, I felt a small flicker of delight in my soul.

A content sigh fell from my lips, but as I inhaled again, I jumped. A distinct rustle rumbled from the woods in front of me. I glanced up and my horrified eyes watched as the treetops silently moved as though disturbed. There was no wind to account for the movement. I began to back away as I looked behind me, but to my horror, I realized that I didn't know how to get back inside the house. My breath quickened as I searched the open field for a place to hide, my mind beginning to accept that this could be it - the moment I was waiting for.

I began to shake as a rush of adrenaline filled my body. It was then I saw something dodge between the trees, and I froze, hoping that it wouldn't sense my presence. I held my breath and knelt close to the ground. The thing emerged into the meadow from the shadows. At first, I was a little shocked that what I saw hadn't exactly been what I'd expected. Still breathing hard, I squinted to be sure my eyes were not playing tricks on me, straightening as my curiosity got the best of me. I took one careful and slow step forward as the figure advanced toward me.

The silence was broken as he spoke.

"What do you think you're doing out here?" the figure boomed, his voice full of sarcasm.

I cringed, finally recognizing the irritating face of from my past.

"Sam?" I looked at his angelic expression in a daze.

He laughed. "The one and only."

I looked at him sideways. "What are you doing here?" There was something about him that was very strange, but my mind was still racing in initial fear, so it was hard to discern.

"Just doing what I came here for," he replied.

I crossed my hands against my chest, my breath escaping in steamy clouds, hot with sudden anger. I wasn't sure exactly what he'd come here for, but I hoped it hadn't been me.

"Oh, come on," he grinned. "Don't be like that."

I snorted.

"Like what?" I glanced at his strong features. His hair was still the same scruffy brown and his face unshaven. His skin was a lot like Edgar's, smooth and young, but much paler and there was a hint of blue under his eyes. I looked down to his clothing and I gawked at the fact he was *still* wearing sneakers, even in the snow.

A sudden, menacing laugh echoed through the field. "I realize their impracticality." He was looking at his feet.

I pushed my brows together and he looked at me, but I

quickly looked away, his gaze electric and somehow invading. How had he read my facial expression with such ease?

"So," he began. "As I was saying, what do you think you're doing out here? I'm pretty sure you were told to stay out of trouble and stay inside."

I shot my angry eyes back at him. "What do you know about my rules?"

He winked. "I know because it's my job to know. I was appointed to watch you."

I threw my hands up in disgust, rolling my eyes and shifting my weight impatiently. So he wasn't a threat, at least not a threat to my life.

"Seriously?" I demanded, my voice reverberating off the nearby trees. "He hired you to watch me?"

Sam smirked at my utter disdain.

"And how exactly are you going to protect me?" I snorted.

His smirk was unchanged. "Well, it's kind of what I'm made for." He walked closer to me, his body now just a foot away, and it was then that I realized what was so strange about him. My eyes widened as I looked over his shoulders at the two large humps that protruded from his back. To my surprise, tucked close to his spine, was a full set of muddied grey wings.

I gasped, quickly stepping around and behind him as I circled his body in amazement.

"Are those..?" I began, but Sam cut me off.

"Yes, Estella. They're wings. I am aware." He sighed, moving them slightly in his attempt to amaze me further.

My mind had been getting sharper over the past weeks, but what I saw before me was still considerably confusing.

I walked back around to the front of him and looked into his golden brown eyes in shock.

"Well, so then, you're like an angel?"

He nodded. "A Guardian Angel, actually."

I raised one eyebrow mockingly. "Are you serious? Really? You've got to be joking."

He spread his large wings and I watched in amazement as they stretched out eight feet on either side of him.

"I don't think these would lie, do you?"

I stared at the layers of feathers, all delicately placed as they fanned out in thick sheets. They were somewhat pearly, but more a metallic silver, and not quite as brilliant as Edgar's. Their warm grey was unlike anything I would stereotypically guess of angel wings. Their sheer size was shocking and surreal.

"Okay, so say I believe you," I finally said.

Sam gave me a hesitant half smile.

"Then, how long, exactly, have you been watching me?" I now felt as though my privacy had been violated. Edgar hadn't even asked my permission and I was angry with him. I thought about that day in class, when Sam had weaseled his way next to me. Edgar had looked so amused by my utter discomfort. Originally, I figured he was going to be furious that some strange and eerily handsome man was treating me with such interest, but now it ends up they were friends, or rather, business partners.

Sam seemed to wait to answer my question until my

thought process was done. I looked at him with an apologetic face, as though sorry that I'd kept him waiting.

He crossed his arms.

"Oh no," he chuckled. "I've been watching you much longer than that. And for the record, I wasn't hitting on you. You were being absolutely impossible, and that's all. Edgar had warned me, but I had to see for myself."

I grumbled at him.

"It's okay, Estella. Just, you know, being that I can read your mind, be careful what you think around me. I don't need all your life details." He was smiling at my dumbfounded face.

You can read my thoughts? I was testing his claim.

He nodded. "It's part of the protection plan. Hearing your thoughts makes it super-easy for me to protect you. No secrets." He smirked again, and I grumbled at him even more.

I spoke without thinking. "The woods that day when I walked to the waterfall… you were there, weren't you?" I was infuriated that he was not only invading my privacy, but also my mind.

He nodded. "Gave you a bit of a start, huh?" he chortled, patting me on the arm.

I grabbed his hand and threw it off me, but when my skin touched his I squealed.

"You're freezing!"

He laughed again, his wings still outstretched.

"I'm dead, Estella. I wouldn't really expect my body to be all that warm." He looked behind him over his shoulder as his wings retracted further until they were hidden behind his back, seeming to be looking for something, or someone.

I glanced over his shoulder as well, but wasn't seeing what he had.

"Guess you're in trouble now," he teased. "Edgar's coming."

I looked at his angelic white face and brown hair.

"I don't care. Let him be mad. I think it's me that deserves to be angrier," I said with false bravado. I was a bit worried that Edgar would be quite angry, but I felt justified enough in my own anger to be defiant.

Sam shrugged. "It's your funeral."

I glared at Sam as Edgar entered the field. When my gaze flickered to meet his, his face was stone-cold and angry, but as soon as he approached Sam, his look had somehow changed to one of amusement.

Edgar put one hand on Sam's shoulder. "See you've got my girl here." They both turned to me with twin glares.

A defiant snort escaped my lips and I crossed my arms in haughty disdain.

"I'm not your girl if you lock me up like a dog," I smarted toward Edgar, realizing Sam had already heard my reply in his mind.

Edgar laughed. "You'll always be my girl, Elle, and you can't deny that."

I glowered at him with sharp eyes, flustered by the truth in his comment.

Edgar turned to Sam and they both snickered about something they were secretly thinking. I felt my blood boil but kept silent.

"Thanks, Sam," Edgar said. "I can take her from here."

Sam nodded and gave me a wink before turning and walking back into the woods, his wings ruffling with his movement.

Edgar's expression changed as he grabbed my arm with a firm grip. My face turned to a scowling frown as he removed his glasses and the full fury of his eyes were now exposed.

"What did you think you were doing?" he snarled under his breath.

He dragged me to the middle of the field by my arm like a mother would with her disobedient child. I gave him a sour face. I wasn't sorry for what I'd done. It was great out here, and besides, no harm had come of it.

"You're really testing my patience, Elle. I don't think you really want to make me angry. It's not safe out here. I'm not just saying that." The iron grasp he had on me was unyielding. He stopped to face me, his eyes still angry, but beginning to soften.

My brows were fixed in stubborn anger.

"Look," he sighed. "I understand…"

Something white popped through the snow over his shoulder and my gaze locked on the cat, peeping over a log.

"Look, look Edgar!" I gasped, pointing one shaking hand toward the cat.

Edgar spun, a look of terror on his face, but the cat was already gone. His body was rigid and his chest rising.

"Estella," the way he said my name sent shivers down

my spine. "Honestly, I'm taking you inside, and that's it!" he hissed.

I was still looking to the log, waiting for the cat to pop its head back up as he dragged me away. After determining it wasn't coming back, I looked at Edgar with a sheepish grin, hoping he'd forgive me.

He sighed.

"I'm sorry," his eyes were now calm. "I just, I can't lose you. This is for your own good. You got your jollies out, now let's just be careful, okay?"

I nodded in compliance, and despite my stubbornness, I knew he was right. I was being stupid, but still. I saw what I saw, and I knew whatever it was, it wasn't dangerous. I had the same feeling about the cat as I did that day in the woods, when something large was following me. Turns out, the giant thing was just Sam, spying on me. I scowled at the thought and I felt like a gullible idiot. This cat, though, there was something about it. It was as though it was trying to get my attention, trying to tell me something important.

I watched him glancing around with a look of concentration on his face.

"What are you doing?" I finally asked.

His eyes locked on mine.

"Just listening to make sure there really isn't something there. Sam would have said something, though. He would have been able to hear its thoughts."

I gave him a strange look. "See, you do believe me."

His lips finally relaxed into a crooked smile. "Elle, I trust you, but I don't think there's anything there. Really, I can't hear anything. I don't want to say it, but I think you're just seeing things"

Suddenly, without a warning from Edgar, everything began spinning and the snow was replaced with the black granite of the front hall. I was fuming as I stormed into the sitting room where I grabbed a book and pretended to read, refusing to discuss the matter any further.

Later that night I noticed Edgar looking at me with a strange fascination. His eyes kept darting to my face, but then glancing quickly away before I looked at him. Biting my nails as we sat on the leather couch in the library, listening to Pavarotti, I thought about nothing but the cat. Its fur was strange and its eyes were so cool and intelligent. I wondered if there was something Edgar had known about the cat, something that had been destined, but that he didn't want me to know.

Edgar dropped his book into his lap with an abrupt slap. He yawned.

"I think it's about time to go to bed," he announced.

My mind was still swimming and my forehead was wrinkled in frustration and residual anger. Edgar reached for me but I shied away, refusing to let go of my anger, pushing away his effective attempts to make me forget about what had happened.

"You could use the rest." Without a warning he scooped me up off the couch.

It wasn't so bad being treated this way, and it was certainly nice to be so lazy. As he walked toward the stairs, I began to think about Sam.

"How is Sam an angel?" My eyes scanned Edgar's smooth and face.

Edgar looked down at me with a soft smile.

"He was human once, in the sixties." He paused. "I was there when he died." He sighed.

"But then, how did he become a Guardian Angel?" My mind was swimming. Typically, humans just died, and that was it. The end, or at least that's what I'd thought.

He was still looking at me as he navigated the stairs.

"He was shot, in New York," he paused as we cleared the top step, turning into my room. "He jumped in front of a bullet, saved a girl he hardly knew, and then as he slowly died, he killed the perpetrator."

My eyes widened with interest. "So that's how he got the job then, huh?"

Edgar smiled. "Yep, self-sacrifice. Hell of an interview, wasn't it?"

I gave him a grave nod. "So that's what he'll do for the rest of eternity?" I asked.

Edgar nodded. "That's why he's a good friend. He will be here as long as we will. It's comforting to know that." He pushed back the covers and slid me inside before removing his own shoes and getting in beside me.

I sighed as Edgar continued.

"He's the best, and I need the best to keep you safe." I felt his hand slide under the covers toward me, and I froze. His fingers grazed my hip and he pulled me toward him, wrapping his arms around my stomach. I drew in a careful breath, relishing the rare closeness. He put his head next to my ear.

"You are my whole world, Elle, and I would do anything to protect that," he whispered.

I turned my head and he put his hand on my cheek, his other hand twisting my whole body to face him. He brushed the hair from my face before pressing his lips against mine. Breathing hard, I put a hand on his chest and felt his heart race. His lips curled into a smile against my lips, but he didn't pull back like usual. He ran his fingers into my hair, gently grabbing a handful. His other hand grazed my belly, and I giggled, opening my eyes to look at him.

He nibbled on my bottom lip.

"You're worth keeping alive," he whispered, his breath sweet against my mouth.

I brushed my fingers across his cheek, feeling his velvety skin react under my touch. His eyes scanned mine. Their sapphire blue was deep and calm. I looked into the glittering depths, searching deep down for my soul, but before I found it, he closed his eyes and kissed me again. His breathing was unsteady as he finally pulled away, and though I tried to kiss him again, this time he held me off. I exhaled in frustration, but he just smirked at me.

With a grumble, I flipped away from him, but this time he didn't distance himself. I felt him wrap his arms around my shoulders as he cradled me. I waited for him to pull away, but as his breathing slowed into measured deep draws. I realized he was asleep, and I smiled, finding myself finally victorious.

HERE KITTY, KITTY...

"Okay, Elle, open your eyes." I had forgotten Edgar was removing my blindfold. The touch of his warm hands on my face was clouding my mind.

Slowly, I opened my eyes to a room of fledgling plants. "Oh, Edgar!" I gasped.

I noticed the room was a new addition to the library. Every wall, including the ceiling, was molded of a crystal green glass with rusty iron grids. My gaze fell to the six large tables propped up on the gravel floor. Each table housed what appeared to be different varieties of plant buds in various pots and planters. I looked to the back of the room where, to my rebellious delight, he'd installed a door. For a brief vindictive moment I thought of my escape until noticing there was a little note attached to the glass in Edgar's writing:

Don't even think about it...

I frowned, but then turned and looked at Edgar.

His face was full of happiness as he watched me.

"I had a little trouble getting things started. It's not the easiest thing to handle something so delicate when you're a life-ending brute like me." His grin turned awkward at the thought. "Everything is probably dead."

Running into his arms, I hugged him tightly.

"Oh I love it!" I squealed. "Besides, I can fix anything you managed to kill already."

He laughed, wincing at the shrillness of my voice. "I hope so, because those purple clovers you left behind in the cabin were impossible to plant."

I turned back on the room and spotted the gnarled blooms by the far left table.

His voice crept up behind me, his mouth right next to my ear. "I figured after the incident last week that if I was trapping you here, it was unfair of me to keep you from your second love."

Twisting my head to face him, I gave him a playful glare.

"Who says they're my second love?"

Edgar's mouth curled into a gorgeous grin.

I smiled as he kissed me on the forehead, holding him tightly before he managed to break my grip.

"So, now you have your greenhouse and I have my library. Merry Christmas, Elle." His voice was smug as he glanced at me over his nose.

I folded my arms across my chest in defeat.

Edgar winked at me before turning and leaving the room. I looked back toward my fledgling plants. Excitement filled my dimming soul. The mid-winter sun streamed in through the glass, touching each box with its brilliant light.

I looked through the blue-green glass to the meadow with a cautious eye. There were still no signs of Matthew, and my body filled with more anxiety at every passing minute. In the last week, the white cat continued to pop up in my peripherals periodically, but every time I caught sight of it, it vanished just as quickly. It was a fast little bugger.

Isabelle and Henry flew into the room and they landed on the edge of a box close to the glass. Isabelle's head was tilted toward the field and I smirked at her. Being in this house gave her an invisibly unfair advantage on hunting. As a magical hawk, she has no need to use doors, so she simply flies in and out as she pleases, wall or no wall. Henry snapped at her as they both fought over something in the field.

She lightly clicked her tongue, fanning her wings in irritation and ducking her head to pounce. Her eyes quickly gazed at me and I gave her a reproachful glare. She ignored my threat as she looked back to the field, releasing her grip on the table with a sudden burst of energy and lunging through the glass before Henry even had a chance to react.

I watched as she soared across the snow, snatching up a frantic field mouse that was desperately trying to tread through the drifts. I winced as my heart went out to the fragile life now hanging in her iron grasp. Henry dodged at her in his attempt to steal the meal, but she shot skyward and out of my view. Shaking my head, I looked back to my plants, trying not to think about Isabelle's lunch.

As I walked down the aisles, the delicate buds leaned toward me. I reached out and touched one. It immediately began to flourish to full size. The beautiful sunflower that now loomed before me made my soul flutter, and I felt the adrenaline in my blood pumping hard. Edgar had left me to be surprised, since it was hard for me to tell exactly what he'd planted. With each bud, I discovered a new secret gift.

There was a pot of dirt in the corner where a small bud reached toward a trellis that climbed the wall. I approached with curiosity as I scanned the ceiling thoughtfully, imagining what I would hope it to be. I knelt down beside the pot and put my face right up next to the bud. I shut my eyes and blew on the tiny leaves. My breath of life tickled the air around it. There were a series of delicate snapping noises, and I stood up, my eyes still shut as the sounds crackled overhead and filled the room with noise like popping popcorn.

There was a sudden burst of fragrance. I finally opened my eyes, my nose tickling filling with a delightfully sweet scent. I looked at the ceiling as the purple clematis burst over half the greenhouse, creating the perfect canopy for my partial sun plants to find shade.

Content, I gazed skyward as I suddenly heard Edgar's soft laugh. Startled, I shot my eyes toward the door. He was leaning against the frame, his arms crossed against his perfect chest and his angelic face plastered with a sly grin.

I suddenly frowned, noticing that he was wearing his

large wool coat.

He snorted at my sulking face. "Just for a little bit, okay?"

I stamped my foot like a two-year old and he laughed, leaning away from the door and stepping down into the greenhouse. He walked down from the door and wrapped me in his arms. I felt small and safe in his embrace.

"But I didn't give you your Christmas present yet!" My voice was muffled by his coat.

He pulled me away.

"You weren't supposed to get me anything, remember? I hope you didn't go outside for this." He eyed me with caution.

Laughing, I shook my head.

"Yeah right, you've hardly given me a moment to look out the window, let alone sneak outside."

He gave me an approving smile. "That's true. So then, what did you manage to find?"

A sly smile crept across my face.

"Well, I was going through all the things in my room and I found something. It looked like something I always meant to give you. Of course, who knows why you need it. I know it's not for me, at least, and besides, it was already engraved."

I pulled a brown box out from the pocket of my sweatshirt.

There was a surprised smile on his face and I was relieved, realizing he really had never seen it before.

"And I thought I knew of everything in this house," he breathed.

I stood proudly, my hands laced behind my back. "I guess not."

Edgar opened the box with care, his large hands fumbling with the string. He slid his fingers under the paper. I saw his hand freeze. A smile spread across his face as he pulled the silver timepiece from within, the chain following in dutiful succession.

"I figured that it was for you. I hate clocks, but you seem to adore them." My eyes scanned his as they began to tear up.

"I never knew," he breathed, his voice cracking. He snapped open the cold silver and read the description inside:

Your heart is my heart. I love you.
Your Elle.

A tear rolled over his pearly skin, glistening in the sun.

"You had said you had something for me, but that day, you..." he paused, his eyes darkening before suddenly coming back with life. "I love it, Elle. I do."

He leaned toward me and kissed me on the forehead before moving away and dropping the timepiece into his pocket. Carefully, I helped him fasten the chain to his belt, my hands grazing his stomach as he shied away, a smile curling onto his face.

Sighing, he wrapped his arms around my shoulders and rested his chin on my head.

"I trust that this time you'll stay inside when I leave? Just remember, Sam is watching." His breath was warm against my hair, and I shuddered.

I smiled, looking up at him. "Yeah, I promise."

His hands laced through my hair and he kissed the top of my head before stepping away. He winked at me as he swiftly left the room. I ran to the glass, pushing my hands against it and feeling the welcoming coolness on my hot palms. I waited as he treaded across the field, his gait graceful and fast, my heart beating in love.

Sighing as he disappeared into the woods, I walked back into the library, where I again looked to the small arched room. My obsession with the painting was insatiable. Their faces were all telling a story and its elusiveness was driving me mad.

I climbed up the new ladder Edgar had found for me after one of the rungs finally snapped. Luckily, he had been there to catch me before I cracked my head on the couch. The event wouldn't have killed me, but it would have been an excruciating and somewhat messy accident.

I ran my hands along the books as I always did. The once dusty leather was now clean from my frequent visitations. I watched as my fingers thudded against the spines, my eyes sharp with childish interest.

My fingers hit a small dent in the stack, and I halted and stepped back a few steps to kneel down. My eyes were level with the books, my attention on one in particular. I squinted as I tried to make out the bright gold lettering. All this time the dust had been hiding its beauty from me, and I wondered why I hadn't noticed it sooner.

Tilting my head, my fingers grazed across the gold stamped words of the spine. I realized with a start that it was written in Italian. I hooked my hand into the binding and pulled it from the stack. I took a deep breath before turning back, blowing a gentle breath across the cover to remove the rest of the hazy film.

I felt a strange pull toward the book. I opened to the first page, attempting to read the Italian. There was a delicately stamped etching of a black crow in a tree that was framing the first words on the page:

Nell'inizio, l'uccello era solo...

I read the first couple words, rolling them around in my mind but finding no translation. My eyes darted to the stamping, inspecting it closely before flipping to the middle of the book. I looked at the pages in shock. They were completely blank. Confused, I grabbed the book by its spine and flipped back through the pages until words again flashed across before my eyes.

I went page by page, taking in the strange images. Mostly, there where just ravens. Some were white and black, in large gatherings and small, but none of it made any sense to me. The images were just snippets of what the words could explain. As I turned to the next page, I was shocked by the eerie images I found there.

The large imprint was unmistakable, its feline eyes dreadfully familiar. My heart rate quickened as I stared at the white cat standing openly in a field. The cat's back was arched and its fur seemed perfect. Its eyes were calm and inviting, but also full of information and knowledge, as though the stories within belonged to it alone. I looked at the words with frustration, angry that I couldn't translate.

I let out an irritated snarl as I looked to the next page for some other clue. As I glanced it over, I was discouraged to find the image was just as vague. The cat was drawn from a distance, entering a cave with caution. Hastily, I flipped to the next page, but I found nothing. The rest of the pages.

I let out a disappointed breath and slammed the book shut in frustration, walking with it under my arm as I entered the small sitting area. I threw myself into the chair, holding the book close to my chest, staring at the group of friends and foes before me.

"What aren't you telling me?" I hissed under my breath, glaring with bitterness at my face in the painting.

My gaze jumped to each male countenance with an accusing glare, even Edgar. Each had the potential to be a killer, but then, as I looked into their eyes, they all had a glimmer that was void missing from Matthew's. Something I recognized to be love, pure and enduring. It had frustrated me that there were no clues in the painting, no hints toward the brutal end besides his sinister glare. I had scanned the thick layers of paint for what seemed hours, day after day, but still nothing.

A warm sensation was filling my chest and I found myself startled as I looked down at the book in my grasp. The feeling had been so subtle that I hadn't noticed it at first, but to my surprise, it was warm. I knew when I had sat with the book that something had been strange, but it hadn't registered as a feeling from the book, but a feeling from me. As the fire in my soul died, the book's warmth was now taking over. I squeezed it tighter to my chest, relishing the feeling as though it were another soul.

I began to doze as I sat there, the comforting space closing in around me like a protective shroud, much like being in Edgar's arms. As things began to fog and my eyes grew tired I was jolted awake. I heard a distant, yet distinct, meow. My eyes flew open. I scanned the room urgently. Sitting up, I tried to discern if what I'd heard was a dream or real. I sat perfectly still, my ears now tuned into the noises around me.

Irritated again by the distracting and inconvenient ticking of clocks, I struggled to pay attention. I jumped as the grandfather clock in the hall began to chime, my breathing heavy and my heart beating like a drum in my chest. Then, between echoing gongs, I heard the meow again, this time long and whiny, as though angry or threatened.

I shot up from the chair, the book dropping to the floor as I rushed to the rail. I listened again, and this time, a distinct growling snarl came from the greenhouse. With a sudden surge of haste and energy, I ran around the perimeter of the library and I stumbled down the ladder, careful not to create too much noise. I skidded to a halt just outside the door of the greenhouse, scanning with wide and wary eyes.

Isabelle was perched in a threatening manner on the edge of a table with her wings spread in a defensive pose. The white cat was cowering on the floor before her with its ears pinned back and its eyes glinting in the sunlight, its pupils a brilliant white. I blinked a few times, allowing the cat to become a real thing, not just a figment of my imagination. The cat spat at Isabelle as it swatted at her with its claws. Its fur was standing on end, and I noticed how it seemed to glow, even whiter than the snow itself.

"Isabelle, no!" I yelled, and the cat broke its iron gaze from Isabelle to me. Isabelle's eyes stayed fixed on the cat, her beak open with hate.

"Isabelle!" I yelled. "Stop that!"

She lunged toward the cat with a fake hop as her talons dug deeper into the wood of the table. The cat hissed, cowering even more before glancing at me with a defeated face and turning to run. It leapt through the glass with a careless effort, its paws splashing through the heavy drifts with ease. Before I knew what I was doing, I took off after the cat, glaring at Isabelle as I ran by, telling her to stay put with my angry eyes.

I burst through the door of the greenhouse, ignoring Edgar's warning as it was ripped from the glass. Suddenly, the house disappeared behind me and my breath began to fog in the frigid air. I scanned the field with frantic eyes, finally catching a glimpse of a bobbing tail leaping into the trees. I took off after it, my new, strong body and sharp sight enabling me to keep up with its rapid gait.

I leapt over the log, shielding my face from branches as I entered the woods. In my desperation, the trees tried to help, lunging their branches at the cat as it dodged over them, as though anticipating every attempt. Edgar's voice boomed across my memory, his angry face contorted as he warned me to stay inside. I pushed the thought away, concentrating only on the cat's tail.

A shadow flew overhead and I pushed my eyebrows together in irritation as I saw Sam looming above me, his giant wings cutting through the air in long delicate strokes. I watched as he cut and dove to the left with a sharp gust of wind, and I looked away, still desperate to follow the cat.

Surprised, I watched as the cat skidded to a stop just ahead of me. It turned to face me, its eyes frantic but harmless. I quickly halted, my bare feet slipping on the snow, fighting for balance as my arms flailed around me. The cat began to trot toward me, its face trying to say something, something foreboding and urgent. The cat then cowered, its gaze diverting from mine as it looked behind me.

The shrill cry of a raven cut through the air and the hairs on my neck rose with instant fear. I whipped my head around, terror paralyzing my body. The cat began to back away, its fur blending with the snow, hiding its escape. I tried to scream as a cloud of a dozen black ravens descended upon me, their talons ready to strike. I saw Sam dive up from the trees, his wings halting as he came down on a group of them, their sharp screams filling the air with a deafening cry. The cat hissed before bolting out of my view, and though I longed to follow, my life was now in peril.

The ravens that got past Sam dove down and hit me hard, their sharp beaks tearing through my skin and slicing me like razorblades. My lungs began to tighten as they had the day in the meadow, and my breath became shallow and short. Their eyes seared through my thoughts, ripping through every memory like a knife, and stealing all I had to give. A scream was caught in my throat, and everything became dark and cloudy. I fell to the ground, the ravens still attacking. Sam's voice was too far to save me as the sounds of shrill death and anger surrounded me.

My mind was screaming the only word it could possibly manage through the thick confusion.

"Edgar!" my thoughts yelled, but my lips failed to form the words. The world went dark and the ground below me disappeared.

FEATHER

When I came to, my body was screaming with pain. I winced and rolled onto my back, groaning and reaching up to clutch my chest. It was very cold and I was shaking with uncontrolled shudders. I was laying on something cold and damp, and the metallic taste of blood was on my tongue.

"Sam?" I murmured, the words catching through the thick bubbles of blood.

"Ahh," a voice rang in my head. "You're awake, you little escapist." The harsh voice hissed like hot coals, the speaker's breath blowing across my ear.

I tried to scream, but my body reacted instinctively, collapsing in on itself. I brought my knees to my chest, curling into the fetal position. What had I done? Where was Sam?

"Estella." The way he said my name was as if it disgusted him to do so. "You were always so naïve!" he yelled. "This entire thing is your fault, you stupid child."

My arms stung and I could feel blood oozing from various wounds. I writhed on the hard cold surface, the pain more than I could bear. My head was fogged and I was weak from loss of blood. Finally, I was able to focus my vision.

"Where have you put it, Estella?" his voice was soft and menacing, measured breaths escaping from his mouth as though attempting to remain calm. I struggled to open my eyes, to identify my captor, but the terror in me suggested I already knew.

Squeezing my eyes shut, I pushed away the pain, my teeth bared in agony. He was looking for my soul, the soul I thankfully did not possess.

"Where!" The voice suddenly boomed, echoing painfully through my empty soul and causing me to arch back in pain, my chest exposed and throbbing. "You can't keep me from my destiny, Estella. My power!"

My hands clenched into tight fists, my mind forcing death away as my fingernails dug into the ground. I felt my body lift from the hard cold surface though no hands were grasping me. I heard Matthew exhale with a sharp heave of his breath, my body now flying like a limp rag across the room. As my shoulder crashed into a wall, my eyes jarred open and I tried to scream. I landed on the cold hard floor and I made a move to pick myself up, but my arms refused to cooperate. I felt a wave of nausea wash over me and wretched blood onto the floor.

"You can't keep it from me, you little brat!" His voice was echoing against the walls. I glanced upward. The light in the room was dark and murky. "You think you're so special, so talented and smart," he spat with a hint of jealousy. "I was promised a grand life for this, and that's exactly what I'll have.

You stand as no challenge to me, and you will not live up to your name."

My blurred gaze fell upon his familiar face, his eyes pitch black and endless, and his skin yellowed and thin. My body was trembling and the pain in my chest almost unbearable. I almost wished to die so that it would end.

He laughed as my pain-filled eyes met his. I could smell my blood as it streamed down my face.

"Estella," he hissed. "You're keeping me from what I want, what I need!" he bellowed. "If you just tell me where it is, foolish girl, then I will let you die quickly. Where is your soul?"

I swallowed hard, trying to clear the blood from my throat, coughing in sharp painful bouts as some more came up.

"You…" I was struggling, holding my upper body off the ground. The pain became so strong that my body felt numb and my limbs dangerously drained of blood. The end was not far. "You won't find it!" I cried, my arms buckled and I slammed back to the floor. My teeth cracked against the stones and sent a searing pain through my jaw.

I felt something grip my neck, lifting me up off the floor.

"You can't win!" he yelled, his eyes storming like a pool of silver mercury as he approached me, his face close to mine, and his noxious breath sucking the air from my lungs. His hairless brows and head were hideous and distorted in frustration. His face was old as his clammy skin glistened with puss, all the youth now long gone.

"Don't you know, you stupid girl?" His mouth was black with tar and his teeth rotted. "That your beloved Edgar won't save you? He didn't last time, and he won't now. I've got a lot in store for him, the most painful death imaginable." His eyes scorched through mine and I tried to look away. "After I kill you, he will be in ruins, and I will prevail. I will be granted the opportunity to advance, to take over!" His voice boomed through the chamber, sending rocks crumbling around us.

I had no way of knowing where I was or how I got here. I looked toward the ceiling as he continued to choke me, but it was difficult to see. Something that did catch my eye made me gasp. There were ravens towering on all sides, all watching me with their soulless and hungry eyes.

"You were all so weak, so useless with your stupid worldly desires." He released his invisible grip on my throat just seconds before I blacked out. "You were all a waste!" he screamed, throwing one hand in the air in his anguish. "We had so much power to learn, so much strength to gain!"

Matthew turned to pace the room as I sat on the floor, my leg aching. I could tell it was broken.

"With you out of my way, with Edgar gone," he paused, taking a deep breath. "I will have no one to stop me. I will kill it all! Take all the energy the world possesses! And no one will be stronger than me." His eyes were filled with a powerful hate. "No one!"

I winced. His voice was high-pitched and piercing. My heart was racing and the adrenaline in my blood was like hot lava, burning its way through my deep open wounds. I tried to listen to his words, but my fear was too intense. My thoughts focused on Edgar. I couldn't do this to him. Why had I let him down?

Matthew laughed again, dark and sinister.

"This is what we all could have done together, but none of you believed me," he spat. "And Margriete." There was a deep, untamed hatred to his voice. "You should have heard her pleas, the way she begged for me to stop all this." I saw an evil smile curl his lips, "Stupid girl."

A veil of darkness shrouded me and I stifled my body's cries to give up. Suddenly, the ravens overhead began to cry, their sharp voices filling the cavern. I recoiled, my ears ringing.

"Ah," he breathed, looking to the sky and holding out his arms as all the ravens flew upward in a sharp rush of wind into the night, "It seems he came for you after all!" His sinister laugh echoed through the now empty cavern.

My body grimaced. "Edgar," I whispered under my breath. "No!"

Suddenly, my body slammed against the wall and my face contorted with pain. Matthew's mind was manipulating me, breaking whatever life there was left inside, and I struggled to remain conscious. As he lifted me off the floor, I shut my eyes, my mind pleading for it to stop. He shot me skyward with one violent thrust. I flew rapidly through the air, Matthew at my side.

We breached the top of the cavern and were now outside. The air was heavy and damp. It was dark, but I could feel the wind against my skin. He threw me to the ground like a used rag and I cried out in pain.

"Matthew!" Edgar's voice echoed over the earth and my heart began to beat hard at the sound.

As I lay there dying, I felt the texture of the fresh dirt beneath me, and I realized we were no longer in the snowy forest. This must be London. The rain that fell on me was refreshing as it washed my blood into the ground. I rested my face in the mud, my cheeks swollen and welcoming of the coolness. Roots began to grow around me in their desperate attempt to protect me. I heard Edgar's voice again.

"You leave her alone! She does not have what you want!" His voice was fierce and closer now.

I whispered his name, but the beating rain hushed my gentle cry.

"So," Matthew sneered, "then I suppose you do." He sounded confident and angry.

I heard Edgar's heavy step advancing toward me, but then there was a sudden explosion of energy and he grunted in pain. I heard his body land several feet away, sliding along the wet ground and leaving a brutal trail of destruction.

The earth began to wrap me in its healing strength, and the grass below me started working to mend my wounds. The stinging began to subside as I felt my deep cuts closing and healing. My leg stopped aching. I felt it crunch back into place. I shuddered as Matthew's angry steps advanced toward me.

I made a move to save myself, my adrenaline taking over and my body again whole. In one quick rush, I rolled onto my back, clenching my jaw as I looked Matthew in the eye, my limbs quickly moving as I saw him looming over me.

The roots that had healed my wounds grabbed at his ankles, holding him prisoner. With all my strength, I kicked him in the face and my boots dug deep into his aged skin.

He fell back with surprising ease, his body hunching over as the roots snapped and the dark rain ran in streams across his mauled profile. He whipped his head back toward me as he pulled what looked like a gold dagger from his coat and lunged, his eyes blazing with fury and skin hanging from his face.

It was then that Sam flew out of nowhere, his wings reverberating in the air like booms of thunder. His strong body slammed into Matthew's side, and together, they slid fifteen feet through the muddy earth, leaving a large trench that quickly filled with water. I looked on in shock as Sam's wings engulfed Matthew. I could no longer see what was happening.

I quickly rose to my feet, my scars fading faster than I had expected and my strength returning. Edgar was standing on the other end of the field, his fists clenched in anger. I took off at a run toward Sam and Matthew as they wrestled on the ground. Skidding to a stop, I heard Edgar yell my name over the beating rain.

"Elle, no! Get away from him!" His voice was sharp and frantic.

I watched in horror as Matthew grabbed Sam by the throat, bringing his arm back and throwing him across the field with surprising strength.

"Sam!" I screamed. Matthew glanced at me, his eyes blazing black.

"You little liar!" he hissed, approaching me with the dagger still in his hand.

I saw Edgar suddenly lunge at Matthew's back. My mouth fell open in horror and my eyes widened in fear that we'd lose it all if Edgar were harmed. Matthew saw my shocked expression and twisted around to face me. Edgar continued to struggle to bring him down, his fist smashing into Matthew's face with ferocity.

I ran at Matthew as he staggered. I tackled him, wrapping my legs around his waist. I slashed at his face with my nails, the roots again struggling to contain him in their desperate attempt to save me. As I viciously tried to take him down, he grabbed my neck like a kitten and flipped me over his head and down to the earth. My breath was knocked from my lungs my body forming a deep crater.

Hot water began to bubble up around me, filling the crater as I stood. I clenched my teeth in fury and hate, Margriete's laughing face was now close at mind. My eyes scanned the field, frantically trying to find Edgar. My eyes found Sam instead, his body hunched down to the ground, ready to pounce with his wings spread into a beautiful fan of fury.

My gaze moved to Matthew as he ran from me, the skin on his face gone and his eyes dark as night. My clothes were heavy and weighed me down as I struggled out of the hole now almost completely filled with water.

When I emerged, Matthew was far across the rocky landscape, headed for Edgar. Sam sprung, leaping down on him with a heavy force. I looked around wildly for something or someone to help Sam. Suddenly, I noticed something that made my heart stop.

Ravens were surrounding me in eerie silence. My throat was dry and hot. I took off at a sprint toward them as Edgar held Matthew at arms length, his other hand cocked back and ready to strike. Sam waited to Edgar's right, again poising himself to attack at the first chance.

As Edgar let his arm go, I watched in horror as Matthew's neck twisted in a gruesome and inhuman manner and his body flew across the rocks, shearing into the earth. Shards of rock flew into the air and speared back down to the ground with a rumble.

"Edgar!" I yelled, running to him. His eyes met mine, his face both relieved and terrified.

I ran into his arms, my soul bursting to life. "Edgar, I'm sorry!"

"This is not the time for apologies, Elle," his voice was frantic. He suddenly tossed me to the side as Matthew lunged at us, his teeth bared in anger and his neck clearly broken. Sam jumped and grabbed me away as the dagger in Matthew's hand went flying by my face.

As Sam saved me from Matthew's lethal aim, Matthew instead plowed into Edgar's chest, his face suddenly searing with pain. Edgar fell back hard and heavy, breath escaping from his lips as his eyes met mine.

"No!" My voice was shrill as they both hit the ground, the Earth rumbling from the impact. I tried to steady myself in Sam's iron grasp as Matthew stood over Edgar, staggering back with blood dripping from the dagger in his hand.

Gasping, I looked at the blood in horror as a malicious sneer snaked across Matthew's face. I screamed in sudden anger, my eyes full of hatred. My soul was suddenly hot with life, the feelings flooding back to me as my soul returned, and Edgar began dying.

I forced myself out of Sam's strong grasp, my breath coming in short gasps. I strode toward Matthew with clenched fists. He stepped back with a sudden fear, realizing what had happened to me as my body seemed to grow with strength. A look of deep terror filled his face as my eyes reflected in his. The roots were suddenly more powerful than before, and they wrapped around his legs in thick knots from which he could not escape.

"You spiteful devil!" I yelled. My voice was so strong that it caused the trees to shake in fear. Matthew dropped the dagger to the ground with a shudder, his body reeling back as I advanced, but his feet were bound. "If you think you're getting away with this, you're highly mistaken." My voice was a deadly hiss. I glanced toward Edgar, his chest was barely moving and the life that had filled his beautiful eyes was waning, and was now alive in mine.

I turned back to Matthew. His face was contorted and bleeding.

"You killed my friends, my family!" My voice was cracking in grief and my heart throbbed with pain. "You underestimate the power of love, of happiness."

I grabbed his throat. My power over him surprised us both. The roots now engulfed half his body, as though pulling him to Hell.

"You had it all wrong, Matthew. We had the power then." My thoughts flashed to the painting: our happiness, or love, and his discontent with it all. "We were the ones with the power, and you," I paused, squeezing his neck harder, his dark, emotionless eyes popping out of his freakishly distorted face. "You're nothing more than a pathetic snake!"

Pulling my arm back, I punched him in the chest and he doubled over, the roots pressing him to the ground in helpless agony. Kneeling down, I grabbed the bloodied dagger from the grass.

"You won't take it from me!" I yelled down at him, my eyes now illuminating the ground where he coiled like a coward. Sam watched me, his gaze looking from Matthew to me.

I raised my hands over my head, both grasping the handle of the dagger as they trembled in fear and anxiety.

"You deserve this! I only hope that the Gods don't take pity on your blood stained soul." And with that, I thrust the dagger down through his chest, stabbing it into his heart and digging it deep into the earth as all the ravens in the field shrieked, taking to the sky in a shroud of black.

His body ceased writhing and his eyes drained of all color, the silver returning as his body began to coil and change. His black feathers pierced through his skin until nothing but a lifeless raven lay dead before me. I heard Sam's heavy breathing behind me, his cold hands now firmly resting on my shoulders.

I stood there as the thick rain washed over my body. I twisted to look back at Edgar as he lay still on the rocky earth.

"Edgar!" my voice was frantic as I ran to his side. "Edgar!" I put my hands to his face, shaking him, willing him to waken. "Edgar, no, no don't!" Ragged sobs tore from my body, but despite my please, his skin was dangerously cold under my touch. Sam arrived at his other side, his eyes scanning Edgar's wound.

As I stared at my dying love, his eyes opened but his breathing was dangerously shallow as Sam worked to mend him.

"Edgar, you're going to be okay," I gasped.

He tried to raise his arm and bring it to my face, but he couldn't. The blood gushed from his chest as the warm liquid drained from his veins. A tear rolled down my cheek as his eyes began to change, the blue filtering out to the edges until there was nothing but a faint grey. The light of life was gone and his gaze was now vacant. Sam continued to work on him, but I knew his efforts were of no use.

I put my head to Edgar's chest, but his heart no longer beat.

"Edgar, no," I whispered. "Please, I love you." I was sobbing with uncontrolled grief, my soul beginning to burn deeper than ever. Sam stopped and grabbed my face, his cold touch like a knife against my chin. His gold eyes searched mine, his face apologizing as he wrapped his wings around us.

The earth around Edgar came to life in a sudden display of light and the roots twined their way around his neck and across his chest. I fell back in horror as Sam's wings cradled me. Though I tried, I couldn't stop the roots from engulfing him as they grew into his wounds and pulled him hard against the ground. I turned away in fear as Sam picked me off the damp, muddy grass, pulling me away from Edgar as he sank under the surface of the Earth. I pushed my face into Sam's stone chest, my warm tears streaming onto his shirt where they turned to icicles when they touched his skin.

"Edgar!" I cried, my nails digging into Sam's skin. Sam cradled me in his arms. I watched the ground where Edgar had disappeared begin to grow. Large branches now reached toward the sky and a giant redwood towered over us.

My body trembled but my head became eerily clear. I squeezed my eyes shut as memories seared through me, like a floodgate opening in my mind. Sam turned me away from the scene, his wings wrapping tighter around our bodies in his attempt to shield me from the rain and sorrow. I winced in pain as I pulled my knees to my chin, my chest bursting open.

I could feel Sam's cold breath against my face as he desperately tried to comfort me, to calm my nerves. As the heat became too great to handle, the torture ceased and everything was silent. I breathed heavily as I opened my eyes, looking into Sam's eyes.

Slowly, he released his grip and my body melted to the ground. My gaze caught sight of a single black feather as it fell toward me from the blackened branches above. I shut my eyes in disbelief, tears pouring through my lashes and streaming hot down my cheeks and onto my neck.

Opening my eyes again, I raised one trembling hand

toward the spiraling black feather, catching it by the quill. I let out one shaky breath as my insides crippled in sadness, my soul blistering with life.

HALF LIFE

Sam's wings cut through the air of the forest. My feet melted onto the ground as he set me down. I stood in the shadows under the evergreens, my breathing steady and shallow and my heart heavy. The familiar field had changed since winter. The smell of spring flowers blew toward us on the mist of the forest wind, reminding me that life still continued, despite my desire for it all to stop.

A defeated sigh escaped my lips. I took one step into the opening as Sam stood back within the trees. The sun glistened down onto my skin, the grasses bowing in obedient appreciation. Isabelle burst from thin air as she flew from the lonely invisible house, her wings flapping with anxiety in her eager approach.

She let out a shrill cry as she crashed into my arms. Her wings flailed as she struggled to right herself. Laughing,

I smiled at her. Her eyes glinted with sorrow as though she already knew that I had come home alone. I watched her grasping onto my forearm, clicking to me and twisting my pearly skin. She glanced at Sam with a thankful wink before turning her sharp gaze back to me.

"Hello girl," I sang. My voice was light and re-born.

Sam's light laugh filtered through the trees of the forest. "She's happy you're back."

Isabelle fluffed her feathers as I walked deeper into the meadow, remembering its beauty and its warmth. As I came to a halt in the middle of the opening, the flowers around me bloomed. I allowed them to welcome me home. Isabelle eyed them with a wary glare before leaping from my arm, spiraling skyward on a gust of wind and meeting Henry as they intertwined. Guilt filled my heart as I saw that Henry held back, mourning the loss of his friend, and father.

Sam walked to my side, his wings now tucked away behind him. As he stood beside me, I noticed how his white skin contrasted with the luscious green grass. The circles under his eyes were dark, but his pupils were a warm bronze. His gaze caught mine as he smiled, the corners of his mouth still shaking with certain sadness.

"Well, Estella," his voice was angelic. "You're home now." His consoling gaze was hard to look into. I still refused to believe that Edgar was gone.

I sighed, placing my warm hand against his frozen face. "Thank you, Sam."

The long winter had been painful, and my return was a long time coming. After my soul found its place back inside the empty space in my chest with Edgar's death, it was hard to find myself, hard to realize where Edgar had gone and what had happened to me. It was as though a life had been gained, but then half was also lost.

After that night, I spent weeks just sitting there, my tears blooming a forest around us and the craters the fight had created gorging into hot springs of life. The redwood where Edgar had died flourished, glowing with unearthly power and strength, the wood almost black.

It was like I'd stored three hundred years of love for him inside my soul, and it suddenly all poured out. He had nurtured that feeling for me, held it within him while I had left him alone. Now it was my turn, and I was going to fight.

Sam had stayed with me, his duties as my Guardian Angel binding him to me for life. As long as I needed him he would always be there, and in his friendship, I hoped to find happiness and strength. I hoped to move on.

I had been angry at the entire world around me in those days. Everything was thriving when half of me was gone. It angered me that despite my continuing sorrow, the cycle of life still dredged on.

Shuddering, I recalled how it felt to burn Matthew's dead body, my soul wrought with grief and hatred. Matthew was gone, hopefully forever, but the future was uncertain. Matthew had died from the same weapon, in the same manner as Edgar, but when he had left this world, he left it differently, as though telling me there was still hope.

Before I left the hillsides of London, I carved two ravens into the redwood that had bloomed over Edgar's body, hoping that one day, he could see that, and remember. Though he was gone, I refused to believe forever. He was the only thing that mattered to me now. I would devote my life to finding an answer, if not an ending.

As I now stood in the meadow of the Cascades, watching Henry and Isabelle celebrate my return, I couldn't help but feel Edgar here. His essence lingered amongst every plant and tree, his intoxicating life remaining as a gloomy reminder. I knelt to the ground, allowing my legs to rest in the tall grass.

Reaching into my belt hook, I retrieved the dagger and held it as the gold gleamed in the sun. A tear fell from my face, and I stabbed it into the soft earth with a promise to avenge my love. My soul was aching with the absence of its warmth, a feeling I used to long to feel, but no longer could. If there was still a way to pass this blame, I would, killing everyone that set it up, and making sure that in the end, this could never happen to another soul.

Sam put one cold hand on my back as he looked skyward, praying for Edgar toward the Heavens. He did not know how to feel love or pain, so in the years since his death, he had felt nothing. Much like I had before. Sam could read my thoughts, and so he knew how to comfort me, but it did little to calm my nerves.

Being back allowed a flood of memories to return. I thought about that day when I was taken, cursed myself for being stubborn and careless. There were so many things that had happened, and I was determined to find out what it all meant, determined to find the white cat. I needed to know exactly why it had lured me out of the house and into imminent doom.

I scanned the trees with a new sense of purpose. My plan was to wait it out, let the white cat come back to me. The cat knew something, and it was my only lead into my new world. Being stubborn has its advantages. I refuse to wait three hundred years for an answer, no matter what it takes.

My body was now reunited with my soul, complete in essence, but not in love. My new senses were going to help me unravel this next chapter of my life. I would fight an eternity for Edgar if I had to, and if eternity comes, then I'll leave this life forever.

Sam knelt down next to me and I lay back against his chest. My mind was suddenly eager for sleep and eager to see Edgar's face in my endless dreams. I shut my eyes to the sun as Sam began to hum in my ear, the same hum my foster mother had lulled me with all my life. He placed his cold hand on my forehead, and slumber washed over me. In my dreams, I remembered.

Just as I had seen in my visions my first days at the college, I was standing in the same meadow. The air was misty and warm, like summer. I felt safe and secure as I peeked down at my body, finding my soul searing with love and my hands even more brilliant than ever before.

My eyes shot up as Edgar appeared from the shadows of the woods, like a ghost within the misty field of my dream. As I noticed him, I smiled, a feeling I'd missed bursting in my soul. The sudden burn made me gasp for air, and I struggled to recognize the warm sensation. As he approached, I brought one hand to my face, feeling a tear roll over my soft skin. I realized he was home, and the feeling was love.

BOOK TWO
GUARDIAN

PREFACE

And though we find that the God's creations were exiled to Earth, what they never expected was the revolt that could ultimately lead to a revolution. When cast to live among the humans, forever bound to a life of sadness and torment, the two halves prevailed, defying all odds and finding each other. Despite their need to destroy all they held dear and self destruct, the breed adapted to their challenge, angering the gods and creating a reunion.

Horrified and driven by a jealous rage, the Gods then set out to kill all those that defied them, finding their amusing game had turned sour. Deep in the roots of Earth they forged a dagger, strong enough to kill their creations forever. This dagger would leave nothing but empty shells of the raven, servants that would hold no heart or soul.

In their greed they ignored the simple fact that such a weapon could be used against them, their hearts too corrupt with power to understand their own demise. Among the Gods creations on Earth, they searched for a worthy soul to carry the weapon and do the deed. They hunted far and wide for one so dark, that they could buy it with the promise of power and barter with his greedy instincts.

When the soul was found, they bestowed him with the dagger, outlining his task to kill and the fruitful future he was promised; a promise that they never planned to uphold. When this soul received the dagger, he turned into no more than a rat, squandering all his riches and killing all his friends, one by one.

The Gods were pleased with the success of their pawn, and as the divine race deceased into legend, they had all but forgotten the game of the human Earth, leaving it to self destruct in a manner that was unstoppable. When they finally turned their attentions away from their greedy crusade and back to the Earth many decades later, the Gods found that the Earth was now dying. The humans they had neglected while hunting for the pure race were now infesting the surface like a plague.

Horrified, the gods ceased their previous plans, finding that now only a few of their divine creations remained as they had slaughtered the rest. These beings that they had previously hunted were now the only beings that could save everyone. Among those left, was the first. She was the original prototype of their experiments, exponentially more potent and powerful than all the rest. She was a proven force that could not be erased, despite their evil pawn's efforts.

In this they knew they needed to recruit her, and though finding they were now locked by her wishes, they would not divulge her importance to her, keeping her power a secret and squeezing all she had left back to the Earth. Content with the new plan, the Gods set it in motion, killing the evil pawn and taking collateral. This is where our story continues...

BABY STEPS

The cold granite felt like steel against my head as I lay on the top landing of the stairs, pondering my next move. I took a few calm measured breaths, allowing my eyes to stay closed. My heart was racing. I hadn't ever gotten this far, not until now. The closest I had gotten to my room was yesterday, when I finally laid one foot on the bottom step. Now here I was, at the top, my body trembling with fear and sorrow like a nervous idiot.

Slowly, I began to draw my eyelids open like a curtain at a play. I felt the granite under my sweaty palms, my arms sprawled out at my sides and my legs cascading down the stairs. I rolled my head to the right, looking at the doors to my room with sad recollection.

It had been nearly two months since I'd been back at the house, but still I could not bring myself to go back to my room and see what I feared would be a scene of sadness and loss. I had taken to sleeping on the couch in the sitting room, despite Sam's attempts to encourage me to face the facts, and move on. He didn't understand how this felt. He didn't know what sorrow was anymore, or fear. He was dead, inside and out.

I drew in a heavy breath and held it as it stung my lungs. Carefully, I rolled my head to the other side, my eyes falling on the doors to Edgar's mysterious room. His room was a place I couldn't even fathom visiting. I had never seen it, at least not in my current recollection. It still seemed like an imaginary place, a place that had never really existed.

Although I had gotten my soul back when Edgar's heart had ceased to beat, it hadn't given me all of my memory. There were certain things that slowly trickled back, like my expert knowledge for chess, and of course my heightened sense of sight, and sound, but not my memory.

I exhaled as I drew my head back to the center, staring at the gold leaf ceiling. I wrenched my tired body up as I leaned my chin into my hands and placed my feet on the top step. Dragging my fingers across my tired eyes, I heard the swift cutting of wings echoing through the large entry foyer.

My hands dropped to my lap as I looked up, seeing Henry and Isabelle circle the chandelier and dive toward me. They landed on the top step as their talons slipped, grinding across the granite like fingernails on a chalkboard. I winced at the shrill noise as they clicked their way back toward me with haste, each rubbing their head against my arm like cats often would.

In the passing months, Henry had grafted himself to

345

me as though he were solely mine. I knew he missed Edgar. There was a glimmer in his eye that was unmistakable and sad. He now looked to me as his foster mother, and that was definitely something I could relate with.

I sighed with a heavy heart as I scratched them both on the head. This trip to my room was always destined to be a failed attempt, but I had at least gotten to the top landing. I looked up as my eyes caught the glimmer of something standing in the center of the entry. Sam was smiling at me as he stood there in angelic silence. It was frustrating that even I could not hear him moving in his soundless existence.

"Wow. Looks like you got pretty far today," he half laughed as he said it.

I wiped the sorrow from my face before he could notice, reverting back to confidence as I prepared myself to take on his sarcastic barrage of emotionless banter. "Thanks Sam." My voice was sharp, but amused.

"So why don't you just do it? Pour salt on the wound so you can move on? I know you're stronger than this, besides, you keep talking in your sleep about how uncomfortable the couch is. And frankly, you're boring." He smirked.

I pushed my brows together. "Do you watch me sleep? Come on Sam, that's creepy."

He laughed. "Of course I watch you. It's my job. And I like being creepy. It goes well with my superhero image."

I pursed my lips and shook my head. It had taken some practice, but I was learning to hide my thoughts away from him. I had found a special room in my head that even he couldn't penetrate, and I was sure it was beginning to frustrate him. He was used to the minds of weak humans; so revealing. But I was more than human now. I was immortal, and my powers could somewhat rival his, though I still wasn't as strong. At least my intelligence and sharp intuition kept him challenged.

I narrowed my eyes. "No, I think you're trying to read my thoughts. You can't stand not knowing my every whim, can you?"

He fidgeted with his hands as he held them behind his back. His wings were entirely withdrawn into his shoulder blades to the point that you would never be able to discern him from a human, other than the fact that his skin was cold as ice and his eyes were heavily shadowed in a light mauve.

He finally smirked, snorting in a delicate manner which suggested he was guilty. "Maybe, I just like to hear your thoughts. It makes me feel alive again. Human thoughts are so boring: what to eat, what to watch on TV, what should I do to poison the Earth today. You on the other hand, your thoughts are fascinating." His eyes suddenly lit up with joy.

I narrowed my eyes even further, exhaling sharply. I pushed myself off the cold floor and stood. Henry and Isabelle trotted toward my bedroom doors, encouraging me. They stopped and looked back as though urging me to follow, but I shook my head. "Not today, guys. Tomorrow, I promise."

They both looked at me as though telling me I'd promised them that a dozen times already. Henry blinked, lowering his head as Isabelle followed suit. It made my heart break to see them that way, but what else could I do? I was a prisoner of fear.

347

Sam snorted. "Yeah, that's exactly what they're thinking."

I turned my gaze to Sam. I had allowed him that thought. "You can't hear what they're thinking, so stop pretending you can. You can't pull that one on me."

Sam shrugged. "True. But I can feel their emotion, and right now they seem pretty disappointed."

"Whatever," I replied tartly. "You're just upset that I can beat you at your own game. You're such a poor loser, Sam."

He chuckled. "Whatever."

I sighed as I darted across the top landing of the stairs to the shelf and grasped the Edgar Allan Poe notebook. I did it as though something was after me, but the only thing chasing me at this point was the ghosts of my past. The thick old leather felt rough between my fingers as I bounded down the stairs. It wasn't that I wanted to run away from reality. I just wasn't ready to face it.

Sam laughed again. "That was some serious Indiana Jones action there, very impressive, but you forgot to replace the idol with a bag of sand. Better watch out! An evil gremlin will likely attack!" He pointed to the stairs behind me with sarcastic humor.

I felt a sudden urge to punch him as my bare feet landed like an expert on the foyer floor, and in fact, that was just what I did. As my fist landed hard against his cold bicep, however, I felt my fingers crunch and a sharp pain pulse through my arm as though I'd punched a marble statue.

Sam looked at me with sly eyes, my punch no more than a brush of a feather to him. "Whoa there missy, better be careful."

I grasped my hand as it throbbed and stung. Glowering at him, I rubbed my broken knuckles in rueful silence as I molded them back to normal in slow gentle strokes.

"I don't get why you choose to inflict pain on yourself like that, time after time. I get the point. You resent me, but get over it. I'm not leaving unless Edgar releases my bond to you." He paused as he smirked, my heart crumbling like rocks as he said his name. "And I don't see that happening anytime soon," he added, an extra twist of the dagger now stabbing at my guilty sad soul.

I growled at him. "Shut up Sam." My hand was feeling much better as I twisted on one foot and stormed toward the kitchen, a sharp angry beat in my step.

He followed like a soundless ghost. "Oh come on Elly. I didn't mean it. I'm not used to being polite."

"Well then get used to it. You're acting like a monster, not an angel." His comment still stung in my heart. Any time he uttered Edgar's name it hurt as though the dagger had stabbed me instead.

"I'm trying, but it's hard to remember what feeling emotion is like. I still don't understand why you chose to get your soul back. All it does is complicate things."

I plopped down on a stool and thumped my elbows down on the copper island. "Well try harder," I spat.

"Ok, let me make you some lunch. What would you like?" the desperation in his voice was working, and I began to feel guilty. He simply didn't know any better.

"How about some sympathy with a side of comfort?" I

smarted.

"What's in that?"

He sounded genuinely confused, and I rolled my eyes at him. You would think he could at least smell his own sarcasm being thrown back at him.

"Just, never mind." I sighed. "Go in the upper cabinet, there should be a box of macaroni and cheese, just follow the directions."

He eyed me with an annoying smirk, I know he knew what I had been talking about, but he was a good actor. I only wished I had been so sarcastic and talented with conversation when I didn't have a soul. Maybe then I wouldn't be as miserable as I was now because I would have never come here, never met Edgar, and I could have lived on in my oblivious depressed darkness.

The box made a dull jingling sound as he tilted it out of he cabinet and the noodles shifted inside. I thought about my eggs and syrup and wished Edgar was here to make it for me; only he knew how. I was never much of a cook, and my appetite hadn't really been great, anyway. I was still sick over the loss, and I wondered if the sinking feeling of sadness would ever leave. Often they say time heals all wounds, but so far, I felt as though my wounds were still gaping, gushing sadness and blood with every painstaking moment that passed.

Sam eyed me with a knowing glare. I had allowed him the torture of that thought as well, letting him know how much I resented his attempts at filling the gap Edgar had left. Failed attempts, like eating sugar when you're starving. Sam was a great friend, but he was no Edgar.

There was an abrupt and odd look on Sam's face and I analyzed it with discretion. I had never seen a look like that before and I almost compared it with real remorse.

I was proud of myself. Fixing Sam had become a sort of pet project, no man should forget what he died for, as he had seemed to. I knew who he used to be, based on Edgar's story of how he gave his life for a young girl he barely knew. I had never confronted him, though. I was afraid of the outcome. Afraid he wouldn't remember why he was here and become frustrated. As hard as it was to admit, I needed him. Otherwise by now, I would have already gone crazy.

Sam was watching me with nervous eyes over the top of the box as he read each direction with diligence, extracting each ingredient and measuring it as though in biology class. Sam didn't eat, either. He didn't need to. He told me he couldn't taste it, anyway. All earthly desires were stripped from him because of his duty to serve. Nothing must sidetrack him from that. But in my stubbornness, I was determined to change that idea.

He had succeeded in making a pot of water boil as it sat very close to the flames of the fire in the kitchen hearth. I was amazed, even I had never succeeded at that simple task and my mac and cheese was rather crunchy due to that fact. He looked inwardly content with himself, as though he'd accomplished something great.

Maybe Edgar had been right when he said it was easier to be the professor than pretend to be the student. A professor led, while a student followed. It was now apparent, more than ever, that there was no one left for me to follow. I had to face

351

the fact that stepping up to my responsibilities was evident.

I had thought about the college and wondered if Scott and Sarah were still there. It was mid-summer, so it was highly likely. It hadn't seemed right, though, to go back. What was the point beyond re-hashing hurtful memories and the doldrums of waiting? And for what? Death? Still, it hadn't escaped my thoughts and I was formulating a time to go, just not yet, not now.

Sam struggled with the packet of fake cheese sauce and I giggled in secrecy. He gave me an embarrassed and reproachful glare before tearing the pack nearly to pieces. He only managed to get about half of its contents into the pot before the rest spilled to the floor.

"Don't worry about it, Sam." I reassured him, surprised to find him upset and angry with himself. Maybe he really was becoming human again.

His face changed from embarrassment to confidence. "Pfft. What are you talking about? I'm not embarrassed."

I could see the attempt to lie crossing his face and I chuckled once, looking down at the copper counter and admiring my reflection. My eyes gleamed like small orbs of luminescent opals, reflecting in sharp rays off the copper and back at me.

"Sam?"

He looked up from the fire, his face pulled together with frustration over the result of his cooking. "Hmm?"

"What happened that day, before I was taken? What did you see?" I had never been able to ask this question, everything else had come first; mostly the fact that Edgar was gone.

"I saw you being stupid," he replied in a blunt and cold manner. His amber eyes scanned my face, trying to pry into my thoughts.

"Yeah, but seriously. You saw the cat, right?" My eyes scanned his and I allowed him to see my thoughts, the blurred memory of the white cat and the vicious attack of the ravens.

His face seemed to be torn, as though he was experiencing something painful. I realized it was a look of failure, failure because he had lost me that day in the woods and had let Edgar die. It was silly that he blamed himself for that. It wasn't even his fault. But, I could see his dutiful point. He had failed at the only thing he did well: being a guardian.

"Yeah, I saw the nasty feline," he spat.

"What was it? Why was it here? Could you feel what it was thinking?" I knew how he could feel Henry and Isabelle and I'd hoped he had felt the cat, too. He had to have noticed something.

"I felt a lot of things, Elly. There were the ravens first and foremost, but I suppose I did feel a strange muted undertone of something. It was strange, as though a mixed signal. I was certain of the fact that it wasn't normal, if you ask me." He shrugged as he pulled the soupy noodles away from the fire. I watched as he contemplated over a plate or bowl, finally settling for a bowl after the sour expression on his face recognized the contents of the pot to be closer to soup than noodles.

"But do you think it was part of Matthew's plan? Do you think it was another strategic move in his game to lure me away from Edgar and into his lethal grasp?" My voice was laced with curiosity.

"No, I don't get that feeling. It wasn't evil. That would be the first thing I would have noticed. To me, the world is black and white, evil and safe." He pushed a plate toward me, his eyes looking at mine with observant curiosity. I could sense he felt nervous that I would judge him for his cooking skills.

"Thanks Sam. Looks great." I smiled.

He narrowed his eyes at me and I could feel him navigating every corner of my brain, coming up empty handed. He grunted, his chest rising as he walked into the sitting room behind me. He threw his body onto the chaise lounge as the furniture yawned beneath him.

I picked at the soggy mass before me, urging my stomach to find it somewhat appetizing. I could hear Sam breathing, though I wasn't sure why he did. Being that he was dead, he really didn't need to. I suppose for the matter of fitting in, however, it made sense. For him, old habits died hard.

I had circled my life around three rooms. When I first came back it was hard for me to get past the front hall. But now, I felt comfortable being in the kitchen, sitting room and entry. Healing was a slow process and my burden to bear. I never understood how humans managed to move on, often so soon after their loss, but I guess love comes down to a choice: You can either get over it and try to be happy, or roll over and rot, all alone. Let's face it, no one likes being alone.

Sam came and went as he pleased, but it didn't seem as though he'd gone into any rooms besides the ones I had, either. I suppose it was out of respect for me, if he even possessed a shred of any. He was so rude, that it wouldn't surprise me if he'd been to every room in the house, let alone sleep in Edgar's bed. But as long as he didn't move anything, I didn't really care anymore.

I worked down another soggy and watered down load of mac and cheese before giving up. I had a new goal in mind. After throwing my bowl in the sink and grabbing the Edgar Allan notebook from where I'd set it on the counter, I tried my best to slink out of the room unnoticed. There was one place in this house I was certain would be easier to visit than my room, and I now set out on a mission to go there.

My hand grazed along the velvety wall paper as I traced toward the library. There was no real reason why I hadn't yet gone there, and I wasn't surprised to find it exactly the same. I gripped my hand around the frame of the door, feeling the familiar spot where I had dug my nails into the wood a hundred times. The memory of those last stressful days with Edgar flashed before me, and I felt the anxiety of the waiting weigh on my conscience.

I took a deep breath and stepped into the room. Sam had not followed me, but I was not so naïve to deny the fact that he knew what I was doing. Even though I had impeccable sight and hearing, he had even better. I noticed how he could watch the air before him when there was nothing there, but to him, there was always something: a particle of dust, a wisp of silk thread. He always knew, but that didn't mean he always told me about it.

I ran my hand along the thick leather of the couch,

finding it cold and uninviting. The notebook of poems in my hand suddenly felt like a ton of bricks as I set it on the coffee table. I looked toward the greenhouse Edgar had built for me. A lump of guilt ached in my throat. That room was still too hard to visit, and even seeing it now was like reliving the death all over again.

As I diverted my gaze from the tables of dead plants, my sight caught the silky mahogany wood of the ladder to the second tier of the library. My breathing quickened, my body now terrified of what I knew was up there. I had tricked myself into coming here, tricked myself into my insatiable obsession with that tiny room, and the painting.

I took a deep breath, placing one hand on the middle rung. Squeezing my eyes shut, the painful memory of Edgar's hands around my waist flooded my mind. My sides began to tingle with the residual touch and the breath was ripped from my lungs. I cursed myself for whimpering like a fool, placing my other hand on the rail. I worked to calm the burning pain in my throat, huffing through my nose in heavy breaths instead. I needed this. It had been long enough. My time for waiting was over and now it was time for a new day. Opening my eyes, I took a deep breath and moved.

Read More At:
www.FeatherBookSeries.com

Stay ahead of the game... Log onto www.featherbookseries.com for changing release dates and order. Also e-mail the author with any specific questions.

In Love with Feather? Also check out the first edition authors copy, available through Amazon and the Website. Each copy is signed by the author and includes a handmade bookmark, depicting the authors journey as a writer, and artist...

Thanks for enjoying, and being a part of my world...

Visit her Blog at:
www.featherbookseries.wordpress.com

And at the website:
www.featherbookseries.com

Also!

Parallel: The Life of Patient 32185
Now Available!

www.ParallelTheBook.com

ABOUT THE AUTHOR

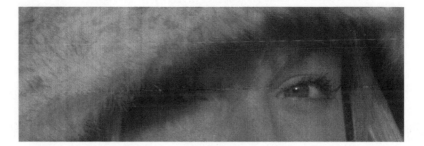

*J*n our world, we are destined to follow a path that we have chosen from birth. For me, life has proven to be a difficult and challenging journey, full of love, hate, anger, happiness, and fear. It is in this that we find who we are, and the power to love, give, and grow. I follow in the footprints of many great minds, including Leonardo DaVinci, Jules Verne, and Edgar A. Poe. I only hope that I can own up to the creative echo they've left for me to follow...

*O*bra Ebner was Born in Seattle, Washington where she still lives with her husband and two cats. She attended Washington State University where she earned her Bachelors degree in Fine Arts and Graphic Design. She also attended the Queensland College of Art in Brisbane, Australia and has traveled to Germany, Switzerland, England, and Scotland where she finds the inspiration for the colorful backdrops of her stories.

7541499R0

Made in the USA
Lexington, KY
29 November 2010